# WOMAN
## OF THE
# PHARISEES

# WOMAN
## OF THE
# PHARISEES

## FRANCOIS MAURIAC

Translated by Gerard Hopkins

A THOMAS MORE BOOK TO LIVE
The Thomas More Press
Chicago, Illinois

This
THOMAS MORE BOOK TO LIVE
edition is made possible in part
by a grant from Andrew M. Greeley

# 1

"COME here, boy!"

I turned round, thinking that the words were addressed to one of my companions. But no, it was to me that the one-time Papal Zouave had spoken. He was smiling, and the scar on his upper lip made the smile hideous.

Colonel the Comte de Mirbel was in the habit of coming once every week into Intermediate School yard. On these occasions his ward, Jean de Mirbel, who was almost always in a state of being "kept in," would move away from the wall against which he had been made to stand, while we, from a distance, watched the arraignment to which his terrifying uncle subjected him. Our master, Monsieur Rausch, called upon to act as witness for the prosecution, replied obsequiously to the Colonel's questions. The old man was tall and vigorous. On his head he wore one of those caps known as a "cronstadt," and his coat, buttoned up to the neck, gave him a military air. He was never to be seen without a riding-switch, probably of raw-hide, tucked under his arm. When our friend's conduct had been particularly bad, he would be marched away across the yard between Monsieur Rausch and his guardian, and the three of them would disappear into a staircase in the left wing of the building, which led to the dormitories. We would stop whatever game we were playing and wait until a long-drawn wail struck sharply on our ears. It sounded like the yelp of a beaten dog (though that may have been due to our imaginations). A moment later, Monsieur Rausch would reappear, accompanied by the Colonel, the scar showing livid in his purple face. His blue eyes would look faintly bloodshot. Monsieur Rausch was all attention. He kept his head turned towards his companion and his lips were stretched in a servile grin. That was the only occasion on which we ever saw that pale, terrifying face, topped by its red, crimped hair, distorted into a grimace of laughter. Monsieur Rausch, the terror of our lives! Whenever we went into class and found his seat still empty, I used to pray: "O God, please let Monsieur Rausch be dead! Blessed Virgin, please let him have broken his leg, or make it so that he's ill—not seriously, but just a little!". . . But he had an iron constitution, and his hard, dry hand at the end of its skinny arm was more to be feared than a slab of wood. Jean de Mirbel, fresh from the mysterious punishments inflicted upon him by his two executioners (vastly exaggerated, no doubt, in our boyish fancies), would come back into the form-room with his eyes red and his grubby face streaked with tears, and make his way to his desk. The rest of us kept our eyes fixed firmly on our notebooks.

"Do as you're told, Louis!" barked Monsieur Rausch. It was the first time he had ever called me by my Christian name. I stayed hesitating on the threshold of the parlor door. Jean de Mirbel was standing inside the room, his back towards me. On a small table there lay an open parcel containing two chocolate éclairs and a bun. The Colonel asked me whether I liked cakes. I nodded my head.

"Well, those are for you, then . . . Go on; what are you waiting for? It's young Pian, isn't it?—know his family well—doesn't look as though he had any more spunk than his poor father. . . . Brigitte Pian, his stepmother, now there's a woman for you—reg'lar Mother of the Church. . . . You, there! stop where you are!"—this he shouted at

2

Jean, who was trying to slink away. "You're not going to get off as lightly as that! You've got to watch your young friend having a good time. . . . Come on, make up your mind, you little fool!" he added, his two eyes fixing me, from either side of the short, firm nose, with a stare in which a glint of anger already showed.

"He's shy," said Monsieur Rausch; "don't wait to be asked twice, Pian."

My friend was looking out of the window. His turn-down collar had come unfastened, and I could see his dirty neck above it. No one in the world had such power to frighten me as the two men now bending down and smiling into my face. I knew from of old the harsh, animal-like smell that hung about Monsieur Rausch. I stammered out that I wasn't hungry, but the Colonel retorted that a boy didn't have to be hungry to eat cakes. Seeing that I was persisting in my obstinacy, Monsieur Rausch told me to go to the Devil, adding that there were plenty of others who wouldn't be so stupid. As I was making my escape into the yard, I heard him call to Mouleyre, an unnaturally fat boy who always ate anything on which he could lay his hands in the dining-hall. He ran up at the summons, sweating. Monsieur Rausch shut the parlor door, from which Mouleyre emerged later, his mouth smeared with cream.

It was a June evening, and still swelteringly hot. When the day-boys had gone home we were allowed to remain outside for a bit because of the heat. Mirbel came up to me. We could hardly be described as friends, and I am pretty sure that he despised me because, in those days, I was a rather spiritless and well-behaved boy. He took from his pocket a pill-box and half raised the lid.

"Look!"

It contained two stag-beetles. He had given them a cherry for food.

"They don't like cherries," said I. "They live on the rotten bark of old oaks."

We used to catch them on Thursdays, near the School Lodge, on our way out. These particular insects always start flying at sunset.

"You can have one of them. Take the bigger, but be careful—they're not tame yet!"

I couldn't tell him that I didn't know where to put the beetle. But I was pleased that he should speak so kindly to me. We sat down on the steps that led to the main block of the school buildings. Two hundred boys and about twenty masters were crowded into what had once been a beautifully proportioned town-house.

"I'm going to train them to pull a cart," said Jean.

He took from his pocket a small box which he fastened with thread to the beetle's claws. We played with it for a while. During these special recreation periods on summer evenings no boy was ever kept in, and there was no insistence on community games. Elsewhere on the steps other boys were busy spitting on apricot stones and polishing them. This done, they made a hole in each and took out the kernel, using the empty shell as a whistle. The heat of the day was still intense within the space surrounded on four sides by buildings. Not a breath of air stirred the leaves on the sickly plane trees. Monsieur Rausch, his legs apart, was in his usual place over by the outdoor toilets, to see that we didn't stay too long in them. They gave off a powerful stench which fought a losing battle with the smell of chlorine and disinfectant. From the other side of the wall came the sound of a cab bumping over the rough cobbles of the rue Leyteire. I was filled with envy of the unknown passenger, of the

4

coachman, and even of the horse, because they were not shut away in school, and didn't have to go in fear of Monsieur Rausch.

"I'm jolly well going to thrash Mouleyre," said Jean suddenly.

"I say, Mirbel, what's a Papal Zouave?" I asked him.

He shrugged his shoulders. "I'm not quite sure, but I think he was one of the chaps who fought for the Pope before 1870, and got beaten." He was silent for a few moments, and then added: "I don't want him and Rausch to die before I'm grown up."

Hatred made him look ugly. I asked him why he was the only one of us who was treated as he was.

"My uncle says it's for my good. He says that when his brother was dying, he swore by God that he'd make a man of me. . . ."

"And your mother? . . ."

"Oh, she believes everything he says . . . or maybe she doesn't dare contradict him. She didn't really want me to be a boarder here. She would have liked me to stay at home at La Devize with a tutor. But he wouldn't allow that. He said my character was too bad."

"*My* mother," said I proudly, "has come to live in Bordeaux for my education."

"But you're a boarder just the same."

"Only for these two weeks, because Vignotte—he's the agent over at Larjuzon—is sick, and my father's got to do his work. But she writes to me every day."

"Madame Brigitte Pian isn't your real mother, is she?"

"It's the same thing, though . . . it's just as if she were."

I stopped at that and felt my cheeks burning. Had my real mother heard? Are the dead always listening to find out what the living are saying about them? But if Mamma knew everything, she would realize that no one had ever taken her place in my heart. It didn't matter how kind my stepmother was to me. It was quite true that she wrote to me every day, but I hadn't even opened the letter that had come from her that morning. And when I cried that night, in the stifling dormitory, before going to sleep, it would be because I was thinking of my father, of my sister Michèle, or of Larjuzon, and not of Brigitte Pian. Still, my father would have liked me to be a boarder all the year round, so that he could have gone on living in the country. It was my stepmother who had insisted. They had taken a little flat in Bordeaux, to make it possible for me to go home every evening. My sister Michèle, who hated our father's wife, always maintained that she had used me as an excuse for breaking the promise she had made when she married, that she would live at Larjuzon. No doubt Michèle was right. If my stepmother never tired of saying that I was "too nervous and too sensitive to be sent to boarding-school," it was because this was the only argument that could persuade my father to stay on in Bordeaux. I knew that well enough, but it didn't make any difference. The grown-ups could settle their own affairs. It was enough for me that my stepmother had had the last word. But I knew that Papa was unhappy when separated from his woods, his horses, and his guns. He must be enjoying himself now. . . . That thought was a great comfort to me during this fortnight of trial. Besides, it would soon be Prize Day, and then Brigitte Pian would have to resign herself to going back to Larjuzon.

"Prize Day soon!" I exclaimed.

Mirbel had a beetle in each hand and was pressing them together.

"They're kissing!" he said, and added without looking at

6

me: "You don't know what a rotten trick my uncle's thought up if I don't get a good report: I'm not going to be allowed to spend vacation with my mother. I'm not to go to La Devize at all. I'm to be sent to board with a priest, the Curé of Baluzac. It's actually only a few miles from where you live. He's been told to make me work six hours a day and to break me in. . . . I gather that's his line."

"Then why not try to get a good report?"

He shook his head. It couldn't be done; not with Rausch. He'd often tried.

"He never takes his eyes off me. You know my desk's just under his nose. You'd almost think he had nothing to do but watch me. All I have to do is glance out of the window . . ."

It was true enough, and nothing could be done to help Mirbel. I promised that if he spent his holidays at Baluzac I'd see a lot of him. I knew Monsieur Calou, the Curé, very well. There was nothing especially terrible about him. As a matter of fact, he was very decent.

"No, he's horrible. My uncle says that bad boys are sent to him to be broken in. I've heard that he drove the two Baillaud boys nearly crazy. But I won't let him lay a finger on me."

Perhaps the Curé of Baluzac was kind only to me? I didn't know what to say to Mirbel. I suggested that perhaps his mother, who never saw him, wouldn't give up the chance of having him home for the holidays.

"She will, if he says so. She does everything he wants!" replied Mirbel in a fury. I realized that he was very close to tears.

"How about letting me help you with your lessons?"

He shook his head. He had too much back work to make

7

up. Besides, Rausch would spot it. "Whenever I hand in a decent exercise he always accuses me of cribbing."

At that moment Rausch put a whistle to his lips. He wore a long frock-coat with stains down the front. In spite of its being summer, he still had his feet stuffed into padded felt slippers. His crinkled, carroty hair grew well back from a bony forehead covered with pimples. His eyes were of different colors and blinked from beneath reddened lids. We marched off in a long line towards the dining-hall. I hated the smell of greasy soup that came from it. It was still broad daylight but no sky was visible through the dirty windows. I noticed that Mirbel was the only boy at our table who did not eat ravenously. The Papal Zouave had hit on the one punishment that could get under his ward's skin—spending the holidays with the Curé of Baluzac, away from his mother. I should be able, with my bicycle, to see him every day. I felt a little stab of happiness. I would speak about Jean to the Curé who was so kind to me and let me gather nuts in his garden. True, I was "young Pian," the stepson of Madame Brigitte, his "benefactress." But that made it all the better. I would ask my stepmother to intercede on Jean's behalf. I told him as much on our way upstairs to the dormitory. Twenty of us slept in a room that was ventilated by one window only, which gave on to the rue Leyteire. At the foot of each bed stood a washstand with a basin. In this we put our tooth-glasses in such a way that the man who came round with a jug could fill both glasses and basins at the same time. In five minutes we were all undressed and in bed. The assistant master, Monsieur Puybaraud, lowered the gas, and in a trembling voice recited three prayers which brought the tears to my eyes. I cried because I was lonely, because some day I should have to die, because I was thinking of my mother. I was thirteen. She had been dead for six years. She

8

had vanished so quickly! One evening she had kissed me, so full of life and sweetness, and the next day . . . the horse had bolted and brought home the trap empty. I never knew how the accident had happened. No one had told me much about it, and my father, now that he had married again, never mentioned his first wife's name. As though to make up for that, my stepmother often exhorted me to pray for the dead woman. She used to ask me each evening whether I had a thought for her. She seemed to believe that Mamma had more need of prayers than other dead people. She had always known my mother, who had been her cousin, and had sometimes invited her to the house during the holidays. "You ought to ask your cousin Brigitte to come to Larjuzon," said my father. "She can't afford a holiday: she gives away all she has. . . ." My mother would do her best to stand out against this appeal, although she professed to admire Brigitte. Perhaps she was afraid of her. That, at any rate, was what my sister Michèle thought. "Mamma saw through her: she knew only too well what an influence her cousin had over Papa."

I attached little importance to such statements. But my stepmother's exhortations made an impression on me. It was only too true that Mamma had had no time in which to prepare herself for death. The sort of education I had had helped me to understand Brigitte's insistence. It was indeed necessary that I should intercede for that poor departed spirit.

That evening, snuffling beneath the sheets, I had begun to tell my beads for Mamma while Monsieur Puybaraud lowered the gas until he had reduced the butterfly of flame to no more than a bluish flicker. He took off his frock-coat and started on a last round of the beds. The rhythmic breathing of the sleepers was already audible. As he passed close by me he must have heard the sob that I was doing my best to smother, for he came close and laid his hand on my tear-stained cheek. With a sigh he tucked me in as Mamma used to do, and then, bending down suddenly, kissed me on the forehead. I flung my arms round his neck and kissed his bristly cheek. He crept away very quietly to his cubicle. I could see his shadow moving behind the thin curtain.

Almost every evening Monsieur Puybaraud consoled me in the same way. "Much too soft-hearted, and dangerously oversensitive," said my stepmother, who had a good deal to do with him, since he acted as general secretary to the Charity Organization.

A few days later when my parents returned to Bordeaux and the butler came at about six to take me home, I ran into Monsieur Puybaraud, who seemed to have been on the lookout for me, in the yard. After smoothing back my hair from my forehead with his rather damp hand, he gave me a sealed letter which he begged me to post. This I promised to do, astonished that he had not given the letter to the censor, whose business it was to take charge of the school correspondence.

I waited until I was in the street before reading the address. The envelope bore the name of Mademoiselle Octavia Tronche, teacher at the Free School, rue Parmentade, Bordeaux. I knew her well. She used to come to the house between her classes, and my stepmother .employed her on various tasks. On the reverse side of the envelope, in a fair round hand, Monsieur Puybaraud had written: *Go, little letter, and bring to my heart a gleam of hope.* . . . Walking a few paces behind the butler, who had put my satchel under his arm, I read and reread this strange invocation. I pondered over it there on the pavement of the Cours Victor-Hugo, just where it joins the rue Sainte-Cathérine, in the dusk of the evening before Prize Day. And in my nostrils was the faint smell of absinthe.

## 2

IT was then that I was guilty of the first bad action of my life—of an action, I mean, the thought of which even now fills me with a sense of remorse. Monsieur Puybaraud had made no attempt to extract from me any promise about the letter, but I knew, nevertheless, that he regarded me as more deserving of his trust than any of my comrades. I tried later to persuade myself that I had not realized what was at stake for the assistant master. That is not true. I understood perfectly well what was involved, and had a pretty shrewd idea of the dramatic touch that his semireligious cast of mind gave to the incident. It was a matter of common knowledge that he belonged to a lay society (now long since dispersed), a sort of Third Order, the members of which were bound by no vows. Sometimes, indeed quite frequently, one or other of the so-called "Brethren" would, with the consent of his superiors, leave the Community in order to marry. But Monsieur Puybaraud's position was rather peculiar. His work kept him in close contact with the diocesan officials of the Charity Organization Society, and with several of the boys' parents. Everyone in the town knew him, and not only the higher clergy and the rich middle-class families. He was a familiar figure in the poorest slums, where the children flocked round him as soon as he appeared at the corner of a street: for he always brought them candy. His frock-coat and the curious high beaver hat that he affected drew no surprised glances. His kindly face looked longer than it was by reason of the short whiskers that stopped at the level of his cheekbones. In summer he held his hat in his hand, and continually mopped his bald forehead and the sparse, silky hair which he wore long behind. His small features were almost too "pretty" for a man. There was about his eyes something of the look of a wounded animal, and his hands were always damp. My stepmother was loud in praise of his virtues, though she held strong views on the subject of his "excessive and morbid sensibility." I, of all people, should have kept myself from mentioning to her the secret of his letter, but it was precisely to her that I burned to impart my knowledge. The possession of it filled me with a sense of self-importance. Young as I was, I wanted to shock, to scandalize. Nevertheless, I was too frightened to say anything so long as other members of the family were present.

I have a vivid recollection of that evening. The flat that my father had consented to lease was on the second floor of a house in the Cours de l'Intendance. On summer evenings the noise of traffic on the cobblestones and the clang of the electric cars—which had only recently begun to operate in the city—made conversation difficult. A fortnight spent in the country had brought the color back to my father's cheeks, and the prospect of the approaching holidays had put him in a good humor. At a word from his wife, however, he left the table to put on a bow tie and a black coat. She could not bear the untidy clothes that he always wore at Larjuzon.

In spite of the heat she had on a high-necked dress with a lace collar that swathed her to the ears. Her large face, with its heavy, lusterless cheeks, was surmounted by a mass of hair puffed out with curls, and kept in place by an almost invisible net. Her black, staring eyes had a hard look, but her mouth was always smiling, though she scarcely ever opened it wide enough to show her long yellow teeth, which were generously filled with gold and stood out firmly from the gums. A double chin gave her an air of dignity which was accentuated by the way she carried her head, by the way she walked, and by her deep voice which was never heard to better advantage than when she was engaged in issuing orders. The right place for her would have been at the head of some Community. After the death of her father, Baron Maillard, who had been Prefect of the Gironde at the time of the Empire, Brigitte had devoted the bulk of her fortune to the purchase and reconditioning of a small convent in the outskirts of Lourdes, where it was her intention to house young women of fashion under a new Rule inspired in part by her Director, the abbé Margis. The material part of the work was completed, but nothing more was ever heard of the scheme.

Brigitte Maillard had more than once, in connection with this undertaking, consulted my father, who in his youth had worked as an unpaid clerk in the office of a Bordeaux solicitor and knew a good deal about the ins and outs of legal business. He dissuaded her from bringing a suit which would have caused considerable scandal and could not possibly have succeeded. He, on his side, valued the advice that she gave him about the domestic difficulties in which he was at that time involved, though they were later to be solved so tragically by the death of my mother.

Those who knew nothing of the events which, at a certain period of my father's life, had led to the forming of a deep intimacy between him and Brigitte Maillard found it hard to imagine how two such dissimilar characters had come to link their destinies. Seen in company with this tall, bilious-looking Madame de Maintenon, my poor father aroused feelings of pity. His appearance was eloquent of weak good-nature. He spoke hesitatingly, there was a greedy look about his mouth, and his drooping mustache seemed as though it should be forever trailing in little "nips" and rich gravies. Overfeeding had given him a red face, and his eyes were prominent.

I can see my sister now as she sat that evening between husband and wife when the Puybaraud affair came to a head. Michèle was at that time fourteen. The general opinion was that her skin was too swarthy. The lower part of her face was abnormally heavy, and her hair grew too low on her forehead. But her really beautiful eyes softened all hearts, and she had very fine teeth which she showed whenever her wide mouth parted in a smile. Some might think that her arms were rather too muscular, but the same could not be said of her legs. They were a matter of great pride to her, and she did her best to show them in spite of the rather long skirts which our stepmother insisted on her wearing even then.

As a matter of fact Brigitte was always extremely patient with her, and as a rule was careful not to get herself involved in arguments with the headstrong little girl. She was always saying: "Since I can exercise no sort of influence over the child, it is my duty to keep peace in the home at all costs." She derived a feeling of triumph from the fact that the Ladies of the Sacred Heart failed equally to elicit any sort of response from Michèle. "The girl is filled with a spirit of contradiction and bad temper," she would remark to our father. But against this sentence he protested. "You are quite wrong, my dear. You do so love to dramatize things! She is willful, that's all, and flares up quickly like my poor mother. . . . But a good husband will settle all that."

Brigitte shook her head with a sigh. She looked on life from a higher standpoint. It was her mission, her glory, to view it from that higher standpoint.

The evening on which the Puybaraud complication burst into flame was a Saturday. We were listening to the sound of the crowds on the pavements of the Cours de l'Intendance where the garrison tattoo was in progress. Michèle and my father were leaning on their elbows at one end of the balcony. I was some little distance off with my stepmother. The sharp-winged swifts were skimming the roof-tops. The flow of traffic was continuous. The walls still held the heat of the day. An occasional gust brought the sweet scent of limes and, with it, that smell to be found only in big cities before the days of motor-cars—a rich mixture of horse-droppings, wet roadways, and circus tanbark. I was still wrestling with the temptation to reveal Monsieur Puybaraud's secret. But I knew that I should succumb. My stepmother was questioning me methodically about the end-of-term examinations. She wanted to know all about the examination in each subject, and how I had answered. I knew that this interest came only from a sense of duty, and that her thoughts were elsewhere. But she said what she had to say. Always, in every circumstance of life and in all her relations with other people, she knew precisely what her words, what her attitude, ought to be.

I made up my mind.

"Mother," I said, "there's something I want to tell you. But"—I added with a touch of hypocrisy—"I'm not sure whether I ought."

A spark of attention began to glow in the black eyes which, till then, had shown no interest in me.

"My dear child, I have no idea what you have to say. But there is one rule which you would do well to follow blindly, and that is, never to keep anything from your second mother. For on her has devolved the duty of bringing you up."

"Even when it is a secret involving others?"

"If it involves others that is all the more reason why you should tell me," she replied sharply. Hungry for my revelations, she asked: "Whom does it concern?—your sister?"

She already suspected the worst of Michèle, although the girl was only fourteen years old. I shook my head. No, it wasn't about Michèle: it was about Monsieur Puybaraud and Octavia Tronche.

She choked back an exclamation. "What's that?" She grabbed my arm. "Monsieur Puybaraud? Octavia?"

I was too ignorant as yet about love to have noticed that my stepmother could never approach the subject calmly, but that as soon as it was mentioned she became, as it were, all worked up. No sooner had I mentioned the letter and the sentence written on its flap than she interrupted me.

"Give it to me, now, at once."

"The letter?—but I posted it."

She seemed to be disappointed. "That was very wrong of you. You should have given it to me. I am responsible for Octavia's moral well-being. She holds an important position at the Free School, and hopes one day to be headmistress. It is not only my right, but my duty, to know everything about her. . . . Never mind, I shall manage to have a look at the letter, somehow or other," she added more calmly.

She saw that I was worried. Monsieur Puybaraud was so fond of me. What on earth would he think? She made it clear to me that I need take no action in the matter. She felt sure that she could persuade Octavia to tell her what it was all about.

"It is not, my dear child, that I suspect anything *wrong*. So estimable a person as Monsieur Puybaraud deserves my complete confidence. After all, if he wishes to leave his Order and go back into the world, he has a perfect right to do so. We must not hold him guilty of anything worse than imprudence. Not, that is, unless we have proof to the contrary. I have always thought that his rather overemotional form of piety might lead him to act rashly. Thanks to you, I can now intervene while there is still time."

In a low voice, from behind clenched teeth, she added, with sudden violence: "Octavia, of all people! But they're all the same—all bitches, every one of them!"

The sound of the brass band playing the tattoo came from the direction of the rue Vital-Carle. The people of Bordeaux were delighted with a recent innovation in the ceremony. The bandsmen had electric bulbs in their caps instead of pompons. My stepmother went back into the drawing-room, while I remained, leaning on my elbows above the heads of the crowd. Boys and girls were marching in step with the soldiers. They walked arm in arm and made a living chain across the pavement. They were shouting and laughing. I struggled no longer with my sense of shame and with the agony of spirit which oppressed me. What was going to happen to poor Monsieur Puybaraud? I was too young fully to understand the paternal instinct that had made him lean over my bed, tuck me in, and kiss me on the forehead. But I did feel that I had betrayed a man whose loneliness was such that he had turned to a boy of thirteen for comfort. I remembered Alphonse Daudet's *Enfant Espion,* and what the German soldiers had said to young Sten: "Not nice, that, not nice." Had I done wrong? My stepmother said that I had

17

done my duty . . . why, then, should I feel so remorseful?

I joined her in the room. She was seated close to the window, trying to read. We could not have any light because of the mosquitoes, and it was too hot to close the windows. A vague longing to "make up" for what I had done made me feel that I wanted to perform some kind action. So I mentioned Mirbel, begging her to speak to the Curé of Baluzac on his behalf. I watched her large pale face in the dusk. It was much too dark to read. She was sitting there quite motionless and very upright. Her early convent training had taught her never to lean back in a chair, nor do I remember ever seeing her cross her legs. I knew that she was only half paying attention, and that her thoughts were busy with the Puybaraud-Tronche affair.

"The Curé of Baluzac?" she said at last. "Poor abbé Calou! —it can't be very easy for him to pose as an ogre! . . . Well, I suppose the extra money helps him to buy a few books. I wonder whether I ought to tell the Colonel how misinformed he has been?"

I begged her to do nothing of the sort. Her words confirmed me in my feeling that the abbé Calou would not be a very terrifying jailer, and I was particularly anxious not to be deprived of the pleasure of having Jean de Mirbel as a companion during the holidays. But she added that, on second thought, she felt sure that the young good-for-nothing could get only what was good from living in the company of Monsieur Calou, and that God's will must be done.

All the next week I watched Monsieur Puybaraud with considerable apprehension. But I was still his "pet" (as the other boys called me), and up to the end of term he was as kind to me as ever. The examinations were almost over, and the heat became too oppressive to make much work possible.

Even Monsieur Rausch relaxed and read *Le Soldat Chapuzot* to us in form. In Senior Yard the carpenters were busy putting up stands for the Prize-giving. Every day we rehearsed Mendelssohn's choruses from *Athalie:*

> *All the world is filled with His glory:*
> *Oh, come, let us adore Him!*

But for Michèle I should probably have known nothing of the opening rounds of the Puybaraud-Tronche scandal. Though her nature was of the frankest, and she, of all people, would be the last to dream of listening at keyholes, her attitude towards our stepmother was defensive. She watched Brigitte Pian with a clear-sighted mistrust which she never for one moment relaxed. Besides, Octavia Tronche was devoted to her, and could not for long hold out against her questions. Consequently, I was kept informed about the deplorable results of my indiscretion.

Octavia Tronche worked at my stepmother's on Thursdays and Saturdays—the only times at which she was free from school classes—from eight to eleven in the mornings. She had thin, lifeless hair, but, though without any freshness of youth, was not wholly devoid of charm. This she owed to her eyes, though they were small and of an indeterminate color, and to the very sweet smile that hung about her rather bloodless lips. The children adored her, and, because of this, she was constantly exposed to the malicious pin-pricks of her jealous colleagues. Her clothes drooped from thin shoulders, and no one could well have had less indication of a bosom. Below the waist, however, she was more markedly feminine, and even her nunlike skirt could not altogether conceal the fullness of her hips.

When, on that particular morning, she entered the small drawing-room where Madame Pian—"Madame Brigitte"—was sitting, Octavia was greeted with an unaccustomed smile.

"I am afraid you are feeling the heat, my dear: I can see it in your face."

Octavia assured her patroness that she was not at all tired.

"And in your work even more than in your face." Brigitte Pian's voice had taken on a sudden note of sternness. "You made several mistakes in addressing when you sent out the last number of the *Bulletin*. I have had complaints from a good many ladies that it arrived late."

Octavia, in some confusion, began to make excuses.

"That, in itself, would not be very serious," went on my stepmother; "but the circular I dictated to you, and neglected to read over (yes, *neglected:* please observe that I do not spare myself when I have been worthy of blame), was full of errors and omissions. Some of the sentences did not even make sense. . . ."

"I am afraid that my head has not been very clear these last few days," Octavia stammered.

"Your head or your heart?" asked Brigitte in a voice whose sweetness was belied by her severe and haughty expression.

"Oh, Madame Brigitte, what *can* you mean?"

"I am not asking you to tell me your secrets, my dear: confidences cannot be forced." And then, as Octavia began to protest that she had no secrets from Madame Brigitte: "You know how scrupulous I am in respecting the consciences of others. You are one of our old girls. I trust you—not blindly, but with my eyes open, and with a sense of almost maternal responsibility. We all have difficult times to go through, my dear."

This was more than Octavia could stand. Falling on her knees, she hid her face in Madame Brigitte's lap. The latter looked at the thin neck beneath the tight little bun into which the girl's hair was drawn, at the pale skin, and at the topmost vertebra which the twisted collar of her dress left exposed. It was as well that the poor creature could not see the expression of disgust that came over the older woman's face. *Even she is no exception, ill-favored though she is,* it seemed to say. Aloud, but quite gently, Madame Brigitte said:

"And so, my poor Octavia, you too think that you have a lover?"

Octavia Tronche looked up, protesting: "That I have a lover? Oh, no, Madame: I am not quite such a fool. It is not that!"

In those few seconds her face had become transfigured. Shyness had given to it a delicate loveliness, something of the adorable charm that comes from utter humility.

"All I ask is that *he* should let me live for him alone and for the children which God in His mercy may see fit to give us."

"Naturally, my dear Octavia, naturally," said my stepmother, helping her to her feet. "Come and sit down beside me and control yourself. That I once looked on you as one called to a higher vocation is no matter. It will make me very happy to think of you with a home and a Christian family of your own. What could be more natural, more simple? The excess of your emotion surprises me."

"But it is not simple at all, Madame—far from it. If you only knew . . ."

I imagine that my stepmother realized, at that moment, what it was to be completely happy. She was tasting the pleasure that belongs, of right, to God alone: the pleasure of knowing to the full the destiny of someone who thought that she was imparting a piece of unsuspected news; of feeling that it was in her power to mold that destiny as she willed. For she did not doubt her hold over the scrupulous conscience of Monsieur Puybaraud. Had she been tempted to do so, Octavia's attitude would have restored her confidence. With masterly skill she let her tone range through every shade of expression from that of confidential friendship to suspicion. At last she said: "I feel your trouble as keenly as you do yourself," and then went on to ask the poor girl, with every mark of anxiety, whether the man in question was married or divorced. At that, her victim hid her face and struggled to conceal her tears. When next Madame Brigitte spoke there was a note almost of horror in her voice.

"Wretched girl! Am I to understand that this man is already bound to somebody whose claims are absolute? Are you setting yourself against the ordinances of God?"

"No, Madame, no! He is free: his superiors have raised no difficulty. Monsieur Puybaraud (you must have guessed already that it is he) has arranged to leave the college at the end of this week. As soon as he has done so, we have permission to consider ourselves engaged."

My stepmother rose, cutting her visitor's protestations short. "You need say no more! I do not wish to *hear* more. The responsibility lies with your respective spiritual directors. It may be that I should not see eye to eye with them in this matter . . ."

"But that is why I am so upset, Madame Brigitte!" cried Octavia between her sobs. "You see, Monsieur Puybaraud will not let himself be convinced that he has the right to act as he wishes. He keeps on saying that you alone can clarify his mind, that you alone are sufficiently instructed to give

22

him peace of mind. But please, please, Madame, understand that the situation is not as you think it. . . . You have only got to look at me to see that. Monsieur Puybaraud is not the slave of mere physical desire. He says the thought that he may one day have a son like your Louis makes him almost sob with joy."

"That I can quite realize," responded my stepmother in gloomy tones. "The Evil One always employs tricks and subterfuges when he sets out to attack men of a frank and upright nature."

"Oh, Madame, surely you are not going to persuade him that this is a trap set by the Evil One?"

Impulsively she seized the hand of my stepmother, who was seated in her usual chair in front of a desk littered with circulars and files.

"Unless he asks me, I shall say nothing at all to him, my child. If he does ask, I shall say only what I feel moved by the Holy Spirit to say. But whatever that may be, I shall speak out fearlessly and directly, as it has always been my rule to do."

Octavia clasped her hands and gazed at the expressionless face with eyes that resembled those of a defenseless lamb.

"But surely there is nothing wrong in his wish to be a father? His director doesn't think so. For years Monsieur Puybaraud has fought against his feelings. May it not be that his failure to overcome them is in itself a sign that he is called upon to follow this particular vocation?"

My stepmother nodded her head. "We should do wrong altogether to dismiss such an hypothesis," she remarked; "though it is not God's way to set the feet of His servants on the heights only to cast them down into the valleys. I shall need more definite evidence before I can bring myself to believe that Heaven has asked of Monsieur Puybaraud such an abandonment of his post, so dire a retreat, so sad a return to a less austere way of life. Nothing should be allowed to shake our faith."

"He says that he has been guilty of the sin of pride, that he has overestimated his strength. It is a blessing vouchsafed him by Heaven, he thinks, that he should have been permitted to see his way clearly before it was too late," urged Octavia in a voice of supplication.

"If he is so certain"—my stepmother interrupted her dryly—"what need is there for him to seek further? Why should I be brought into the matter at all?"

Octavia realized that this was precisely where the trouble lay. He was *not* certain: his mind changed from day to day. Bursting into tears she declared that she could see how it was: Madame Brigitte's mind was made up, she would be inexorable.

At this my stepmother became more human. "You are wrong, Octavia. You must not think that I am hostile *in principle* to these promptings of nature. There are others concerned, besides Monsieur Puybaraud. It would, indeed, make me very happy to know that you, at least, had been called upon to fulfill the duties of a wife and mother. Yes"— she went on, her gaze fixed upon her humble suppliant (and perhaps seeing already in anticipation the swollen figure beneath its smock, the plain face made plainer still by pregnancy)—"it may be that the intentions of the Almighty on your behalf have made necessary this deviation of Monsieur Puybaraud from a higher vocation. I realize that he may have to be humbled if you are to be saved."

Thus it was that Brigitte Pian attributed to our Father in Heaven the complexities and perversities of her own nature. But Octavia Tronche, snatching at this straw of hope, was already recovering like a flower in water. She raised her gentle, suffering face.

"Oh, Madame Brigitte!" she exclaimed in tones of exaltation. "Now indeed you are speaking with God's voice. You know everything, I admit everything. Unworthy though I am, it is for me that Monsieur Puybaraud is willing to renounce the joys of a higher vocation, to turn his back on the peace which might await him within the walls of an institution on which he has already brought so much credit."

"And you would quite calmly accept such a sacrifice, my child?" asked Brigitte Pian sharply.

Octavia was nonplused.

"I am not saying that you ought to refuse it. All I wish to point out is that, all other considerations apart, you have to ask yourself this question: Have you, or have you not, the right to accept such a sacrifice? Are you willing that a man like Monsieur Puybaraud, who is infinitely superior to you in spiritual gifts and in the degree to which Grace has been accorded him, should, for your sake, abandon the fruits of his apostolic mission, and lose the glory he enjoys in the sight of God as well as the honor he has won in the eyes of men? For it is no good disguising the fact that if he deserts his present post he *will* suffer a loss of credit, even (and especially) in the opinion of his neighbors. You must face the facts. Every door will be closed to him. No one could well be more helpless than he in all that pertains to the day-to-day struggle for existence, and you must realize that, owing entirely to you, he may find himself condemned to a life of care and even of poverty. . . ."

Octavia Tronche's face was irradiated, not for the first time, by a smile of pure humility.

"*That* does not trouble me, Madame Brigitte. I am strong and healthy. So long as there is breath in my body he shall lack for nothing, no, not even if it means that I have to work by the day. He shall want neither for the necessities nor yet for the luxuries. . . ."

"You know perfectly well that you are *not* strong. Why, even your secretarial work here (which amounts to practically nothing) is almost too much for you when added to your duties at school: though I don't want you to think that I am complaining."

It was true enough that Octavia Tronche could not stand up to long hours, and that the work of organizing charity sales, coming on top of her teaching, very soon exhausted her. My stepmother repeated that it was her duty to face that aspect of the problem, however painful she might find it to do so. When Octavia shyly suggested that they had hoped he might get some appointment on the staff of the Charity Organization, in which for years he had been doing unpaid work, Brigitte expressed surprise that she should have been guilty of such an offense against all tact and propriety. How could she dream that any such thing was possible? There are certain facts, surely, that need no explanation.

"You must be out of your senses, my poor child. Quite apart from anything else, it is not customary to use money that belongs to the poor to pay for work which can be performed by almost any priest, to say nothing of pious laymen. No, the most we shall be able to do will be to recommend Monsieur Puybaraud—so far, that is, as we can recommend *honestly* any man who has sunk so low through no fault but his own, and who, so far as I know, has no particular qualification and holds no diploma."

Whenever my stepmother had cast a fellow human creature into the depths of affliction, it then gave her pleasure to raise the victim by a spontaneous act of mercy. Since, in

26

her view, Octavia had been driven to the lowest level of despair, she was now at pains to bring her slowly back again and to give her grounds for hope. It was only later, on the evening before Prize Day, and from the lips of Monsieur Puybaraud himself, that I learned what had been decided between them.

We had been working hard all day, hanging banners and grouping the Papal and Republican flags. Monsieur Puybaraud appeared, walking across the yard, and I hastened to join him. This I always did. It was a special privilege that none of the other boys ever thought of disputing. He made me sit down on the steps of the platform, and told me that he was on the point of making a very grave decision. Madame Brigitte, "who, like all real saints, conceals much true goodness of heart beneath a forbidding exterior," realized that he needed a period of calm and solitude in which to collect his thoughts and decide what it would be best for him to do. She had had the great kindness to suggest that he should spend the vacation at Larjuzon.

"At Larjuzon!" I exclaimed in amazement. There are places into which certain persons do not fit. I found it impossible to think of one of my schoolmasters in the country surroundings which were the background of my summer holidays.

The official explanation of his presence at Larjuzon would be that he was there to coach me in Latin.

I tried to imagine what Monsieur Puybaraud would look like in his frock-coat and high-hat on a blazing summer's day walking the garden paths at Larjuzon. I asked him whether he would wear the same clothes that he always did. He told me that he would have to invest in a country outfit, and that he might therefore not arrive for a few days.

Monsieur Rausch had moved from his usual position and

now, in his shirtsleeves, perched on a ladder and armed with a hammer, he was expending his natural ferocity on a nail. The boys were exchanging addresses. The school orchestra was busy in the Hall rehearsing the opening bars of *Travels in China*. Jean de Mirbel, leaning as usual against the wall, though punishments were over for the term, even for him, had his eyes fixed on the ground. His hands were in his trousers pockets, and he wore his cap untidily (his appearance did no credit to the school) on the side of his head. The slight down on his cheeks made him look much older than the rest of us (he was two years behind in his school work). It was probably his age even more than his bad behavior that cut him off from his companions. He lived alone in a stormy world, with no one to give him a helping hand, the victim of some mysterious fate which seemed to hang over his future. What it might be he did not know, and there was no one whom he could take into his confidence.

# 3

THE hired victoria from Langon stopped in front of the presbytery garden. The Colonel was the first to get out. The luncheon which he had just devoured had had the effect of heightening to an unusual degree the mottled purple of his face, so that the scar looked white by comparison. His cap was tilted slightly over his left ear. The short fawn top-coat, reaching only to his thighs, had a faded red rosette on its lapel. His skinny legs, clad in very tight trousers, were like those of a cock. He wore white spats.

Jean, encumbered with a suitcase and a haversack, followed him into the garden, where it was almost impossible to tread without stepping on serried rows of vegetables. The presbytery was surrounded—jostled is the better word—on all sides by potatoes, beans, tomatoes, and green-stuff of every description. Currant bushes and peach trees lined the narrow path that led to a low doorway surmounted by a St. John's cross made from the pith of an elder tree.

Neither the nephew nor the uncle had the slightest idea that from behind a dusty window on the ground floor somebody was watching them. As soon as the abbé Calou heard the sound of the knocker he opened the front door. He was a head taller than the Colonel. He wore over his soutane a blue gardening smock. He had not shaved for several days and the stubble on his face reached as high as his cheekbones. His forehead was low, and his wide blue eyes gave him the look of a child. He had a cleft tip to his nose and strong, healthy teeth. But the only thing that Jean de Mirbel noticed on the occasion of this first meeting was that the priest's huge hands, with their square-tipped fingers, were covered with hair.

"I've brought you your young boarder. Can't say he's a present most people would like to have. . . . Take your hat off to the Curé! . . . Come on, quicker than that! I don't want to have to tell you twice. . . . True to type, you see, from the word go!"

Jean, his beret in his hand, bowed his head without so much as uttering a word.

"A reg'lar young hooligan! I'm not sorry to have you see him in his true colors—gives you an idea of the sort of ill-conditioned cub you've got on your hands. . . . Won't get a how-d'ye-do out of him without a flogging!"

"We've plenty of time to get to know one another," replied the Curé.

29

There was something cold and impersonal about his tone. Without another word he led them upstairs to the boy's room on the second floor. It was a whitewashed attic, with the bare minimum of furniture, but very clean. The window looked on to the church and the graveyard, with, beyond it, a valley through which, behind a screen of pine trees, ran the Ciron, a minor tributary of the Garonne. The fresh green of willows marked its course.

"I sleep and work just below. There is nothing but these floor-boards between us. I shall almost be able to hear him breathing."

The Papal Zouave expressed his complete approval of the arrangements. The boy, he said, was up to all sorts of tricks. "Doesn't do to let him out of your sight for a single moment, day or night."

They went downstairs again to the large apartment on the ground floor which the Curé dignified with the name of drawing-room. It was furnished with a small table and four armchairs. The lime, working out of the walls, had eaten away most of the paper. The Colonel whispered to their host:

"I'd like a word with you in private. Run along, you, and stay in the garden till I tell you to come back—now, then, quick march!"

At this point the Curé interrupted quietly: "If you don't mind, Colonel, I would rather he remained here and heard our conversation. It is part of my system that he should do so. You must have complete confidence in me. I consider it important that the young man should know precisely what it is that you complain of in his behavior, and what it is that we have to correct."

"I warn you that such a step may have serious consequences. You don't know him. I should feel freer. . . ."

The Colonel was displeased, but the Curé would listen to no objection. Jean, therefore, remained standing in the middle of the drawing-room floor, his eyes fixed upon his uncle.

"Don't quite know how to tell you what I want to say. Young hooligan's about the length and breadth of it. Incorrigible, no other word for him—in-cor-ri-gi-ble," he repeated in an acid tone.

It was perfectly true that he could find no other word. Like many people who regard themselves as being above the common herd, he had a very limited vocabulary which he enriched with pantomime, cliché, intonation, and gesture.

"Rather be killed than do what he's told. Usually gives in in the long run, however . . . gets sick of being flogged. . . . No fool, though . . . got abilities. . . . Trouble is, won't do as he's told . . . won't learn his lessons."

"What does he like doing? I mean, what are his special tastes?"

"Like doing?" The Colonel seemed to be taken aback. "Well, what *do* you like doing? Nothing, eh? I know all about that. But what else?—come on, answer, now. . . . You see, not a word—just like him. Answer me, boy, or I'll box your ears!"

The Curé laid his hand on the arm raised to strike. "Let him be: I'll find out soon enough what his tastes are."

"And he'll find out soon enough what your system is . . . nothing very mysterious about it, I don't mind betting"— and he gave the Curé a wink. "Only two ways of getting the better of a vicious horse—spur and whip. At least, *I* don't know any others. . . . And when I say vicious, I know what I'm talking about. . . . There are one or two things I'd have liked to tell you in private. . . ."

Jean de Mirbel's face had become scarlet. So low did he

31

hang his head that the Curé could see nothing but his hair.

"Need I add that I speak as his guardian and in the name of the Comtesse de Mirbel, the young scoundrel's mother? You are at liberty to use any means you may think proper, provided you break him in, *any*—you understand me—short of injuring his health."

"I quite understand," replied the Curé, his eyes still fixed upon the shamefaced object before him.

"To go back to what you were saying about his tastes. He likes reading—and not unnaturally his choice in books is pretty low. Young though he is, he knows a thing or two. Don't think I need say more about that. . . . And he's not always as dumb as he is now—can argue the hind legs off a donkey when he likes. D'you know what he was brazen enough to maintain last Easter to Monsieur Talazac, our Curé at home?—that not only oughtn't Combes to be blamed if he acted sincerely in kicking the Religious Orders out of France, but that he had acquired merit in the eyes of God by doing so!"

"Did he really argue that?" asked the Curé with a show of interest.

"Should damn well think he did. . . . Fine state of affairs, eh? And nothing would budge him—not Monsieur Talazac's reasoning, not the shocked looks of the ladies, nor yet the thrashing I gave him!"

"So you actually argued like that?" repeated the Curé. And he fixed a thoughtful gaze upon the little fox trapped there in his drawing-room, who, with his hair bristling, seemed to be hunting for a way of escape.

"If you have some private recipe for getting brains to work as they should, the family will be eternally grateful. You see, our name, our fortune, and the future of our line are all dependent on this young devil. He says he'd rather be seen

32

dead than take the St.-Cyr entrance examination, or volunteer for service with the colors, as the Mirbels have always done. Anyhow, he's so behind in his work that it's too late now for him to start thinking about the professional Army. He has the cynical effrontery to say that he'll do nothing, that he doesn't want to do anything, not even to look after his estates. You see, not a word of denial from him!—just a grin. You, there, stop grinning, or I'll let you feel the weight of my hand!"

Jean had retreated towards the wall. His lips were parted in a smile that showed his side-teeth which, though white and pointed, were irregular. He put up his arm to protect himself—the familiar gesture of a boy who knows what it is to be frequently beaten.

"Please don't get worked up, Colonel. From now on this lad is my concern. You can leave him here with an easy conscience. I will send regular reports on his progress to you and the Countess, and he shall write home himself."

"Not if I know it!" exclaimed Jean. They were the first words that he had uttered.

"Till our next meeting, then, young feller-me-lad. I am leaving you in good hands"—he shook the Curé's enormous fist—"in good, strong hands. I am told that they have done wonders in other cases."

He burst into one of his surprisingly shrill guffaws of laughter.

The Curé went with him as far as the carriage. "And no coddling, mind," was the Colonel's final injunction. He handed the priest an envelope containing the first installment of fees. "You're not dealing with a young girl. He's got a hide like a rhinoceros. You needn't be afraid of treating him rough. I'll back you up. Whatever happens, just ignore anything that my sister-in-law may write. I'm captain of this ship, and it's for me to decide what's to be done."

The Curé went back into the drawing-room. Jean had not moved from where he had been standing. He started back as the priest approached, and once again his arm went up as though to ward off an expected blow.

"Come and help me lay the table," said the Curé.

"I'm not your servant!"

"In this house everyone is his own servant . . . except in the matter of cooking. Maria looks after that, but she is seventy-one and suffers from rheumatism. When I said lay the table, I meant for your tea. I never take it myself. Your friend Louis Pian and his sister are bicycling over to see you. They'll be here any moment now."

He opened the dining-room door.

"There's a fruit tart and some plums in the sideboard, and an opened bottle of orange syrup. If you want some water, you'll find a jug in the scullery. See you again this evening, my boy. . . . One thing more. My study, as you know, is just under your room. There are plenty of books, though probably not the kind you like. Still, if you look carefully, you may come on something. . . . You can root about there to your heart's content. You won't disturb me."

Jean listened to the Curé's heavy footsteps on the wooden stairs. Then he heard the sound of a chair scraping on the floor above his head. There followed an interval of complete silence broken only by the noise of grasshoppers, the cluck of fowls, and the buzzing of flies.

"If he thinks he's going to get round me like that! . . ."

Nevertheless, he pushed open the dining-room door and sniffed the odor of fruit tart. The room was better furnished than the rest of the house. It contained an old-fashioned

34

clock, a long Louis-Philippe sideboard, a table of waxed cherry-wood, and several wicker chairs. It felt cool and the air was filled with the faint scent of fruit. Beyond the French windows there was a view on to the low roofs of outhouses and, beyond them, to a sloping field in which the hay stood ready stacked.

Someone may ask: "But how do you know so much about events of which you were not a witness? What right have you to reproduce conversations which you cannot have heard?" Well, if the truth must be told, I have outlived most of my characters, several of whom played an important part in my life. Besides, I am the sort of man who keeps old papers, and I have at my disposition not only a private diary (Monsieur Puybaraud's), but various notes made by Monsieur Calou which Mirbel found after the priest's death. At this very moment, for instance, I have before me the very letter which the abbé was reading—not for the first time— while Jean, alone in the dining-room, was wandering round the table and yielding to the temptation to take an occasional bite at a plum . . . and while I and my sister Michèle were bicycling to see him along the white and dusty roads which, in those days, were still innocent of tar. (At Vallandraut we had seen the Comte de Mirbel driving home in the victoria, his cap perched over one ear, his thin legs crossed. Michèle had drawn my attention to his scar, and to the faded red rosette on the lapel of his fawn top-coat.)

I don't deny that I have exercised my right to arrange my material, to orchestrate the reality which it records—that cross-section of existence which will live for as long as I live, with memory unimpaired, and upon which the passing years have had no effect. I may have given literary form to the talk that went on, but at least I am guiltless of changing so much as a syllable of that letter from the Comtesse de Mirbel

35

which the abbé Calou had received the day before Jean's arrival. It was signed, in a spidery hand, "La Mirandieuze-Mirbel" and was written in blue ink. It ran as follows:

*I am venturing to write to you direct because I understand from Madame Baillaud that your methods of educating the young are very different from those attributed to you by my brother-in-law, the Comte Adhémar de Mirbel. I thank God that it did not occur to him to pay the Baillauds a visit, and that he still believes in the reputation you have gained for taming difficult boys and, as he puts it, of using an iron hand with them. Unlike him, I did not stand upon ceremony. It is not easy for me to be on calling terms with the family of a retired druggist whose forebears were my forebears' servants. Nevertheless, I did not hesitate to get into touch with them, and any effort it may have cost me has been amply rewarded by the knowledge I have gained of the kind of man I am dealing with, and by the certainty I now possess that I can have complete confidence in you.*

*It is essential that I should tell you certain things which will help you to get a clear picture of my unfortunate son. In the first place, you should know that his love for me is very much more violent than that which a boy of his age usually feels for his mother. Jean is convinced that I do not return his affection. He believes that I judge him in the light of his uncle's attitude. To be perfectly frank, he has some reason for so thinking, since it must look as though I were abandoning him without a struggle and handing him over to the tender mercies of a butcher! I trust that you will forgive my choice of phrase. When you have seen the Count you will understand what I mean.*

*And at this point, I think, I must make a rather painful confession. I do so with the greater readiness because I*

36

realize that I am addressing a priest—a man trained in the duty of forgiveness. I am powerless where my brother-in-law is concerned, partly because by my husband's will he was given complete charge of my son, but chiefly because he has a hold over me. My husband, during his last illness, put into Adhémar's hands certain documents which are terribly damaging to me in more ways than one. I will not go so far as to say that I was ever a "guilty" wife. In whatever I have done my conscience has been clear. I have but exercised my rights as a woman. Imprudent, incapable of deceit or calculation, I may have been. It would have been easy for me to deceive my husband, and it is only fair to myself to say that I should have had every excuse for doing so. What I suffered as a young woman—the bullying and incarceration to which I was subjected as a result of my husband's jealousy, the secret punishments and acts of vengeance that were wreaked upon me with impunity in the solitude of our Armagnac château—would make a novel in themselves. Some day I may write it. For I can write. In a sense writing has been my undoing. Adhémar has in his possession a number of unfortunate letters sent to me by a certain person, together with my replies. I was a fool not to have destroyed them, for, urged on by the demon of literary composition, I expressed on paper, and in extremely passionate terms, sentiments which, in the eyes of the world, a woman may be forgiven for yielding to, though never for putting into words.

That is my secret. Though I no longer believe in the mysteries of religion, I still trust in the virtue and discretion of its ministers. It is necessary that you should know all this. Adhémar has complete power over Jean only because my honor has been betrayed into his hands. If I so much as stumble on the road in which he has set my feet, I am lost.

37

*My saying this will show you what manner of man he is.*
*But he fears that his hold over me is insufficient. He would*
*like me to be his wife. My very considerable fortune is an*
*added temptation, but it is only fair to say that it was my*
*husband's dying wish that he should marry me. It was one*
*of his favorite maxims that a woman can be tamed only in*
*marriage. It never occurred to either of them that a Mirbel*
*who was also, on her mother's side, a La Mirandieuze could*
*ever so much as dream of divorce. Adhémar exercises over*
*me a sort of indirect blackmail. He hints that in the event*
*of my consenting to become his wife, he would give his per-*
*mission for Jean to be brought up at home, here, at La*
*Devize. I gather that if such a course were taken, I should*
*have the deciding vote in all matters affecting his education,*
*and be free to spend part of each year with my parents.*
*Madame de La Mirandieuze, as you probably know, has*
*influential connections, nor have I abandoned the idea that*
*I might even now be able to take a staggering revenge for*
*everything I have suffered through the medium of a literary*
*success.*

*What am I to do? I have not given my brother-in-law a*
*definite "no": I am playing for time. Adhémar is well over*
*sixty and gets very red after meals. The irregularities of his*
*present way of life—over which I am generous enough to*
*draw a veil—would be sufficient to encourage in me certain*
*definite anticipations, were it not for the fact that I am not*
*that sort of woman. I may have been foolish, but I am in-*
*capable of baseness. I have told you all this because I thought*
*it necessary to do so. I venture to hope that you will judge*
*me, not by those narrow standards which I know are abhor-*
*rent to you, but by the touchstone of an enlightened and*
*humane religion, and that you will not withhold from me*

*the forgiveness which you alone can confer. It is my dear wish that you should prevail upon Adhémar to allow me to pay a visit to Jean while he is at Baluzac. If you write to him that in your opinion it would be good for the boy, he will not refuse. Tell him that you can let me have a room in your house. Not that I intend to impose myself upon you. Rather than cause you any inconvenience, I will sleep at the inn at Vallandraut. I have a mother's heart, and it waits impatiently for your reply. I beg you to believe that I am already deeply grateful to the benefactor of an only and much-loved child.*

The Curé took a red pencil and underlined the words—*I will sleep at the inn at Vallandraut.* Those marks of red crayon, scarcely faded by time, lie before me as I write. . . . Did the Curé, even then, realize that those words formed the very heart and kernel of the letter?—that all the rest of it was merely an elaborate preliminary? I thought so once, but, truth to tell, I very much doubt whether he could have had so prophetic an insight. I am inclined to believe that the words were underlined later, after the events had occurred which gave them such significance. But he must have realized at once that nothing would ever have induced Adhémar de Mirbel to use against his sister-in-law a document which would inevitably have brought disgrace upon his family. Nor was it very probable that the Colonel, nearly seventy, and the possessor of a handsome fortune of his own, should be playing with the idea of marrying the Countess.

Monsieur Calou took from a drawer a folder on which were written the two words—"False Women." In this he placed the letter, put it back, and closed the drawer. He listened for a while to our voices in the room below, to our

39

laughter, to the clink of plates. He stood there motionless, his elbows resting on the top of the desk, his face hidden in his enormous hands.

4

"KIDS' stuff," said Jean, emptying his glass of orange syrup. "I want something stronger than that."

He started rummaging in the sideboard. I felt pretty sure that it was just swagger meant to impress us, but I was shocked for all that. Might it be true, after all, that Mirbel really was the kind of boy with whom nothing could be done? He brought out several half-empty bottles, uncorked them, and sniffed their contents.

"Probably black-currant or angelica cordial or nut wine—old maid's tipple. . . . But the Curé's not the man to drink that sort of muck. . . . Ah, this is more. like it! Here's what he fills himself up on!" he exclaimed suddenly, brandishing an already opened bottle of Armagnac—"1860, too" (he made a clucking noise with his tongue), "the year Uncle Adhémar got his wound at Castelfidardo."

Michèle protested. . . . Surely he wasn't going to drink Armagnac in the afternoon?—you drink it with dessert.

"But when the dessert comes in the Curé will be here."

"Jean, you *can't* do that!"

"Can't I!—and no liqueur glass for me, either!"

I found it difficult to decide just how much was mere play-acting. This noisy boaster was so different from the sullen schoolboy who was always in trouble with the authorities. I did not realize at once that his foolhardy mood was the result of having Michèle as an audience, for he hardly addressed a word directly to her, and answered her when she spoke in monosyllables only. He scarcely seemed to be aware of her presence.

"It's too much, Jean: you'll make yourself ill!"

"And at one gulp, too: just you watch!"

He tilted back his head, but choked and started to cough. Michèle slapped his back. The room was filled with the smell of spirits.

"Monsieur Calou will notice," said I.

"We'll fill up the bottle with water: he'll just think the stuff has gone flat."

"But the smell. Jean. You stink of it, and so does the whole house."

We heard the scraping sound of a chair being pushed back, and then the abbé Calou's heavy tread upon the stairs. As soon as he entered the room he sniffed and looked sharply at us.

"So the young rascals have discovered my Armagnac, have they?" he said in high good-humor. Then, turning to Jean—"You must admit it's not bad, eh?—and you ought to know. I don't mind betting there's good brandy at La Devize —the best of it comes from round there. . . . Louis, you ought to take your young friend down to the Ciron. Does he like fishing?—He does?—Well then, show him the good pools. The pike are doing a lot of damage, but I expect you'll find something."

He opened the French window which led straight out to the back of the house. We stood for a moment looking out, then started across the half-mown meadow. The storms of this wet summer had interfered with the hay harvest. We walked towards the line of willows. Darting blue dragon-flies announced the proximity of the stream even before we could see it. We trudged on across the marshy ground. It

41

was an afternoon of moist, stifling heat. The brandy must have made Jean bold, for he walked beside Michèle, and far enough behind me to be out of earshot. I led the way. I was conscious of a vague uneasiness. It was the first symptom of that mental and emotional pain which was to infect my whole existence. But I am not telling the story of my own life, and I have no intention of isolating its single thread from the woof of the various destinies with which I am concerned. Still, I can scarcely pass over in silence that consciousness of being hurt of which, as a child, I then became aware. Nothing is so common as ordinary jealousy. But the jealousy which swept over me that day as, a boy of thirteen, I walked through the sodden fields, straining my ears to catch what my friend and my sister were saying, was not of the common kind—at least, I hope not, if only for the sake of humanity in general, whose shoulders already have to bear more than enough of the curses to which flesh is heir.

I did not know then which of my emotions was mainly concerned—my love for my sister or my friendship for Jean. It was hateful to realize that she was talking to him in the low, intimate voice which, till then, she had kept for me alone. Michèle belonged to me. So far I had never shared her with anyone, and now here was Jean taking her away from me, making her laugh; Jean whom, for the last fortnight, I had loved to picture in imagination on the roads about Larjuzon; Jean, who had played a part in all my holiday plans, whom I had dreamed of having to myself. He, no less than my sister, had suddenly broken away from me. Why hadn't I realized that things would turn out like this?

*They're treating me like a kid: they're hiding from me,* I told myself. Sometimes I had to stop to let them catch up.

42

Now and again, at a twist in the path, I lost sight of them altogether and had to turn back.

"What are you two talking about?"

They looked at one another, laughing but saying nothing. Jean was chewing a piece of grass. Michèle was rather red in the face. The brim of her straw hat was so broad that she had to tilt her head back in order to see me. I pressed my question: what were they talking about? Things that couldn't possibly interest a little boy, Michèle said. Jean's lips approached her ear. This time I caught what he said. "D'you think he *knows?*" he asked.

Now, to *"know"* meant, in our language, to be informed about the facts of life, the mysteries of generation. My face flushed scarlet, and I stalked on ahead, turning over this further grievance in my mind. They were hiding from me in order to discuss forbidden things. Their guilty secret was another barrier between us.

My stepmother had given me permission to ask Jean to lunch with us next day at Larjuzon. I had looked forward to this, but now decided suddenly not to pass on the invitation. I was terrified at the thought that the day was approaching when either Michèle would take Jean from me, or Jean would take Michèle. Rather than have this happen, I would deprive myself of Jean's company. Let him stay alone at the presbytery and be bored stiff! After all, his uncle probably knew what he was doing when he put the screw on. The general view at school was that Mirbel was a dirty beast. He was allowed to stay on only because his guardian had been one of the heroes of Castelfidardo. Probably at this very moment he was telling Michèle what I called "one of his dirty stories." Michèle mustn't be allowed to see him. I would warn my stepmother. It would be far better for me to give him up, never to see him again, than to

43

experience this tightness in the throat, this feeling in the pit of the stomach, this pain, this misery for which there was no cure, since any possible cure was beyond my power to control, and lay within the will, the heart, the hidden thoughts of my friend and my sister who were now in league against me! The torments I was suffering were more acute than any words of mine could express. To be sure, here beside the Ciron, looking down on the swirling stream, leaning against the trunk of a pine tree which had grown to a great height by reason of the water that fed its roots, I did not fully realize that I could find no words for all that I was feeling. It was pride alone, I thought, that compelled me to hide my vexation. Without waiting for them to come up with me, and in the hope of putting them off my trail, I had walked quickly. I dried my tears, got back my breath, and composed my features. They were laughing, and I could hear their laughter long before they came in sight. I caught a glimpse of Michèle's straw hat above the bracken which their movement had set waving. At last I saw them. My sister asked me how Jean de Mirbel was going to get to Larjuzon next day, seeing that he had no bicycle.

"That old beast has confiscated it!" he said.

The old beast was his uncle. I answered coldly that there was nothing I could do about it.

"I was thinking of lending him mine," said Michèle. "I could ride yours this evening and take you back on the frame."

"Five miles on the frame? No, thank you. I have no intention of getting my bike smashed up. Mirbel will just have to walk from Larjuzon. If he's so keen on coming, five miles will be nothing."

"I knew he'd say that!" cried Michèle in a sudden fury.

"His wretched old bike's sacred. I knew he would raise a row!"

"Oh, no, he won't," said Jean, taking my arm, half coaxing, half bullying. "You'll let me do it, won't you, Louis?"

I shook myself free and sat down on a root. "He's sulking," said Michèle; "it'll be ages before we can get him to say yes."

But I wasn't sulking, I was suffering. I watched the water-spiders struggling against the current. Long weeds were swaying in the clear stream. Minnows were darting about near the banks. I could see their shadows on the sandy bottom. Till my dying day I shall have in my nostrils the smell of trodden mint and river plants. They symbolize for me the memory of that moment in which I said good-bye to the happy summers of my childhood, when I made acquaintance with sorrow and the torment of a boy's love. No, I was not sulking, I was wrestling with the miseries of a grown man. The others must have sat down too, some way off, for I could still hear them whispering though the bracken hid them. Suddenly I heard Jean's voice raised. I realized that he was talking loud on purpose.

"Don't worry: he'll come round all right. If he doesn't we'll take matters into our own hands. . . ."

I got up and ran over to them. "How are you going to do that, you great brute? Just you try!"

He seized my wrists. He was hurting me, but I clenched my teeth so as not to cry out.

"Are you going to lend your sister your bike, or aren't you?"

"Let me go, you're twisting my wrists!"

"Don't want to ride home on the frame, eh?"

Suddenly I was free, Michèle had attacked my tormentor. In a furious voice she shouted: "Leave my brother alone!"

45

"All right, all right, I wasn't going to hurt him!"

They glared at each other. I was conscious of a sudden sense of calm. They were quarreling, they were going to be enemies. Michèle liked me better than him, and he wasn't in love with her after all. It was because of me that they were fighting. It was lovely to feel the tightness in my chest loosen. As always happens with me, as soon as the trouble grew remote, I thought that it had vanished for good. I no longer hated them. My old affection for them both returned. Of course Michèle and I would go back on my bike. But I wasn't going to give in at once, wasn't going to deprive myself of the pleasure of seeing them walk with a space of enmity between them. Now it was Mirbel's turn to go ahead, chewing his piece of grass, while I followed some distance behind, holding my sister by the hand. So on we went, I clutching Michèle's hand and looking at Jean as he marched ahead. It was pure happiness. The grass was wet. A great storm-cloud darkened the sky above the trees, but there was no thunder. Several men and women were busy round a wagon half piled with hay.

"Really, you know, Mirbel *is* just a great brute," I said.

"Still, he's rather nice. . . ."

"Doesn't alter the fact that he's a brute. . . ."

"But we'll fix it up, won't we, so he can come over to lunch tomorrow?"

Again I felt that tightness in my throat. I asked Michèle whether she was terribly keen on having him come.

"Larjuzon's a bit queer this vacation, don't you think, with that Puybaraud of yours looking like a great white worm, and Brigitte always fussing round him?"

"Oh, Michèle!"

"If she's not careful, she will make life at Larjuzon impossible, even for Papa. Of course I'm going to lend my bicycle to Mirbel."

"Then you'll jolly well walk back!" I said with a flare of temper. Jean had turned. This sudden storm of words between Michèle and me gave him a sense of triumph. That was what came of not letting him show me who was who. *He* knew how to treat kids. . . .

We walked round the presbytery, all shouting at the same time. .

"Well, it's my bike, isn't it?" I protested.

"I call it frightfully nice of you to have asked his permission at all," said Jean to Michèle. "Just you jump on it before he can do anything. If he doesn't want to ride on the frame, well, he can do the five miles on foot, that's all!"

I got in before them and seized my bicycle. But Jean did not let me get far. He hung on to the handle-bar and stuck his foot in the wheel, so that I fell off. Monsieur Calou, who must have seen us, came hurriedly out of the house, ran towards us and picked me up. I had merely grazed my arm. He turned to Mirbel.

"Go up to my room and bring down the iodine and the package of cotton that you'll find on the washstand."

He issued this order in his usual quiet way, but his voice held a threat of thunder, and he kept his eyes fixed on Mirbel, who stood there with his great fists half clenched. Still, he obeyed at once. When he came back again the abbé proceeded to bathe my injury at the pump. Without turning to Jean he said:

"Dab it with cotton. . . . Now, put on some iodine—not too much. Stings a bit, doesn't it? What's been happening, Michèle?—tell me."

She embarked on a confused story. She said we were both

47

to blame. Mirbel had been rough, but I had gone out of my way to irritate him.

"Shake hands," said the abbé.

I took Jean's hand and he made no effort to withdraw it. Monsieur Calou then said that he would settle the matter. He wouldn't hear of letting two of us go back on the one bicycle. He said that he'd lend Jean his next day so that he could get over to Larjuzon. It could be spared for a few hours, for there was no one seriously ill among his flock. But something unexpected might turn up, so he asked Jean to be sure to be back before four. "And you two can come with him. In that way you'll be able to spend the rest of the afternoon together."

The threat of thunder had gone from his voice; there would be no storm. The wind had swept the sky clean. He asked us to water his vegetables for him, and advised us to do it barefoot so as not to get our shoes wet. As a reward, he said, we could take as many currants as we liked. Maria had finished her jam-making.

As soon as the abbé had gone back into the house, Jean said that he hadn't come there to do manual work, and wouldn't be treated like a servant. But no sooner had Michèle and I taken off our shoes and stockings than the temptation was too much for him. He got out of his sandals and took one of the watering cans that my sister was carrying. Such is the power of happiness that I remember as a time of calm, unclouded happiness that summer's day when we ran barefoot over the gravel which hurt our feet, and did all we could to splash one another as much as possible. But all the same, my pleasure was streaked with pain because it was Michèle whom Jean splashed. She had tucked her skirt up to her knees and, though pretending to be angry, gave vent to little shrill gusts of laughter which were quite unlike any

48

sound I had heard her make before. But I refused to let myself suffer. Deep within me I carried a load of dumb agony which a trifle would have served to waken, and I shouted louder than either of them to keep it from my mind. When the sun disappeared behind the pines it was time for us to think of going. Jean asked at what hour lunch would be at Larjuzon.

"Twelve, but come early," said Michèle; "we get up at eight. Come as soon as you can get the abbé's bicycle."

I protested that he mustn't be deprived of it for too long. He might be called to some sick-bed. Jean replied in his "nasty" voice that "people could die without the help of a curé." Michèle seemed shocked at this, and I noticed that there was a certain coldness in her tone when she said good-bye. But she turned round twice to give an answering signal to his waving beret. He was wearing a sailor's peajacket over a striped red-and-white jersey. His feet were bare, his trousers rolled above his knees and kept in position by an elastic.

Later, he told me about his first evening at the presbytery. For a while he had wandered round the house, not knowing what to do with himself. Baluzac could hardly be called a village. It consisted of a single inn and a drugstore kept by a man called Voyod, with whom the Curé did not wish his charge to have anything to do. In fact, the only order he had issued was that he should keep clear of the place. The abbé Calou had also spoken about the books in his study. In Jean's life books occupied a place which no one who had had to do with him suspected. On his father's side he belonged to a family which would have viewed a taste for reading in a young boy as a disquieting symptom. His guardian and his mother were convinced that he was interested only in scabrous and obscene publications, and, to tell the truth, their suspicions were not wholly without foundation.

Jean could not resist his desires. The knowledge that the house was full of books, even if they were only books for a priest's reading, that there was a library of which he had been given the free run, exercised over his mind a power no less than many worse temptations. But he stood out against it. He did not want Monsieur Calou to think that he could be won over so easily. He was cautious about putting his head into so obvious a trap. Nevertheless, he went upstairs to the first floor, taking care not to make the stairs creak.

There was a strong smell of pipe tobacco. Jean hesitated to approach the door. His pride held him back. He felt quite sure that the Curé had been listening, had caught the sound of his padding footsteps, and was waiting with as keen a sense of expectation as any fisherman watching the trout circling a waiting snare.

Monsieur Calou could contain himself no longer, but opened the door. "Anything you want, you young scamp?"

Jean shook his head.

"A book, perhaps?"

The boy entered the thick haze of smoke. He had never seen so many books. They were ranged in rows from floor to ceiling: they lay scattered over chairs and on the mantel-piece. There were books everywhere, bound in paper covers. There was a set of steps mounted on wheels for reaching the upper shelves, and a desk at which a man could read and write standing. Never had he seen so many marvels! The books must be pretty boring, of course; still, one never knew, and no book, thought Jean, could be wholly boring.

The Curé went back to his table without taking any further notice of him. Jean climbed on to the steps. How tiresome it was that he felt so sick, and had such a pain at the back of his neck. . . . The Armagnac that he had drunk out of bravado was giving him a lot of trouble, and the smell of the Curé's pipe was the last straw. Hurriedly, he returned to the floor, picked up a volume at random and read the title: *A Treatise on Concupiscence—A Letter and Some Maxims on the Theatre—Logic—A Treatise on Free Will,* by Bossuet. Was he going to be sick? Was he going to faint, here in the Curé's study? On no account must he do that! In an effort to forget his qualms, he opened the book and forced himself to read.

*The woman in Proverbs who boasted of the perfumes scattered about her bed, and of the sweet odors that regaled the visitor to her chamber; who said, "Let us take our fill of love, let us solace ourselves with love," showed by her words whither may lead those cunning scents which are prepared with an intent to ensnare the Will, and draw it to an indulgence of the senses through an employment of that which seems not directly to attack the stronghold of our modesty. . . .*

"You're very pale, my boy: almost green. Don't you feel well?"

Jean protested that it was nothing, just a little attack of sickness.

"Lie down."

The boy refused. It would pass off of itself. He felt better already. He made another effort to concentrate his thoughts on the page. . . . The abbé heard the sound of Jean's body striking the floor, though not violently, for the sufferer had kept hold of the steps. The boy felt himself lifted by two strong arms, and retched uncontrollably. The Curé, without showing the slightest sign of disgust, handed him a basin and supported his head with his great hand. Jean opened his eyes and asked to be allowed to go down to the garden. He was in despair at the thought that he had been betrayed, unexpectedly like this, into the hands of the enemy.

"I'm coming down too," said the abbé. "I want to finish reading my breviary in the church. You can join me there. It's a lovely little church, built by Bertrand de Gouth, who afterwards became Clement V. I don't suppose you know that he, was a fellow countryman of ours—born at Vallandraut, though there are some who say it was at Uzeste, where he is buried. . . . It wouldn't do to have many Popes like him."

Jean replied that he was not interested in old stones.

"Never mind, come along anyhow, and pay our Lord a little visit."

Aha!—that was the priest for you! Jean muttered that he didn't believe in all those old wives' tales.

"Really?—that's interesting." There was no hint of outrage in Monsieur Calou's tone.

"Does it surprise you?" Jean's tone was smug.

"Why should it?" said the Curé. "The really surprising thing is that a man *should* believe. . . . The really surprising thing is that what we believe should be true. The really surprising thing is that the truth should really exist, that it should have taken on flesh, that I can keep it a prisoner here beneath these old vaults that don't interest you, thanks to the strength in these great hands of mine which your uncle Adhémar admires so much. Yes, you little oddity, I can never get over feeling how absurd, how utterly mad, it is that what we believe should be precisely and literally true!"

Was the Curé laughing at him? Jean tried another fling: "Oh, well, anyhow it doesn't mean a thing to me!"

He tried to carry off his attitude with a swagger, staring

52

his adversary straight in the face. But, in spite of himself, he had to lower his eyes.

"That may be so now, my queer little scrap of humanity, but you may feel different later."

"You shan't get me!" cried the boy defiantly.

"It's not a question of my getting you. How could it be?"

"Well, who else could? There's no one else here, is there, except you and Maria?"

The Curé said nothing. He seemed to be thinking. "How do you manage at school? I don't suppose you're allowed to trifle with Confession or Communion there?"

Jean replied complacently that he had never let that bother him. They had Confession every Saturday. He just said anything that came into his head. And every Sunday they had to go to Communion. But what did it matter whether one believed or not? It didn't make the slightest difference.

He had expected an outburst, but it did not come.

"You really think so?" asked Monsieur Calou.

Jean presented an insolent face to his gaze. But he felt shamed by its gentle sadness.

"Every Saturday and every Sunday, for Heaven knows how long . . . two years at least, O Lord!"

Monsieur Calou looked at the handsome face, at the unsullied brow beneath the mop of dark hair in which one lighter lock shone like a flame. He could say no more than: "Lie down a little before dinner, my boy." Then he hurried off towards the church without looking back. His bent shoulders made him seem less than his real height.

# 5

I FIND it difficult, looking back, to distinguish the first occasion on which Mirbel lunched at Larjuzon from those that came later. All through August we were constantly together. When he didn't come to us, Michèle was forever hanging about him at Baluzac, and nothing would have induced me not to go with her, since my peace of mind would have been utterly destroyed had I known that they were together away from me. My whole life centered round the need I felt to be always the third party in their meetings.

Nor, at first, was it very difficult for me to be with them. The bad days, when they managed to give me the slip, were far fewer than those on which Michèle railed against us two boys and had to protect herself against the tricks which we invented at the expense of my "kid sister." There was never entire harmony among us. Either she or I had to be the victim. I was never happy unless I was defending Michèle against Jean and his often ill-natured teasing. But almost always, just when I thought that they had quarreled for good and all, they would quite suddenly make it up. It was precisely when I felt myself most safe from any possible hostile coalition of my sister and my friend that inexplicable scenes would occur which had the effect of putting me to the torture—such as the occasion on which we sent her off into a temper by alluding to "the story of the cakes" which, as Mirbel said, had united him and me till "death should us part."

"What story of what cakes?" asked my sister.

We winked at one another, put our fingers to our lips, and swore our most solemn oath that never, no, never, would we let her into the secret. We began to run round her in circles, pulling her hair, snapping our fingers, and chanting: "Cowardy, Cowardy Custard! . . ." I was careful to keep my distance, but Jean jumped about like a dancing dervish, touching her and then springing back out of reach. . . . Suddenly Michèle leaped at him, her fingers clawed, and made a dash at his face. He did not attempt to defend himself, but stumbled and measured his length on the grass. When he got up we saw that his cheek was bleeding from a scratch. We stood there appalled. Michèle looked quite pale.

"Oh, Jean, wipe your face! I haven't got a hanky."

But he did nothing to stanch the blood. I thought he was going to rush at her, but instead, he stood there grinning. It was so unlike him to act that way that it seemed almost as though he had some hold over her, and she over him, as though he didn't mind her hurting him. Children though they were, they had become, unconsciously, free of that world in which blows mean the same thing as kisses, and insults may express more of love than the tenderest endearments. A sort of curtain seemed to drop between us. They passed from my vision, leaving me, an outsider, on the wrong side of the curtain—a small boy lost in a universe peopled by that inconsequent race of monsters whom we knew as "the grown-ups."

If Mirbel showed signs of becoming less wild, the credit was due entirely to my sister and not to Monsieur Calou (at any rate, until the end of August, when an event occurred which I shall describe in due course). True, the Curé had won a signal victory over his charge on the very day of his arrival, but, during the weeks that followed, he made no noticeable progress in his campaign.

*I have a cat here with me in the house* [noted Monsieur Calou in his diary that summer]: *a cat that slinks in and out of the library without so much as moving a chair, sniffs round the books, pads into the dining-room, settles itself at the table, and gobbles its soup. It never shows fight, works an hour each day without complaining, and, on Sunday, goes to Mass. I showed my hand too soon. The boy hates my gentleness . . . that "professional gentleness of yours"—as the young spark from Bordeaux put it one day in accents of repulsion. I don't want there to be anything in my looks or speech to put him off. The great thing is not to sicken him by the slightest hint of unctuousness. How harsh the unction of Christ is! To cleave their hearts, one must be as hard as a diamond! Jean would have felt far less dislike for me if I had been rough and stern. He expected that, and was ready armed against it.*

It may be that the abbé Calou had stumbled on Jean's secret, but of mine he had no suspicion. Could anyone really have understood it and explained me to myself? No man can bear a child's cross. It is something beyond the comprehension of the fully grown.

Monsieur Puybaraud watched over my studies and the good of my soul with an ardent singleness of mind for which I was not at all grateful. That he loved me there could be no doubt, and the accepted view at home was that I adored him. To this game of make-believe I willingly lent myself. "Louis swears by Monsieur Puybaraud: he takes no notice of anyone else. . . ." As a matter of fact, I shouldn't have cared greatly if I had been told that I was never going to see him again. The degree of indifference shown by children to grown-ups, even to those to whom they seem to be most attached, is seldom realized. Except for Jean and Michèle and, in quite a different way, for my father and my dead mother, no living creature was altogether real to me. Those who could be collectively described as "the others" were, for me, a mere anonymous crowd. They served to fill the stage. They stood about the center of my heart when it leaped with happiness or wallowed in despair according to my relations of the moment with Jean and Mirbel, but its condition meant nothing to them.

When I walked in the park with Monsieur Puybaraud, and he talked to me in a moral or a learned strain, I answered him in proper wise, responding to his advances with that rather knowing gentleness which served so well to win me the affection of others whenever I took the trouble to employ it. The poor man had no idea that my heart was suffering a thousand miles away, that the words I uttered had no connection with my thoughts or real feelings, that effortlessly and without the faintest sense of shame I hid my true self from him, substituting for it the mere image of the solemn and attentive child on whom he lavished the treasures of his kindly spirit.

I was in the advantageous position of knowing all about his private life. Not that it really interested me. That summer was Monsieur Puybaraud's molting season. He was halfway back to the world. He wore a panama instead of his top-hat, a short jacket in place of his frock-coat. But he was loyal to his black trousers and his starched shirts, no matter how stiflingly hot the day might be. His attitude to me was that of a Christian schoolmaster, though he was led to confess more intimate matters than are usually thought fitting for young ears. Today, after such a long interval of time, when Monsieur Puybaraud has long been dust, I can read his diary and find excitement in the struggle he was waging, in the drama of which I was then the disinterested spectator, because it touches on problems with which I become the more obsessed the older I grow.

During the first week of Monsieur Puybaraud's stay, Brigitte Pian had plenty to occupy her. The days were too short for her happy task of helping a man to straighten the tangled skein of his private problems. She felt that she was not wasting her life, that she was not running counter to her true vocation, which was to make clear to others what God had planned for them from the beginning of time. Here, at her very door, was an unrivaled opportunity for her to show her mettle, though she fully realized the dangers involved. She was, perhaps, too satisfied in the part she felt called upon to play. Not that she was guilty, even in the smallest degree, of self-indulgence: still, at first she did seem to be deriving too much satisfaction from Monsieur Puybaraud's way of listening to her as to an oracle. But, alas, his meekness was superficial only. Very soon it was borne in on Brigitte Pian that she was dealing with a less submissive sheep than she had at first supposed. "He is a wandering soul," she told herself in the course of the second week. She even went so far as to accuse him of deliberately setting his face against the operations of Grace—by which she meant her own advice.

It was Brigitte Pian's way to drive reluctant souls on to the mountain tops (that was how she phrased it), and she made it her duty to open Monsieur Puybaraud's eyes to that especial trick of the Devil which takes the form of enlisting against a Christian sinner the very sense he has of his own humility. My master was convinced that previously he had

had too high an idea of his own strength when he had felt himself called upon to eschew the normal destiny of mankind. He felt that it was his duty, while there might yet be time, to find his way back to the beaten track marked out by those who had gone before him and, like them, to take to himself a wife, have children, and watch over them as a bird watches over its brood. But Brigitte Pian knew well that it is sometimes necessary to tear from human souls that mask of spurious humility behind which they take refuge. She declared, as though she had been the very mouthpiece of God, that Monsieur Puybaraud had been taken from his school work only because, from all eternity, he had been destined for the life of the cloister. She assured him that he had to face one problem and one alone—at what door should he knock? to what Order should he make his submission?

Not only, however, did Madame Brigitte fail to make progress in her struggle with Monsieur Puybaraud, although she was fighting him on ground of her own choosing; she was forced to admit that she was at grips with an influence considerably stronger than any that she could bring to bear —and what an influence! for what was defeating her was the persuasive power exercised by Octavia Tronche, who inspired in my stepmother a feeling which the world would have described as contempt. But she knew that we should feel contempt for no human creature, and that even the soul of Octavia Tronche had value in the sight of God.

It was a matter for astonishment to my stepmother that Octavia at a distance had a greater hold over Monsieur Puybaraud than when, back in the city, she had been seeing him every day. The reason for this was that though separated from my master she wrote to him daily. Madame Brigitte devoured the outside of these letters with her eyes. Monsieur Puybaraud read them in her presence at breakfast-time, bringing to the task a degree of concentration that had to be seen to be believed. The truth was that his former occasional dissatisfaction with Octavia's rather homely appearance (responsive though he always was to the spiritual charm that shone out from her) yielded wholly a feeling of admiration and tender respect during this time of her absence, when her contact with him was confined to the pages that she wrote each night before going to bed.

Their correspondence—which I found among Monsieur Puybaraud's effects—could not possibly be published here, not because it does not deserve publication, but because I doubt whether there are many readers capable of appreciating the charm of true humility, which takes no heed of itself and seems completely ignorant of its effect on others. I cannot, however, pass it by in silence, seeing that Octavia's victory over my stepmother had tragic repercussions on more than one person.

Although Octavia thought highly of Madame Brigitte, she was encouraged by distance to resist her influence, and to warn her lover against indulging in an excessive distrust of the dictates of his own conscience. "No matter how superior in virtue another person may be," she wrote, "her views cannot supersede your own vision of the Divine Will, since that is the fruit of complete surrender to God. . . . My own opinion is that we should most certainly pay attention to the advice of others, but that we should never let it divert our attention from the ever watchful respect which we owe to our own inner voice. Don't you agree, my dear, that it is in the secrecy of our own hearts that we most truly hear the bidding of God? I find it impossible to believe that what I feel for you so strongly can be contrary to His will. Light, for me, is where you are. If I struggle against the instinct which leads me to you, I see nothing but darkness. I am the more convinced that what I say is true, because I know that if your temporal or spiritual welfare depended upon my giving you up, I *could* give you up, not, indeed, without pain and suffering, but certainly without a struggle. Selfish though I am (and God alone knows how selfish that is!), I love you too much to consider my own feelings. So wholly do I love you, that I would not, no, not for a single moment, fight against the influences to which you are exposed at Larjuzon, if I were sure that they are making for your happiness, if I did not feel that too much subtle reasoning may be brought to bear upon what is really a perfectly simple and very ordinary situation. Perhaps a poor creature like me has no right to judge, but I *do* think that there is one point in particular about which Madame Brigitte is wrong. She does not realize, as you and I do, that all flesh, imperfect and corrupt though It may be, is holy; that, in spite of original sin, the birth of a child is still God's loveliest mystery. I have heard her say things on this subject which I may perhaps have misunderstood. What I love most in you, my darling, is that fondness for children which God has implanted in your heart, for those little children like whom we must become if we are to gain the Kingdom of Heaven. We cannot become like them, but at least we can bring them into the world, and that is no small thing. No doubt there are higher vocations . . . still, I do not believe that in becoming your wife I shall be resisting Christ's summons to His flock, His insistence that we should leave all and follow Him. For in you, and through you, beloved, in and through the children who may be born to us, I submit to that Will which it is our chief delight to honor. . . . The mere thought that this is so sets me trembling with happiness. . . ."

Monsieur Puybaraud did not show these letters to me, and

I could judge of my stepmother's defeat only by the increasing gloom of her demeanor, especially at mealtimes, the atmosphere of which soon became almost intolerable.

I had a feeling that his affairs were going badly, that his relations with Madame Brigitte were becoming embittered, but I was far too unhappy myself to pay much attention to what was going on. Ever since Michèle had scratched Jean's cheek, the friendship between them had grown closer and closer. Gone were the happy times when my friend, a child once more, had plotted with me to tease my "kid sister." Whenever Jean came to the house they thought of one thing only—how to be alone together. They were as clever in their efforts to avoid me as I was in trying not to let them out of my sight. I was ashamed of my persistence: it became hateful to me. Yet I dogged their footsteps, pretending not to notice the glances of irritated impatience that passed between them.

If my stepmother called me, if Monsieur Puybaraud had a corrected exercise to give back, if I had to be absent for no matter how short a time, I knew that when I got back Michèle and Jean would have vanished. In the garden path where but a moment earlier Michèle's laughter had echoed, or my friend's loud and breaking voice as he called to the dog, I now heard nothing but the sighing of wind in the branches left dripping by the recent storm. I cried their names, "Michèle! Jean!—where are you?" and then fell silent, knowing full well that even if they had heard, the only effect of my appeal would be to make them lower their voices still further, walk on tiptoe, and hide their tracks.

I had no clear idea of the nature of the attraction that held them in thrall. My senses were not yet awakened: I had felt nothing of the kind myself. What causes jealousy is a vision of the delight that a beloved person gives to, and

62

receives from, another. I do not think that I was capable then of any such emotion. But their happiness, conditioned as it was in part by my absence, hurt me to such an extent that I could have cried aloud.

I remember the day when Monsieur Puybaraud suddenly decided to leave us. At luncheon scarcely anybody said a word except Monsieur Calou, who had come over to Larjuzon with Jean. Monsieur Puybaraud answered his questions, but Madame Brigitte never opened her lips. Her great face was gloomy enough to have frightened me. Opposite her, my father sat huddled over his plate, chewing his food and paying not the slightest attention to anybody. Jean and Michèle, with the whole length of the table between them, exchanged wordless speeches with their eyes. I, sitting next to Monsieur Puybaraud, pretended to be absorbed in his remarks. But I was aware of nothing but that silent interchange between my sister and my friend, was conscious of nothing but the happy peace of mind that I knew Michèle was feeling just because Jean was there. For her, I was merely part of the rest of the world, which meant that I didn't really exist at all. I was a part of nothingness.

Because of the storm we could not drink our coffee under the trees. My stepmother apologized for her silence. She had a headache, she said, and asked me to fetch an antipyrine tablet from her room. The two minutes during which I was away sufficed for Jean and Michèle to make their escape in spite of the bad weather. I wanted to follow them, but the rain had grown heavier, and my stepmother forbade me. "If Michèle wants to get wet, that is her affair. You will stay indoors."

Could it be that she had noticed nothing? Michèle's behavior ought to have filled her with horror. But she had eyes for no one but Monsieur Puybaraud. Her headache, which was genuine enough, forced her to go to her room. No matter what the company, my father would never give up his siesta. So I was left alone in the billiard-room, watching the drenched countryside through the French windows. In the drawing-room Monsieur Puybaraud and the abbé Calou were talking. At first they kept their voices low, but after a while I could hear every word of their conversation. Monsieur Puybaraud was complaining of the tactless tyranny to which he was being exposed. Monsieur Calou, I gathered, was laughing at him for being so timid, and was advising him to slip his moorings without any further delay.

"They must be hiding," I told myself, "in the abandoned farm." I conjured up a picture of Michèle and Jean in the kitchen where only an occasional shepherd ever lit a fire, and where the walls were scribbled over with pictures and words that made Jean laugh, but which I did not understand. They were kissing. They were delighting in one another. Michèle was never gentle with me. Even when she was kind there was a rough quality in her kindness. Jean, even when he was in a good mood, always spoke to me as though he were my master. A hulking great brute, but not to Michèle. He would say to her, "Your hands are cold," and hold them in his for a long while. He was never kind to me. I have always wanted people to be kind. . . .

Looking out on to the rainy fields, I suffered.

Monsieur Calou wanted to take advantage of a break in the clouds to go back to Baluzac. He asked me to call Jean. I rang the great bell, but in vain. There was no sign of Jean. The abbé Calou decided at last that his charge was old enough to get home alone. He rode off on his bicycle after saying good-bye to Madame Brigitte. Her headache had gone, and she took a stroll in the avenue with Monsieur

Puybaraud. Standing on the steps, I could see them pacing up and down. My master was doing all the talking. There were only the briefest of interchanges between them, and, although I could hear no high words, something told me that all was not well. Monsieur Puybaraud, on his way back into the house, stroked my hair. He was very pale.

"I am going away tomorrow morning, Louis. I must see to my packing."

I scarcely heard him. Where were Michèle and Jean? They had not come back to tea. I could remember no previous occasion on which they had been alone together for so long. It was not annoyance that I most felt now, but anger, a desire to hurt them. I became a prey to all the nastiest instincts that flourish in us at that period of life when the man we are to be is already fully formed and fully dowered with his individual portion of inclinations and passions.

The rain had left off. I walked quickly beneath the dripping trees. Now and again a raindrop splashed on my cheek or ran down my neck. It was a sunless summer and the grasshoppers were silent. If only there had been some other boy or girl at Larjuzon with whom I could have played on my own . . . But no face, no name came to my mind. At a turn in the path I saw my stepmother walking toward me. She saw me standing there, my hand pressed to my forehead. I could not restrain my tears, and for a while could make no answer to her questions.

"They're running away from me," I managed at last to stammer.

She thought that I was referring to some childish game. "Pretend not to notice. Then they'll have to be 'out.' . . ."

"No, no—that's what they want."

"What *are* you talking about?"

"Yes," I insisted, almost whispering, "to be alone."

65

She frowned. "What do you mean?" she asked. Her suspicions had been awakened, but as yet they had no definite object. She was too much preoccupied, too wholly confined within her own circle of pain. Still, the seed I dropped had fallen on good soil. Sooner or later it would put forth shoots.

"One is always punished when one attaches too much importance to other people," murmured Brigitte Pian on a note of bitterness. "I sometimes wonder, dear child, whether I don't give too much of myself when I work for the salvation of my neighbors. Oh, I know that the least among them is of infinite worth. I would give my life that one might be saved. But there are moments when I am frightened to think how much time I have wasted (at least, it *seems* wasted, but of that God alone is judge) over insignificant, nay, evil persons. It is the cross laid upon the great-hearted that they shall exhaust themselves in darkness and uncertainty on behalf of the spiritually mean and inferior. . . ."

She uttered the last word from between tightened lips. I realized that when she spoke of the spiritually inferior she meant Monsieur Puybaraud. Why was she so interested in him? Was she in love with him? If she wasn't in love with him, thought I, why did she get in such a state at the mere mention of his name? How can those we do not love affect us for either good or ill?

I caught sight of Michèle in the distance seated on one of the stone steps. Without waiting for me to ask her what she had been doing, she said that she had been for a ride on her bicycle, and that Jean had gone back to Baluzac without returning to Larjuzon. She must have come straight from her room. She had tidied her hair and washed her face and hands. She looked at me, trying to guess what I was thinking. But I pretended not to be interested. I found pleasure in feeling at the same time acutely miserable and completely master of myself.

I went upstairs early, meaning to read in bed, but this I could not do. Through the floor I could hear the rumblings of a violent dispute. Michèle told me next day that my stepmother had lost control of herself and had been very harsh to Monsieur Puybaraud. He too, finally, had lost his temper, exasperated by the fact that when he tried to explain to my stepmother why it was that he had decided to marry Octavia, she had replied, raising her eyes to Heaven, that this was the cross she had always known was reserved for her, and that she willingly accepted the sacrifice.

"But, Madame Brigitte, there is no question of your being sacrificed. This is my affair, and mine only. . . ."

But Madame Brigitte would not listen. She had been wounded, but forgave the hand that held the weapon. She always behaved like this when people told her that she had been wrong or had committed some injustice. Instead of frankly admitting her fault and sitting in sackcloth and ashes, she turned the other cheek, protesting that it was well she should be thus misunderstood and vilified. In this way she added another link of mail to the armor of perfection and merit in which she went clad from head to foot. On such occasions her interlocutor was driven to speak angry words, and this gave her a feeling of still greater excellence at the bar of her own conscience and in the sight of God.

On this particular evening, however, she had given full rein to her fury. She must have exceeded all decent limits, for next day at breakfast (which was earlier than usual, because my master was taking the eight o'clock train), she humbled herself to the extent of apologizing to him in my presence.

"Such behavior was unworthy of me," she said, not once,

but many times, in an access of humility, "and I want Louis to hear me acknowledge my fault. When I have reason to believe that a fellow human soul is straying and in danger of damnation, I can contain myself no longer. . . . But excess of zeal is no excuse for the violence of my words. He who would tame the old Adam must never sleep. I realize, in all humility, that I have a fiery nature." This she said with every sign of satisfaction. "My friend, you must forgive me."

"No, Madame Brigitte," Monsieur Puybaraud protested, "I cannot bear to see you abasing yourself in this way. I am not worthy."

But she would not listen. She wanted to revel in the grandeur of her attitude. She had paid the price asked of her, and it cost her nothing now to tread the path of humiliation to the end, since, by so doing, she forced her adversary to lay down his arms, and increased her own sense of personal merit (one link the more added to the armor of perfection).

"My conduct to you and to Octavia shall prove that I bear you no grudge. What I have said, I felt in conscience bound to say. But that is all over now, and I confide you both to God. You will have no trustier friend than me in the new life, so beset by snares, so full, I fear, of ordeals, which is opening before you."

Monsieur Puybaraud seized her hand and kissed it fervently. What would they do without Madame Brigitte? Octavia's position at the Free School, and his own in the Charity Organization, depended upon her. One word from her . . . He raised his eyes to the face of his benefactress, which suddenly emptied itself of all expression. Brigitte Pian's words became vague. She spoke of the necessity of trusting in Providence, that ever-sure protector that wrapped us in its loving care when we suffered most and felt our-

68

selves abandoned by the world. And then, since Monsieur Puybaraud insisted on mentioning the subject again, she said that she could decide nothing as yet. She had, she remarked, only one vote in the Organization, like every other member of the Committee.

"Oh, but, Madame Brigitte," he urgently replied, "no one knows better than you that if only you would take our side . . ."

But my stepmother this morning was in humble mood, and the more Monsieur Puybaraud assured her that she was all-powerful in the matter of assuring continued employment for Octavia and himself, the more she retreated, taking a delight in minimizing her influence and stressing her utter unimportance.

# 6

AFTER Monsieur Puybaraud had gone, Larjuzon knew peace for several days. My stepmother scarcely ever left her bedroom. She both wrote and received a great many letters. It had now turned hot and fine, but though the thunder had ceased to crack and crash behind the trees, it still rumbled deep down in more than one heart. That week Jean bicycled over only once. He spent the whole afternoon with me, but I got no pleasure from his companionship. That sixth sense of suffering which I have never yet found misleading warned me that he was not following his own inclinations, but was acting in conformity with some plan of action drawn up in advance by him and Michèle.

She made no effort to come with us when we set off intending to idle our time away on the bank of the stream.

Jean was kind to me that afternoon, just as kind as I had long wanted him to be. But in spite of this I had never felt so sad, the reason being that his kindness derived from the same source as my own sense of irritation—from the influence that Michèle had acquired over him. That he who but yesterday had been a misunderstood and tormented child should now be basking in happiness was for me a cause of suffering.

We talked very little. He was deep in a daydream and I was brooding over my suspicion that he had arranged to meet Michèle somewhere else. Almost every day now Michèle went off alone on her bicycle while I was working. There must be some place on the road between Baluzac and Larjuzon where they met. . . . He had come with me today merely in order to put me off the scent. I watched him whittling away at a willow branch. He said he was making a whistle. His swarthy face was radiant with good humor.

"Monsieur Calou is really pretty decent, you know. He's actually written to my uncle suggesting that Mamma should pay me a visit, and Uncle has given his consent. She's coming next week. She's going to stay at Vallandraut."

"Oh, I *am* pleased!"

And I was. It was the thought of his mother's visit, then, that had caused his happiness. Michèle had something to do with it, of course, but it wasn't only because of her.

"You've never met Mamma, have you? She's lovely"—he made an appreciative noise with his tongue. "Lots of well-known artists have wanted to paint her portrait. But you'll see for yourself. She's planning to call on your stepmother to thank her. She'll enjoy it here, though she doesn't ordinarily go in for paying visits. I've told her a lot about you and Michèle. I'm sure she'll like Michèle. Mamma loves natural people. There's only one thing I'm afraid of, and that is that Michèle will be too careful. You know what she's like when she wants to be thought a perfect young lady —the way she minces when she speaks—and it's not her style, really. I don't think her hair ought to be too neat, do you?"

I said nothing. Actually, he was talking to himself. I didn't really mean a thing to him. He looked at his watch, yawned, suddenly grasped my arm, and gave me a hug. He was overflowing with tenderness, and I had come in for a drop of it because I happened to be available. But I knew that the hug had been meant for Michèle.

That day they said good-bye to one another with a decidedly frosty handshake. But when he had mounted his bicycle they exchanged a few words in a low tone. At dinner my stepmother talked of the Comtesse de Mirbel and her coming visit. To hear her speak one would have thought that Jean's mother represented in beauty of soul and loveliness of body all that was fairest in contemporary society. Of course, she *had* given occasion for a good deal of gossip, but charity should forbid us to believe everything we hear, and certainly she, Brigitte Pian, gave no credence to the abominable stories that were going round. No one should say things like that except on the evidence of his own eyes. Besides, however great the scandal may have been, it could not be denied that, ever since her husband's death, Julia de Mirbel had lived a very retired existence at La Devize. Except for the few months that she spent in Paris with her Mirandieuze relations, she had never left it. Her general conduct had been a perfect example of quiet dignity.

From what was said it became perfectly clear that the daughter of the former Imperial Prefect attached considerable importance to the behavior of a lady whose parents would not have condescended to recognize the existence of her own. The coming visit stood, on the worldly plane, for the only piece of snobbish gratification which, in those days, was available to my stepmother. For no one could deny that she belonged to the highest circle of local society, less by reason of her family background and considerable wealth than because of the mysterious power she wielded among church-going folk, and her reputation for shining virtue. There could be no doubt that it was the name of Mirbel that had opened the doors of Larjuzon to Jean. Normally, my stepmother would have been loud in her disapproval of him, and certainly the boy had always been spoken of in our family as both headstrong and undesirable.

After dinner the moon rose, and Michèle wanted to go for a walk in the park. My father woke from his doze just long enough to repeat, word for word, the phrase that our mother had always been in the habit of using on such occasions: "Cover up well: there's a damp chill from the river."

I noticed in Michèle the same sort of happiness as that with which Jean had been overflowing that afternoon, the same excitement, the same appearance of intoxication. The moon lit up her face with its slightly underhung jaw. The full, projecting lower lip gave her a hungry, almost animal, expression which to some extent was an index to her character. Nowhere have I ever met with anybody who had such an appetite for happiness. It had always been marked in her and showed itself by the greedy way in which she bit into fruit or buried her face in a rose, and by a complete surrender to sleep, which was like an enchanter's spell, and came upon her at times as she sat beside me on the grass. But she never waited passively for happiness to come. She was constantly tormented by the urge to fight, to conquer,

and of this she gave me proof that evening when she spoke
of Jean. For it was in order to talk about Jean that she had
suggested taking this walk in the park. Just before we began
to skirt the mist-drenched meadows, she decided to broach
the subject. She put her bare arm round my neck, and I
could feel her breath on my ear. What she had to tell me
was quite mad, so amazing indeed that I could scarcely believe her.

"We're engaged, you know. . . . I mean it. It's terribly
serious, though he's not yet seventeen and I'm going on
fifteen. . . . I know everyone'll just laugh and not believe
it . . . so we're not telling anyone except you—only you,
dear, darling Louis. . . . Why are you crying? Don't you
think it's marvelous?"

Marvelous!—it was her favorite word. I hid my face
against her shoulder, and she let me cry, not asking me anything. For she was accustomed to my tears, which were apt
to come on the slightest pretext. I was conscious of a feeling
of peace. No need to ask more questions: everything was
settled now; there was nothing left for me to hope for,
nothing for me to look forward to except playing the rôle
of confidant for which they had cast me. Never again should
I be the only, the prime, concern of Michèle's heart. From
the meadows came the quiet, cold gurgle of water. Michèle
smelled of warm carnations. She wiped my eyes with her
handkerchief, talking all the while in her low voice.

I had guessed right. They were in the habit of meeting
several times a week behind Monsieur Du Buch's mill. They
were terrified lest my stepmother should discover them.
Michèle made me swear to say nothing that might put her
on their track. When she said that, I remembered what I
had told Brigitte Pian about their hiding from me. I had
spoken with no thought of making mischief. (Though was

73

that really true?) Perhaps her suspicions had already been aroused.

"I'm frightened of her, Louis. She hates people to be happy. I have a feeling she's always got it in for me because I don't look miserable. We must be very careful. But Jean is so reckless!"

She spoke to me of him with a freedom of which I should never have been capable. She knew perfectly well the risk she ran. He was much, much worse even than his uncle imagined. I ask myself today why she thought that, because he has told me himself that he would have regarded as sacrilege any attempt on his part to give her more than the most chaste of kisses. Perhaps it was that she knew he would not always be so lamblike. . . . Whatever the reason, she was not frightened of him. She would marry him and nobody else. She had chosen him, and he her, children though they were. If she lived to be a hundred no other man would ever mean anything in her life. That was a truth on which there could be no going back. He was so intelligent, so strong.

"And so handsome, too—don't you think?"

No, I did not think that he was handsome. What meaning can a child attach to the word? He knows strength, of course, when he meets it—physical power. But the question must have made an impression on me, because now, at the end of a long life, I can still remember that spot in the path where Michèle asked me about Jean. Am I in any better position today to say precisely what I mean by the word handsome, beautiful? Can I say by what signs I recognize it in a human face, in a landscape, in a stretch of sky, a color, a word, a tune? All I know is that beauty troubles the senses, for all that it concerns the spirit, that it breeds in one a sort of despairing happiness, leads to a contemplation that never wholly finds its object but is worth a world of kisses. . . .

"Look here, Michèle," I said. "I suppose you know that the boys at school say that Jean is a dirty beast?"

"Yes, I think I do. . . . But Monsieur Calou doesn't think he is. What I am going to say may startle you, but *I* think it's better to be a dirty beast than to have Brigitte Pian's brand of virtue!"

"Oh, Michèle!"

"I mean it. I'd rather be in Hell without her than in Heaven with her!"

"But, darling Michèle, it's blasphemous to say things like that," I protested. "It'll bring you bad luck. Ask to be forgiven, now, at once; make an act of contrition."

Obediently she made a quick sign of the cross, and murmured a few words: *I repent with all my heart the sin which I have committed against Thy adorable Majesty*—then she burst out laughing.

"D'you know what Monsieur Calou said to Jean about Brigitte Pian? He said that there are some people who choose God, but that perhaps God doesn't choose them. . . ."

"Monsieur Puybaraud," said I in shocked tones, "thinks that Monsieur Calou has too much intelligence for a priest: that he is too acute, and that his ideas smell of the stake."

Michèle did not know what the expression "to smell of the stake" meant. She asked me, but I did not answer, for my whole attention was fixed on an idea that had just occurred to me.

"Listen," I said sharply, "there's something I want you to tell me. Don't be angry. . . . Does he kiss you?"

"Of course he does . . . passionately," she said. "You wouldn't understand, but it's marvelous. He doesn't do anything else, though, Louis . . . not anything. . . . You mustn't imagine . . ."

Gracious Heaven! what worse could they do than kiss?

My cheeks were on fire. I looked at Michèle, who was my senior by just a year (but she was already a woman, I, still a child), and thought how old she was, how heavily burdened with experience and sin!

"You *are* a silly, Louis: haven't I just told you we're engaged?"

She, too, was trying to reassure herself. Her conscience was far from easy. But a fresh wave of happiness swept suddenly over her and she started humming in that voice of hers which was as yet "unplaced," was still capable of astonishing breaks. The tune was an air of Gounod's which our mother used to sing on just such summer nights as this:

*"The darkness brings the silence back. . . ."*

It was a long while before I could get to sleep: not that I was more unhappy than usual, but that I was tormented by a sense of remorse. I tried to remember the expression on Brigitte Pian's face when I had complained that Jean and Michèle were hiding from me. I knew her too well to feel comforted because she had shown no overt sign. I was not without experience of her self-control, and was aware that she never yielded to sudden impulses. She buried her grievances and dug them up weeks later when no one remembered what had caused them. I was often scolded for something I had done in such and such circumstances a year earlier, and about which she had never spoken until then.

Certain slight changes in my stepmother increased my anxiety, and I warned my sister. I pointed out to her that Madame Brigitte kept less often to her room than was usual, despite the heat; that one was likely to come across her at all hours of the day on the stairs or even in the park. She would enter the drawing-room unheralded by any creak of footsteps. Michèle did her best to reassure me by pointing out that our stepmother no longer had Monsieur Puybaraud to get her teeth into. But the very first day that Jean came over to Larjuzon again, I knew from certain signs that he had entered the world of Brigitte's preoccupations. One morning she expressed surprise that Michèle should walk about on the roads during the hours of siesta, when even the farm animals stayed in the barn.

Such remarks were the sharp flashes of lightning that announced the coming storm. But I, at least, had the consolation of being able to tell myself that my fears had been groundless, that, so far as the present unease was concerned, I was without guilt.

I have already mentioned Vignotte. He was the estate agent at Larjuzon, where he had been installed with his wife for only a short while. They had been imported by my stepmother, and it was about them, I feel pretty sure, that my father and she had had their first serious disagreement. Very shortly after her marriage Brigitte had fallen foul of old Saintis, who had been born on the place, and with whose rudeness, drunkenness, and dishonesty my father put up uncomplainingly. People who settle in the country after having spent all their lives in cities soon find themselves at odds with the local folk and make enemies of them. The theme is as old as the hills. Balzac made use of it. But in this case the story had not followed the usual course of fiction, for the country dwellers of Larjuzon had been worsted by the lady from the city. One day, when Saintis had been drinking heavily, he was so rude to my stepmother that my father was compelled to get rid of him. But he never forgave his second wife for having driven him to take this step.

The Vignottes, who regarded Brigitte as their benefactress, were very grudgingly accepted by my father. He could not abide his new agent and regretted old Saintis for all his drunkenness and his thieving propensities.

Ours was a district in which any wagging tongues were feared, but those of the Vignottes most of all. Madame Vignotte, with her lips and cheeks sucked inwards over her toothless gums, looked like nothing so much as a walking proboscis straddled by a pair of spectacles and surmounted by shiny strands of false black hair. She never returned from her shopping expeditions without having some morsel of gossip for Madame Brigitte. She rarely made direct assaults upon the reputations of our neighbors, but delighted in hints and sly jokes at their expense. The odd thing was that nothing ever seemed to shock the pious old dame, who had never in her life been a step from the village. Adultery, needless to say, she took in her stride. But she knew all about, and was quite willing to discuss, incest and every kind of sexual aberration, not excluding the crime of sodomy, chuckling and winking the while.

The market was her happy hunting-ground, and she left the woods and fields to the tender mercies of her husband who, from his pony-trap perched high on its big wheels, dominated the countryside as he drove from farm to farm. Many were the couples philandering in fancied security during the heat of the day or when darkness fell who were marked by his hawklike eye. Sometimes the actual prey was hidden from view, but the sight of two bicycles, symbolically entwined beneath a bush, would fill him with a wicked joy.

Now it so happened that one day, not far from a hut used for pigeon-shooting, he noticed a tall, dusty bicycle, and, close beside it, looking tiny by comparison, the very machine which Mademoiselle Michèle had asked him, the day before, to oil (as though it was his business to oil bicycles!). True to her usual methods, Brigitte Pian at first made no use of

78

what Vignotte told her. She pretended not to believe him and, by so doing, put him on his mettle. The more she refused to be convinced, the coarser became his charges. He went so far as to say that Mademoiselle Michèle and the young fellow over at Monsieur Calou's . . . All this he asserted to an accompaniment of resounding oaths. He had seen them with his own eyes, or as good as. Nothing was going to persuade him that a young scamp like that would stay for over an hour with a girl in a shooting-hut without . . . Still, one mustn't be too hard. After all, one had been young oneself, and these things happened . . . even to young ladies . . . why, one had only got to look at her to see . . . Abeline Vignotte had got wise to it all right, not that it much surprised her. "But I said, 'No, Abeline, fun and games, perhaps, but . . .' 'Get away with you,' she replied; 'just you look and see how her figure's developing! . . . It's sad, all the same, a girl like that, with the example of Madame Brigitte always before her eyes. . . .'"

Brigitte had decided to do nothing until Madame de Mirbel should have paid her expected visit. But the situation was serious from more than one point of view, and extremely delicate. Monsieur Pian adored Michèle, and it was difficult to foresee the nature of his reactions. I gather from a notebook kept by Monsieur Calou, which is relevant to this incident, that my stepmother had certain scruples (for at this time she searched her conscience with avidity, though never to the point of fanaticism). What troubled her was that she could not disguise from herself the fact that she found considerable pleasure in the thought of a disaster that ought to have brought her nothing but shame and consternation. For was she not like a second mother to Michèle? But faced by a difficulty of this complexion, Brigitte Pian set herself to apply the only solution to which she attached any value.

She must conquer her scruples by force of logic, must find some reason that would make her pleasure seem legitimate and fit it into the pattern of her moral perfection.

She was helped, on this occasion, by letting her mind dwell, for the space of a few seconds, upon the alluring prospect of a marriage into the Mirbel family—though such a prospect, it is true, was distant and by no means certain, considering the boy's age. Madame Brigitte rejected the temptation without much difficulty, but she gloried, all the same, in her renunciation, and wove it diligently into the mail corselet of her merits. Had she been a worldly woman, she told herself, she would have taken full advantage of a scandal of this kind. But no, she would turn it into a weapon with which to achieve the wretched girl's salvation. That the child should have come as close as she had done to the edge of the abyss was disaster enough, even if she had not actually taken the final plunge into the depths, but a rescue was still possible. The situation should be painted in its true colors. The scales would fall from Monsieur Pian's eyes, and the whole spiritual atmosphere of the house would be transformed. There would be nothing but profit for Michèle in being made to drink this cup of humiliation to the dregs.

Where Michèle was concerned, Madame Brigitte did her utmost to encourage thoughts of mercy in herself, for mercy is a virtue that must not be neglected. How could she help feeling indulgent when she remembered whose daughter the poor child was? The first Madame Pian had been precipitated into outer darkness through a sudden and terrible death over which had hung the well-founded suspicion of suicide. Brigitte had in her possession a file of documents which only charity had prevented her from opening in the presence of her husband, who insisted on remaining so willfully blind to the truth. So far she had not done so, in spite of the odious, the actually insulting, comparisons that he allowed himself at times to draw between her and her predecessor. Only the highest kind of virtue—heroic virtue, as God well knew—had kept Brigitte silent. But perhaps the time was coming, was even now at hand, when, for the sake of the girl, she would have to display to the eyes of the outraged father and husband written proofs that the wife he mourned had been far from deserving of his tears. But if the papers proved that, they would prove, too, that the foolish rather than blameworthy daughter should be pardoned because of the heavy legacy that lay so crushingly upon her.

In this way did Brigitte Pian color the pleasure she savored in anticipation. She was a logical-minded woman who kept to a straight road marked out by clearly labeled principles. She never took a step that she could not immediately justify. Later she would yield to the onset of those obscure anxieties that she now put from her without excessive difficulty, would leave the highroad to beat the undergrowth of guilty motive.

A day was to come when the memory of deeds that could never be undone would prove her torment, showing her their true face—till then undreamed of and horrible beyond words. But that time was far off. Many were to be her victims before the true vision dawned on her of that love in whose service she thought herself enrolled, but of which she was in fact wholly ignorant.

# 7

THE only thing that I remember at all vividly about the
Comtesse de Mirbel's day at Larjuzon is that Jean appeared
to my eyes in an entirely new light. Up till then I had always
seen him as the bad boy of the school who knew rather too
much about "life" for his age; as the dunce on whom Uncle
Adhémar and Monsieur Rausch had to use physical force;
as a dangerous sort of chap, though he could be kind enough
when he liked—almost gentle, indeed, in his dealings with
me. That was the trouble. I was fond of him but could not
respect him. As the result of a logical contradiction which
I can't say worried me a great deal, I thought less highly of
my sister when I knew she was in love with him.

But when his mother was there, Jean seemed a different
person. His eyes never left her face except when he glanced
round at us to see whether we were sufficiently admiring.
Every time the Countess produced a verbal sally, he looked
at me with a laugh, as though fearful that I might have
missed the point, or might not show myself responsive to
such wit. From the very moment of their arrival he showed
how pleased he was at our surprise on finding that the
mother of this great lout of seventeen was both elegant and
young. Today there is nothing particularly miraculous about
the preservation of a youthful figure. It is a thing that can be
had by all who are willing to pay for it. But at the time of
which I am speaking, it was a matter for astonishment to
find a mother who still retained the figure of a young girl.

At first, therefore, we were more struck by the apparent youth of the Countess than by her beauty, which, though almost perfect so far as features went, was lacking in brilliance. She was afraid of the sun, and went to as much trouble to avoid it as she would today to expose every inch of her body to its rays. The veil in which her face and straw hat were swathed did not, in her opinion, afford sufficient protection, and whenever she had to cross the tiniest patch of sunlight she was most careful to open her elegant parasol. She never so much as half removed her gloves, except at luncheon. In her anxiety to produce a good impression on us she achieved an effect of rather affected simplicity.

When coffee had been served under the oaks, Jean took her off for a stroll along the path which made the circuit of the park, that she might have an opportunity of talking to Michèle. During their brief absence, the abbé Calou and my parents exchanged a number of acid remarks.

"In her own way she's a very superior sort of person, of course," said my stepmother; "but I need hardly add that it's not a way I particularly like, even judging by worldly standards. Don't you think there's something almost idolatrous about the cult of the body when it's carried to quite such extremes?"

Although at that time she still regarded Monsieur Calou as a good and learned priest, though rather on the simple side and quite without ambition, she held that his judgment was both childish and eccentric. She kept, as she said, "a careful eye" on him, for she regarded it as her privilege to watch over every soutane that came within her orbit.

"The Comtesse de Mirbel," said the priest, "is a lady of letters"—and his sudden laugh was out of all proportion to the very mild humor of his remark. "Did you know that she has written novels?"

"Has she ever had any of them published?" I asked.

"No," snapped my stepmother in her most sarcastic tone; "she finds it sufficient to live them."

Heavens!—backbiting, and in front of a child too, who might well be scandalized by such a remark. One link—two—sprang loose from the carefully wrought armor of her perfection. But almost immediately she set herself to repair the damage. She spoke, she said, without any real knowledge, and regretted that she had not resisted the temptation.

"I give you absolution, Madame," said the abbé Calou.

"There are some things about which a priest ought not to joke," replied Brigitte, frowning portentously.

We could see the Countess in the distance, coming towards us flanked by Michèle and her son. Jean had his face turned toward her as he walked. He was laughing and leaning forward in his anxiety to hear what my sister was saying. He did not see us: the two adored creatures at his side completely blotted us out from his consciousness. I suffered, but there was no jealousy in my suffering. I felt I wanted to cry. Jean was not what we had thought him. He was good, though at times he might give the impression of naughtiness. Brigitte gazed at the group as it moved towards us. The corners of her mouth were drawn slightly downward; her large face was like a mask, and I could learn nothing from its carefully assumed expression of composure. The abbé Calou, like her, never took his eyes from them. He seemed preoccupied and sad. By the time they had come within hearing, an argument had broken out between mother and son.

Jean was begging to be allowed to go back with her to Vallandraut. She shook her head. They must be careful to observe every detail of the arrangements made by Uncle

Adhémar. It had been agreed that she should have an early dinner with Jean at the presbytery, and then go back in the carriage to Vallandraut in time to get to bed early. The train left at six, which meant that she would have to be ready at dawn. They must say good-bye at the abbé Calou's.

But Jean would never give up anything on which he had set his heart. His mother's arguments went in one ear and out the other. They made no impression on him. Nothing mattered to him except his longing to spend part of the night with her. He had secretly planned to sit up in her room and watch the day break.

"But we're *always* apart: I never see you: and now, when I've *got* a chance, you grudge me an evening—a night."

He was speaking in the obstinate tone I knew so well, and his face had assumed the mulish look that Monsieur Rausch found so exasperating. But his mother was as determined in her refusal as he was in his request. Michèle tactfully left them to themselves. The argument grew noisier. We could hear Madame de Mirbel's last words, uttered with a dry finality.

"I said no, and I mean no. You always ask for more than you are given. You're spoiling the whole day for yourself. No . . . I'll not listen."

She came toward us with a smile. Though it seemed to light up her whole face there was something about it that was strained and tremulous. Jean watched her surreptitiously, a look of defiance in his eye. The Countess, after my stepmother had served her with currant syrup and barley water, went back to the carriage, telling her hostess once more how *very* kind she had been, though we got the impression that she was more distant and more preoccupied than she had been when she first arrived. I watched the victoria out of sight. Jean occupied a little let-down seat, and had his back to the horses. He looked obstinate and far from happy, but his face was soon hidden from us by the parasol that the Countess suddenly opened.

What I am now going to relate owes nothing to my imagination, though Jean rarely spoke of it to me. But one whole volume of the abbé Calou's diary is taken up with the details of what happened.

Scarcely had the victoria reached the main road when Jean returned to the attack. At such times he was like a hound on the scent. But it was no good. His mother maintained her refusal with an air of irritated firmness. When she had exhausted all her arguments, she half turned to the abbé Calou, who was looking on in silence.

"You're in charge of Jean: please make him be sensible."

He answered her dryly that today he had "transferred his responsibility." To this she replied, with a touch of insolence in her tone, that now if ever was the time to show that strong hand about which she had heard so much. At this Jean, white with anger, sprang up and, taking advantage of the fact that the horses had slowed down for a hill, jumped from the carriage and narrowly escaped falling under the wheels.

The driver tugged at his reins, the horses reared. By the time the Countess and the priest reached Jean, he had got up. He was unhurt. For a few moments mother and son glared at each other in silence, standing there on the deserted highway. It was an overcast day with occasional bursts of sunlight. The grasshoppers were scraping away at a sort of intermittent prelude. The coachman had the greatest difficulty in holding in his team, and kept slashing with his whip at the horseflies which were proving troublesome.

"I am forced to agree with your uncle. There's no doing anything with you."

But Jean started to argue again. He hadn't seen her for three months: she had made this trip for his sake, and now she wanted to spoil the one evening that they might have spent together.

"My dear boy," she said, "I promised your uncle, I gave him my word. . . . Next time I will keep a whole night for you . . . and I won't wait until the end of the holidays, either. But we mustn't set your uncle against us. Now, get back into the carriage and sit between us. If that won't be too uncomfortable for *you*," she added, turning to the priest. Then she put her arm round her son. "Snuggle up to me . . . like a baby," she said.

He stopped fighting, gave up the battle. He had surrendered at last! The shadows of the pines grew longer, spanning the road from one side to the other. The abbé Calou turned away his head.

"This is the best time for catching grasshoppers," said Jean; "they come down the trunks when the sun sinks, and start making their noise when they're about a man's height from the ground."

The Countess heaved a sigh of relief. He was talking of other things. He had loosened his grip. When they reached the presbytery, she told the coachman that it was not worth while taking the horses out, because she was going to start for Vallandraut before eight. But the man would not listen to her. He meant to feed and water his animals. In hot weather like this they needed a rub-down, too. All the Countess could get from him was a promise that he would leave their harness on.

When they sat down to dinner she complained that Madame Pian's too lavish luncheon had made it impossible for her to do honor to Maria's chicken. It was only seven o'clock, and the horizontal light was flooding the small presbytery dining-room although the blinds were drawn.

"How pleasant it is here!" she said. "Jocelyn's dining-room must have been just like this." *

She took scarcely a thing on her plate, and kept glancing toward the kitchen. The service was slow because Maria had no one to help her. More than once the Curé had to get up and go into the kitchen for a dish, but this he did gloomily and with a grudging air. Perhaps he was still upset by what had happened in the carriage. Jean was not surprised that the priest should remain proof against his mother's charms. It was only to be expected. "They could never get on together," he thought. And then, she made no effort to conceal her anxiety to be gone. She was aware of this herself, and tried to find some excuse. The coachman, she said, had made her feel nervous: he had the look of a jailbird.

"I don't want to be out late on the roads with a man like that."

Jean interrupted her: "I'll ride back with you, Mamma, on my bicycle."

She bit her lip. "You're *not* going to begin that all over again! You promised me . . ."

He hung his head. Maria brought in the "pastry," which was her masterpiece.

"You won't taste many better," said the Curé.

The Countess did her best to swallow a few mouthfuls. That was the best she could manage. But she liked making herself popular, and did not want to leave with a feeling that she had disappointed her host. She tried, therefore, to be friendly with him, and gentle to the boy. But the gloom on

* The reference here is to Lamartine's novel in verse, *Jocelyn.*— Translator.

88

the Curé's face remained unlightened. As soon as dessert had been served, he left the room in order to read for a short while in his breviary. The Countess realized that he had done this in order to give her an opportunity to be alone with her son before she took her departure. Jean realized it too, and came closer. He could have given a very accurate account of her thoughts at that moment. He knew that she was in a hurry to be off, yet was ashamed to let her anxiety be seen. She forced herself to stroke his hair, but kept on glancing surreptitiously at the clock that hung over the mantelpiece. Jean caught her doing this, and reassured her. "It's fast," he said. She replied eagerly that she could spare him a few more moments. She embarked on some advice, speaking in a rather preoccupied tone of voice. The abbé Calou was quite nice, really. . . . Jean wasn't unhappy, was he?

"No, Mamma, no . . . I'm happy . . . honestly I am—very happy," he added with shy warmth.

She did not see the blush that came to his cheeks, nor feel him tremble. The day before, he had made up his mind to confide in his mother, hoping she would not laugh, would not mock him, would treat the matter seriously. . . . But he had let the right moment slip, and it was too late now to pour out his feelings. . . . Much better to keep Michèle's name from this last-minute conversation. Thus he argued to himself. But there was another reason which he dared not admit: that it was no use giving himself away to someone whose mind was elsewhere. Many years later, when we were seated by my fire in the rue Vaneau in Paris, and Jean was telling me about the saddest moments of his life, he could still remember those few minutes of twilight after the stifling day, with himself sitting in the presbytery dining-room at the side of his adored mother, their knees almost touching, and watching her as she kept on glancing at the clock. Through the glass door he could see the Curé moving up and down in the kitchen garden, intent upon his breviary.

"I'll come back before the end of the holidays, darling: that's a promise. And next time you shall have a whole evening."

He made no reply. She told the coachman to close the hood of the victoria. Jean jumped on the step and touched her neck with his lips.

"Get down! Don't you see he can't hold the horses in? . . ."

A cloud of dust rose and then subsided. Jean waited until the carriage had disappeared round the last bend, and then went back into the garden. He took off his shoes and stockings, got a watering can, and began to water the chicory that he had transplanted the day before. Monsieur Calou said not a word, but went off to the church to make his devotions. When he returned, Jean had gone to bed, and called out "good night" sleepily through the door. The Curé, before himself retiring, went down again to make sure that he had bolted the front entrance. Contrary to his usual custom, he did not leave the key hanging on its nail in the passage, but put it under his pillow. Then, kneeling down beside the bed, he prayed at greater length than on other nights.

Monsieur Calou thought at first that it was the wind that had waked him. It was blowing hard, though the night was fine and moonlight lay along the floor. Somewhere a shutter was banging. Leaning out of the window he saw that it belonged to the room above his own, where Jean slept. The fastening must be broken. He slipped on his soutane, reached the attic landing, and opened Jean's door as quietly as possible, meaning to shut the window. A violent gust over-turned a vase filled with heather picked by Michèle, standing on the table. The abbé saw at once that the bed was empty. He waited a few moments to get his breath, then went downstairs and tried the front door. The bolt had not been drawn, nor the lock forced. The young lunatic must have got out through the window by hanging on to the gutter. The Curé took the key from under his pillow and went out.

The night was given over to wind and moonlight. All about the house was a great murmuring of pines. It was not like the intermittent moaning of the sea. No wave, no crash of foam broke the green swell and surge-of the trees. He went first to the shed where the two bicycles were kept (he had hired one for his pupil at Vallandraut), and found that only his own was there. At the corner of the house, where the gutter ended, he could see in the sandy soil the marks of a fall. Jean must have jumped from a fair height because the indentations of his two heels were clearly defined.

The abbé went back to the shed, took out his bicycle, and then hesitated.

It was almost midnight—too late now to do anything. The harm was done! What harm? . . . No use letting himself get into a state. Why make a tragedy of the furious midnight scene that was probably taking place in the inn at Vallandraut? What, in any case, had it to do with the Curé of Baluzac? True, he was in charge of the boy, had made himself responsible for him: but the truant would return before morning, and the simplest thing would be to notice nothing. There were some things that were better ignored. The really wise man never let himself be forced into the position of having to take disciplinary action that might destroy at a blow all the advantages he had previously gained. . . . But that was precisely the problem! The Curé paced for a while among the currant bushes, pushed open the gate, and gazed down the road which lay empty beneath the moon.

There was no way he could be of help to the boy whom he loved so dearly, who, perhaps at that very moment, was receiving a mortal blow. His mother had had good reason for wishing to be left alone at night. Her opposition to Jean had been obstinate, fierce—almost, it had seemed, inspired by hate. The abbé Calou tried to make himself believe that his thoughts were nonsense. But he knew the type too well! The exigence (which Jean had inherited), the frenzy which would not stop, if need be, at trampling a son into the mud. . . . Perhaps, though, he was exaggerating the danger just because he loved Jean so dearly.

It was the first time he had ever become attached to one of his pupils. Since he had begun to specialize in "difficult cases" no such opportunity for affection had come his way. He had not taken on the work because he had to. His brother, a landed proprietor in the Sauterne country, to whom he had surrendered his share of the family estate, sent him each year a sum of money, the amount of which varied according to the harvest, though it was never more than six thousand francs. This, with his stipend and the small sums that came to him from parishioners, was a great deal more than he needed, for he lived off his own poultry and vegetables and occasional gifts from the neighbors.

If, then, he had decided to undertake the training of boys whom their parents could not manage, it had not been from any desire to make money. No, he just spread his nets and patiently waited, never abandoning hope that some day the one wild bird who might really prove worthy of his care would drop plumb into his house. If that should happen, he would make a man of him. He thought he ran a better chance of finding the right one if he confined himself to the unruly. This predilection for "bad lots" was doubtless due to the strain of romanticism that still remained in him, to the heritage he had brought with him from the seminary. But it responded, too, to some deeper and more secret yearning, to a desire to help young creatures who might be threatened, who might already have been hurt, by life, who did not care whether they were saved or not, who needed a sponsor at the Father's throne. It was not a matter of virtue so much as of preference and inclination.

Until now he had put up with his charges because he was in love with young life and adolescence. But in every case so far, the ephemeral charm of youth had overlaid a solid bottom of vulgarity, stupidity, and boorishness. A superficial grace often lent a glow to the most ordinary and insensitive little middle-class oaf. In Jean de Mirbel the abbé Calou had found for the first time what he had always hoped that God might some day send him. At last a child had come his way who had a soul.

But that soul was hard to reach. Not that it mattered. The abbé Calou was one of those people who, from their earliest days, are vowed to a life of disinterested labor, whose affections ask nothing in return for what they give. The trouble was that Jean would not let himself be loved or protected. Though he had had the boy there under his hand, and just a little watchfulness would have served to make all well, the abbé had not been able to avert the danger of this nocturnal meeting between mother and son. What would happen to Jean when he had left the presbytery and was at large upon the highways of the world? (For the abbé could not imagine that he would ever be content to vegetate in a country château.) Even when he had left his roof, the abbé would feel himself still bound by the responsibility he had undertaken. . . . Where was he now? How follow him? How reach him? Doubtless he would be home before morning. If he were not, the abbé would simply go out and look for him. Meanwhile, there was nothing to be done but to make some hot coffee. He went back to the kitchen, and, after opening the shutters to let the moonlight in, lit a few twigs. This done, he sat down in Maria's low chair, took from his pocket a rosary made of olive stones, and stayed there motionless. The moonlight touched the back of his head and shone upon his rough, untended hair. He sat there with his arms resting upon his thighs. The enormous hands, hanging down between his legs, took on a strange, exaggerated significance.

# 8

JEAN had waited to put his plan of escape into action until he heard the sound of the Curé's regular breathing through the floor. The clock had not yet struck eleven when he started off down the moonlit road. The wind was at his back, and he rode without effort in a state of tranquil intoxication, certain now that nothing in the world could keep him from accomplishing what he had set his mind upon. He would see his mother this very night, would watch by her pillow until break of day. He was as sure that this would be so as that one day he would hold Michèle in his arms. Never before had he ridden at dead of night by the light of a moon spun by the wind above an empty world. He felt no nervousness about the coming interview with his mother. In the presence of a third person she had seemed to be the stronger: alone with him she would be at his mercy.

He traveled swiftly and was soon enveloped by the river mist where the road dropped into a hollow just before it reached the first houses of Vallandraut. At once he lost his self-assurance. He conjured up a picture of the locked and bolted inn. How could he explain his presence there? How manage to have his mother wakened? What excuse could he contrive? Not that it much mattered. He would say that the thought of not seeing her again had made him ill, and that Monsieur Calou had advised him to take a chance. At dead of night, and in a public inn, his mother could scarcely scold him overmuch, for fear of scandal. He would attack her hard hostility; yes, in the long run, he would soften it. He would not fly into a rage, whatever happened. He would hide his face in her skirt and cry; he would kiss her hands.

He reached the market-square where a few carts with up-tilted shafts cast on the ground a shadow as of horned animals. The waning moon shone straight on to the flaking plaster of the Hotel Larrue, picking out the black lettering of a sign that said: "Lodging for Man and Beast." There was still a light in the bar, and he could hear the click of billiard balls. He leaned his bicycle against the wall, and asked the plump young woman who was dozing in a chair by the deserted counter for a glass of lemonade. She answered him with an ill grace that it was too late, that the hotel ought by rights to be shut, and that no drinks were served after eleven. Then he put to her the question he had long prepared: was the Comtesse de Mirbel staying there? He was the bearer of an urgent message.

"Countess?—what Countess?"

The girl was suspicious and obviously thought that her leg was being pulled. She said that she had other things to do than listen to tall stories, and added that at his age he'd be better off at home than wandering the roads.

"But I know there is a lady staying here" (perhaps, he thought, she had not given her name). "A fair lady, wearing a straw hat and a gray tailor-made suit. . . ."

"A fair lady?—wait a moment. . . ." A flicker of intelligence showed in her stupid eyes.

"In a tailor-made costume," she went on, "and a spotted veil, and carrying a handsome dressing-case which she left here to be taken care of?"

Jean interrupted her with some impatience: where was her room?

"Her room? But she's not sleeping here. She only came in to leave her luggage. She's staying at Balauze"—the girl was insistent—"she gave me a telegram this morning addressed to the Hotel Garbet, reserving a room."

Jean reflected that Balauze was the county town, and that probably his mother had thought she would be more comfortable at the Garbet than here. But, then, why had she told him that she would be sleeping at Vallandraut? He asked how far it was to Balauze. Seven miles? . . . less than an hour's run on his bicycle.

"She meant to sleep at the Garbet," went on the girl, who had suddenly become talkative (and was probably moved by an instinct of hostility towards a lady who had scorned the Hotel Larrue). "But I shouldn't be surprised to hear that she'd spent the night in a ditch. . . ."

Jean became anxious.

"Why? Did she have bad horses?"

"Horses!—I like that! She came in a motor-car. The whole town turned out to see the sight. You've no idea the row it made, and what a stink of gasoline and oil and dust there was. . . . And it ran over Madame Caffin's chicken, though it's only fair to say that they paid her much more than it was worth. . . . You ought to have seen the gentleman in a pair

96

of goggles that almost covered his face—a regular mask it was, enough to frighten one to death—and a gray duster down to his heels. . . . The things they wear nowadays!"

"Then she's at the Hotel Garbet at Balauze, close to the church? You're quite sure?"

He thanked her, jumped on his bicycle, and turned right from the Baluzac road. Now the wind was in his face, and he struggled against its unseen strength, against the hostile power (or was it pity, perhaps, and not hostility that inspired it?) that was doing its best to slow down his approach to Balauze. Had he been with the young Pians he would never have dared confess his weakness, but since he was alone, he dismounted as soon as the road began to rise. In spite of the cool night wind, his face was running with sweat, and his backside was sore. He could think of nothing but how tired he was. For all his boast of manhood, he was still a child about anything that concerned his mother. It would never have occurred to him that she could have any connection with what he vaguely thought of as human crimes and passions. Both his father and his uncle figured in his imagination as brutes. From his earliest years at La Devize he remembered his father's shrill voice, could see him now, looking like an angry little turkey-cock strutting round his mother where she sat, an image of silent martyrdom. Uncle Adhémar, who had the same kind of voice, had always shown a certain amount of courtesy in his dealings with his sister-in-law. Never for a moment had Jean entertained the idea that she might have deserved their hatred. But, for all that, he had scarcely ever spent a whole day with his mother without being made aware that she was not in the least like his private idea of her. He was constantly noticing her lack of warmth, her insincerity. The way she had deceived them all about spending the night at Balauze ought not to have surprised him. At La Devize, as in Paris, where she always stayed with her grandparents, the Mirandieuzes, from January to June, Jean, home for the Easter holidays, had more than once caught her in an inconsistency, for the Countess never bothered to give plausibility to her various lies. She would say, for instance, that she was simply *longing* to go to some play of which everyone was talking, quite forgetful of the fact that she had ostensibly been to see it one evening the week before, and the next day had given them an enthusiastic, if rather vague, account of its plot. Often and often had Jean, with the terrible logic of childhood, disconcerted her by his never-varying comment—"But, Mamma, you *said*"—never dreaming of taking her words at other than their face value. What she had said did not always—did not, indeed, very often—agree with the story she was telling then. But she never troubled to think up an explanation. "Did I *really* say that? You must have dreamed it, darling. . . ." But if ever Jean had been visited by the hint of a suspicion, it did not survive their separation. How should he have dreamed that her soul was less lovely than her face? In his memory of her the idea of sin must ever be a stranger to that serene brow, to the set of her rather too short nose, to those heavy lids veiling eyes that held the color of the sea (*glaukopis:* he had underlined the Greek word in his lexicon), above all, to the thrilling contralto voice, with its occasional hoarseness: that unforgettable voice that casts its spell over me even today whenever I go to see the old lady whose hand alone seems to show the ravages of time, for the structure of her face has remained unaltered beneath the flaccid skin, like some marvel of Greek statuary that has survived the centuries, and her eyelids are like the trampled edges of those same green pools with their reflections of sea anemone and weed.

Jean pushed his bicycle up the last hill on the road to Balauze, not at all worried by what he had heard, but nervous at the thought that the interview between him and his mother would have a witness at the Hotel Garbet. Which of his mother's friends had a motor-car? It must be Raoul . . . for that was how the famous dramatist was known to the Mirandieuzes, who, like all people of fashion, enjoyed being on familiar terms with so well-known a man. He was not in fact called Raoul, but I am not going to set down the real name of a man who was once as celebrated as Donnay, Bernstein, or Porto-Riche, though today he is entirely forgotten. If nothing now remains of a body of work which was once highly considered, if the very titles of his most famous plays have passed from human memory, it remains true that he once exercised a profound influence on many who are still alive and who, like the Comtesse de Mirbel, are dragging out the fag-end of their existence before taking the final plunge into nothingness.

It would never have occurred to Jean that there could be any bond between his mother and this fat gentleman in his forties. "She probably thought it would be amusing as well as convenient to do the journey by motor-car," he reflected. "But it was not nice of her to deprive me of a treat that I should have enjoyed so enormously."

He rode down a dark, narrow street that debouched onto the Cathedral square with its arcaded pavements. It was empty. He went round it and had some difficulty in making out the hotel which stood in the shadow of the church. It had been contrived from the outbuildings of the former bishop's palace, and only a narrow alley separated it from the Cathedral. The front door and the entrance to the stable-yard were both closed, and all the shutters were fastened except on the first floor, where two windows seemed to be half open. Should he ring, knock at the door, wake the household in the middle of the night? What excuse could he give? He might ask them to take him in, but he had scarcely any money. Would his mother pay for him? He stood hesitating. Though his mind was innocent of all suspicion, something told him that he had better do nothing of the sort, that it would be wiser to advance no farther along the path on which he had so foolishly set his feet. But he couldn't go back to Baluzac: that would be tantamount to admitting that he was beaten, and for nothing in the world would he have done that. He decided to lie down on a sort of low ledge that he could see between two of the buttresses of the Cathedral, and to wait for morning. The alley was so narrow that this meant he would be as good as directly under the windows of the hotel. When his mother came out, he would give her a hug and say nothing at all. She would be so surprised that it would not occur to her to question him. The fact that he had ridden all that distance through the darkness, that, worn out and hungry though he was, he had kept his vigil there just in order to be able to give her one more kiss, would prove how much he loved her. Within these walls she was sleeping now, doubtless on the first floor, behind those unfastened shutters—she always kept her bedroom windows open.

By this time the moon had disappeared behind the apse of the Cathedral, but its diffused light still cast a pallor on the sky, so that only an occasional twinkling star was visible. Jean was cold, and the stones hurt him. He lay down on the grass, but some nettles that he had not noticed stung him, and he got up again with an exclamation of pain. A dog that had been keeping late hours was wakened by the sound and barked, but soon left off again. The hour of cockcrow was still far off. Jean began to think of Michèle, and his thoughts were chaste, no matter what his life may have been. In imagination he held her in his arms, though seeking no other pleasure in the contact than that of finding peace in the nearness of a faithful heart. And all the time, close to him, on the other side of the road, behind the half-closed shutters . . .

Later, he was to know everything about his mother. All this man's affairs were public property, all were marked by the same horrible character. There are many novels that bear, or might bear, the title: *A Woman's Heart;* more than one professional psychologist has plumbed the secrets of the feminine mind. . . . The man who was sharing tonight the Comtesse de Mirbel's bed at the Hotel Garbet lived for no other object than to reduce this mystery to its true and rather squalid proportions. His victims knew precisely what they might expect of him. Those whom he had possessed all bore about with them the same indelible sign—the sign of a lust that could know no satisfaction. They became moral wanderers on the face of the earth, creatures wholly detached from all human responsibility, obsessed by the experiences they had shared with him. "You don't know yourself," he would whisper to each in turn; "you are ignorant of your potentialities and limitations: you have no idea what perspectives lie before you. . . ." Though he might leave them later, they still retained from their contact with him the rudiments of that dangerous science of bodily pleasure which is more difficult to learn than the virtuous think, since beings who are genuinely perverse are almost as rare in this world as saints. One does not often meet a saint by the roadside, but neither does one often come across anyone capable of dragging from one's vitals that particular kind of groan, that cry expressing horror no less than delight, which becomes sharper as time lays its hand upon a body already threatened by decay, already undermined as much by desire as by age, by the passage of the years, and by passions that can no longer be assuaged. No one has ever written of the torment that old age brings to women of a certain type. In it they taste of Hell before death touches them.

Jean slept for a considerable while, his head resting against the corner made by the wall and the buttress. The discomfort of his cramped position woke him, or maybe it was the cold, or perhaps the sound of a man's voice speaking at the window above.

"Come and look. I don't know whether it's the moon or the dawn that makes the sky so pale."

He was speaking to someone in the room behind him, whom Jean could not see. He was standing a little back from the window, with his face turned sideways to it. He wore a dressing-gown of dark-colored silk.

"Put something on," he added; "the night is chilly."

He leaned his elbows on the bar of the window, and made room beside him for the woman. But he occupied most of the opening, and the white, light figure could barely squeeze between the wall and his powerful torso.

"What a wonderful effect of loneliness!—and how still it is! . . . No, darling, I'm not cold."

"But you must be: throw my overcoat round your shoulders."

She disappeared and came back wearing a man's ulster. It made her body look larger and her head very small. The two of them remained there for a long time without speaking.

"How unimportant it makes one feel," said the man. "Do you think that the people now asleep in all these houses have ever seen one of my plays?—that they so much as know my name?"

"They've probably read them in *l'Illustration*."

"That's true," he said more cheerfully; "the Supplement to *l'Illustration* goes everywhere. They must have seen it, if only at the hairdresser's. . . . What a stage-set this square would make, eh? But the open air's not really my line. The stuff I write needs four walls."

She made her answer in a low voice, choking back a little laugh. He, too, laughed, and added:

"With one of the four walls cut away. That's what a play ought to be, the masterpiece of which I dream. . . ."

"And with no dialogue: isn't that what you're thinking?"

They whispered. Jean could hear nothing but the throbbing of the blood in his own ears.

One o'clock sounded.

"No, no . . . really, we must get some sleep."

Once again there was the sound of a choked-back laugh. The woman leaned her head against the shoulder at her side. Jean looked at the gable that crowned the front of the building. The door of the stable-yard must be very old. A horseshoe was nailed to one of its sides. He read: *Hotel Garbet. Weddings and Banquets Catered For.* He compared in his imagination the man standing at the window, every note of whose voice he recognized, with the middle-aged person with the dyed hair combed across a bald, white pate, whom the Mirandieuzes knew as Raoul. The comfort that a child seeks instinctively deep down within itself when threatened by some terrible pain, he now expressed out loud. "It's comic!" he said in mocking tones; "it really is . . . just too comic!" And then: "All right, my fine lady!" He heard the faint sound made by the window being closed. "Oh, well, I suppose it amuses you, and it doesn't do anyone any harm. . . ." And suddenly he was seized with panic at the idea that he might be discovered, might have to listen to her explanations. How awful! He had a sudden vision of his mother's face, could see her look of shame, could hear her stammered words. . . . He jumped on to his bicycle, crossed the square, unconscious at first of his fatigue, so happy was he at the idea of increasing the distance between himself and that room at Balauze. But at the first hill his legs felt weak. He dismounted, dragged his bicycle to a near-by mill, dropped into some hay, and lost consciousness.

How hot it was in the hay! He felt as though he were on fire in spite of the cold dawn wind. His head ached. That must be a lark singing there above him in the mist. Close by his ear a hen and her brood were scratching the earth and clucking. He tried to get up. He was shivering. "I'm feverish," he told himself. He took his bicycle and tried to resume his journey. About a hundred yards farther on, at the crossing where a road led off to Uzeste, a pine branch over a door announced an ale-house. With great difficulty he reached it and ordered some hot coffee. An old woman looked at him curiously, muttering something in the local dialect. The sun was hot upon the seat beside the door onto which he dropped. What if the motor-car suddenly appeared? But no, they would get up late. They had the whole day before them, the dirty beasts! . . . Because they *were* dirty beasts . . . not because they were lovers, but because they were so horribly mincing and affected. . . . Well, that was the last time he'd make a fool of himself . . . for anyone. Everyone slept with everyone else: that was what life was. With whom did Uncle sleep? and Monsieur Rausch? and Monsieur Calou? . . . It'd be fun to see the old Curé on the job. He'd ask them, all of them . . . that is, if he didn't die before he got the chance.

He moistened his lips with the coffee, swallowed a few mouthfuls, and then turned round and was sick. He leaned his head against the wall and closed his eyes. He no longer had sufficient energy even to brush the flies away from his burning face. A bicycle passed and slowed down. He heard an exclamation, and then the sound of his own name repeated several times. The huge, anxious face of Monsieur Calou was close to his own. If he made an effort perhaps he would be able to understand and answer. But the Curé was there, so why struggle any more? why not just let himself go? He felt himself lifted like a little child, put into a bed in a dark room that smelled of manure. Monsieur Calou wrapped him in his old black cloak, after which he had a long argument with the landlord, who didn't want to rent him his cart because it was market-day at Balauze. "I don't care how much you charge," said Monsieur Calou in an impatient voice. At last came the clip-clop of a horse on the cobbles of the yard. Some straw had been laid in the cart. Jean was asleep when the Curé lifted him, and his head bumped against the old man's shoulder. The priest laid him in the straw and covered him with his cloak. He took off the knitted jersey that he had put on under his soutane in the chill of the dawn, and rolled it up under the boy's head.

The attack of pleurisy was serious. For a fortnight Jean was in danger. The Papal Zouave spent forty-eight hours at the presbytery and agreed with Monsieur Calou that it would be better not to upset the Countess; she was merely told that the boy had a bad attack of bronchitis, and she didn't worry. Mountain treatment was not then in vogue, and was only very rarely prescribed. The doctor summoned from Bordeaux said that the smell of pines was the best possible thing in such cases, and advised the Colonel to accept Monsieur

Calou's offer. The Curé had undertaken to coach the boy for his examination, and to get him through in two years without any danger of overworking him. But what ultimately decided the Papal Zouave was his dislike of the idea of sending his nephew back to a school that had recently been dishonored by "the scandal of Monsieur Puybaraud's marriage."

The evening on which it was decided to leave Jean at Baluzac, the Curé wished ardently that God was still incarnate, so that he might have kissed His hands and embraced His feet in token of gratitude. Jean maintained a hostile silence, and never opened his mouth except to ask imperiously for what he wanted. Monsieur Calou knew nothing about what had happened at Balauze, but he could see that the boy had suffered a terrible shock. How the wound had been inflicted and with what weapon he would learn later. Or perhaps he wouldn't. It did not matter. What mattered was to prevent the infection from spreading. At dusk he sat by the dozing boy and asked him whether he didn't dread a winter at Baluzac. Jean replied that anything was better than Monsieur Rausch, but that he was sorry he couldn't "bash his face in," as he had meant to do.

The Curé pretended to think he was joking. "Just you wait till you see what a lovely blaze I get going when we're working and reading in the evenings. We'll take notes and drink walnut juice, while the west wind roars in the pines and flings rain against the shutters. . . ."

In a voice quite unlike his own, Jean said that "there wouldn't be much love knocking around."

Monsieur Calou replied very gently that what was important was to love in one's heart.

"You don't say so!" (The voice was still the voice of another, of a stranger.)

Without any sign of dismay, the Curé returned the rosary to the pocket of his soutane, took out his pipe, and set to sniffing it (he wouldn't let himself smoke in Jean's room).

"I'm an old man," he said, "and I've found my way into port."

"Oh, of course: God and all that. You needn't tell me."

The priest got up and laid his hand on Jean's forehead. "Yes, God first, last, and all the time, naturally."

It was as though he had a son of his own, a naughty son, or rather, a son who would have liked to be naughty, but *his* for all that.

Jean threw himself back on his pillow and exclaimed: "Don't go getting ideas. If you want to know, I loathe and detest everything you stand for!"

"You'll make your fever worse," said the Curé.

How terribly the poor boy was suffering! "He takes it out on me because I happen to be at hand and there's no one else he can snap at." The abbé sat plunged in thought, his elbows on his knees, deliberately keeping his face in shadow because Jean, from the depths of his pillows, was trying to see the effect of his outburst. But even if the lamp had been shining full on it, the sick boy would have seen nothing, so empty of expression was it. Suddenly he felt ashamed of what he had said.

"I wasn't talking against *you*," he muttered.

Monsieur Calou shrugged his shoulders. "Much better to get it off your chest. . . . Very soon, you know, you'll be able to have visitors."

"I don't know anyone."

"What about the Pians?"

"They haven't come near me: they haven't even written."

107

"They've sent over every day for news."

"But they haven't come," Jean said again, and turned his face to the wall.

One of our farmers who lived at Baluzac and brought us milk every morning did, in fact, bring us news of Jean. But the Curé was surprised that we hadn't given any more definite sign of interest. He was pretty sure that Mirbel felt hurt by this neglect, though he could not know how deeply wounded he had been by our seeming indifference. The Curé of Baluzac, however, firmly convinced that "that Brigitte woman" was behind it all, made up his mind to go over to Larjuzon as soon as his patient was a little better, and have it out with her.

# 9

At Larjuzon the postman always arrived while the family was gathered round the breakfast table. My stepmother, whether she had come back from Mass or had only just emerged from her room, was, even at this early hour, invariably dressed and buttoned up to the neck with formal precision. On the morning when I read out the letter from Monsieur Calou announcing Mirbel's illness she was in one of her bad moods. Her face was set and hard, and she was frowning. At eleven o'clock she was due to take a confirmation class in its catechism, and, to judge by the way she spoke of the children, they were without exception stupid, incapable of learning anything, and interested only in pinching one another's behinds. In addition to which they were dirty, given to leaving tracks on the floor, and they smelled. As for the least sign of gratitude—well, one might wear oneself to the bone for them and not get so much as a word of thanks. If their parents only got the chance, they would think nothing of looting the house and murdering everyone in it.

We knew that on these catechism days the least shock was enough to set a spark to that inflammable temperament with which Heaven had seen fit to endow Madame Brigitte.

"We must go over to Baluzac at once!" cried Michèle, as soon as I had come to the end of the letter; "and I'm not dressed yet."

My stepmother's voice broke in on a high note: "Am I to understand that you are proposing to go over to Baluzac this morning?"

"Of course I am!"

"I forbid it!"

"Why shouldn't I go this morning?"

"You'll go neither this morning nor this afternoon!" snapped Madame Brigitte, white with anger.

We looked at one another dumbfounded. Strained though her relations with my sister were, she had always, till now, avoided an open breach.

"What's the matter with you?" replied Michèle, stung to insolence. "There's no reason why I should wait until tomorrow."

"Nor tomorrow either. You're never going to Baluzac again!" said my stepmother. "And don't look as though you'd no idea what I mean, you little hypocrite!"

My father glanced up nervously from his newspaper. "Brigitte, dear, what are you in such a state about?"

"I ought to have asserted myself sooner." Her voice had become solemn.

Michèle asked what it was she was being accused of.

"I am accusing you of nothing. I never believe evil of anyone until I see it with my own eyes."

My father got up. He was wearing an old brown dressing-gown. A few tufts of gray hair showed through the unbuttoned collar of his shirt. "All the same, you seem . . ." he began.

She fixed upon her husband a look of angelic patience. "It hurts me to hurt you: but it is necessary that you should know the truth. I am told that she is in the habit of meeting young Mirbel behind Du Buch's mill."

Michèle replied in a firm voice that it was perfectly true that she did sometimes meet Jean. What harm was there in that?

"Don't look so innocent: it ill becomes you. You have been seen."

"*What* has been seen? There was nothing *to* see."

My father drew her tenderly to him. "Of course there is no harm in your meeting young Mirbel at Monsieur Du Buch's mill. But though you are still only a child, you look older, and the people of this town, especially the women, are a lot of poisonous snakes."

Brigitte cut him short. "Poisonous snakes, indeed! Don't you go taking Michèle's part against me! I am interfering now, before it is too late, simply and solely in order to protect her from idle gossip—though I am prepared to admit that it may have no foundation. Young Mirbel is a bad lot. May God forgive me for ever having had him in the house!" In a lower voice she added: "The important question is, how far has it gone?"

She had become very gentle all of a sudden. My father

took hold of her by the wrist. "Come on now, out with it! What *is* all this nonsense?"

"It's . . . let me go!" she exclaimed. "You seem to forget who I am! . . . If you want the truth you shall have it."

She was furious, and moved back to the other side of the table where, entrenched behind the china and the silver, she stood with her hands on the back of a chair. Her eyes were closed, and, under cover of their veined lids, she seemed to be concentrating her thoughts.

"Michèle is a young girl who is in love with a young man. There you have it in a nutshell."

In the silence which followed these words we none of us dared to exchange a glance. Madame Brigitte, suddenly sobered, fixed her eyes with a look of pain on father and daughter.

Octave Pian had risen. He looked very tall, and more as I remembered him before Mamma's death. He had been wounded in his tenderest feelings—the affection of a father for his daughter, in which respect plays a large part, as well as a modesty so sensitive that the least affront to it is unforgivable. He had been jerked out of his normal mood of black gloom, and the memory of his dead wife had for the moment been driven from his mind by the presence of that other woman who was so terribly real, so horribly alive.

"A child who is not yet fifteen? How ridiculous to talk like that! You ought to be ashamed of yourself!"

"Ashamed of what? I am not accusing her of anything," replied my stepmother, with an obvious effort at self-control. "I want to believe that she is innocent—or comparatively so: I said it before, and I say it again." But girl-mothers of fourteen and fifteen *had* been known. It was only necessary to visit the poor to realize that! . . .

I can still hear the sound of her voice as she pronounced

the words "girl-mothers." Never had two words contained such a concentrated accent of disgust. In a low voice I asked Michèle what girl-mothers were. She said nothing; perhaps she did not know. With her eyes fixed on her father she said: "You don't believe her, do you?"

"Of course I don't, my dear, dear child!" and he drew her to him again.

"Do you wish me to produce her accusers?" asked my stepmother; "the people who say that they saw her with their own eyes?"

"Yes, produce them!" cried the girl.

"I can make a pretty shrewd guess: it's the Vignottes," said my father, suddenly quite calm. "We all know what the Vignottes are like! . . . So you're ready to swallow the tittle-tattle of a pair like that, are you?"

"Who says that I'm *ready* to do anything of the sort? I repeat that I am accusing no one. I am performing a painful duty. I am reporting something that was told me—no more. It is your duty to satisfy yourself whether it is true. *My* task finishes where yours begins."

Brigitte Pian folded her arms. She stood there, impartial, invulnerable, justified in the sight of God and all His angels.

"And what, may I ask, do the Vignottes say that Michèle was doing?"

"You must ask them that yourself. You can hardly expect me to soil my lips. . . . It is bad enough to have to listen to such things. But if it is absolutely necessary, if you insist on my being present, I will find the needful courage in that love which I have vowed to all of you, and especially to *you,* Michèle. . . . Oh, you can laugh if you like! But I have never loved you so fondly as at this moment."

A few tears started to her eyes. She was careful to wipe them away only when she was sure that we were looking.

My father, without the slightest show of heat, told me to go and fetch the Vignottes.

Vignotte came in holding his beret in his hand. His right eye, which had received a charge of slugs out shooting, was closed. The other had a sort of look of concentrated stupidity. Round his mouth with its few stumps of decayed teeth was a growth of untrimmed beard. He was bandy-legged. He had left his wooden clogs in the hall, and padded through the half-open door, his feet encased in list slippers that flapped as he walked. No one had heard him enter. We turned our heads, and there he was, obsequious, grinning, stinking of sweat and garlic.

He realized what was in the wind as soon as he had crossed the threshold. My father ordered me out of the room, and told Michèle, very gently, to go upstairs and wait until she was summoned. I went to the drawing-room, but stayed near the door in a state of considerable excitement. My chief sensation, I remember, was one of rather shamefaced hope. Michèle and Jean were going to be separated. My function would be to act as the link between them. They would be able to communicate only when *I* was willing, and under *my* supervision. I had no very clear idea of all this: I just felt it, sensed it with extreme vividness. I had run like a mad creature to find Vignotte, and had hurried back with him. Though haste was no part of that prudent man's make-up, I had made him follow me at once without giving him time even to put on his "overcoat," as he called his jacket. Now I could hear him through the door.

"I never said no such thing. . . . I sees what I sees. . . . Not but what I was in that there hut all right. . . . I can't tell how long *they'd* been there not saying a thing . . . and what was they doin', all silent-like? That's what I asks meself. . . . Didn't have to use my eyes to know as they was there. . . . S'pose they was just *lookin'*. . . . Well, I only hopes they was. . . . Though it don't matter to me."

My father asked some questions which I could not properly hear. He did not raise his voice, but spoke in his normal slow drawl. Every now and then he used some word of local dialect, stressing it in an odd sort of way. Those parts of his talk I understood better than the rest. He had become once more the master who has no need to shout, who can make himself feared by the turn of an inflection. He interrupted my stepmother, cutting her short in the middle of a sentence. "Let me finish what I have to say to Vignotte."

It was not an argument, not even a discussion, but a summing-up. When my father had finished speaking, I heard no more save the trumpeting sound made by Vignotte when he blew his nose. Then my stepmother opened the door, and I had barely time to get out of the way. She never so much as glanced at me. With her garden hat stuck well at the back of her head, her hands concealed in white mittens, she reached the hall, took a parasol and went down the front steps, looking not so much angry as plunged in thought. I learned shortly afterwards from my sister that our father had just shown some of the firmness which had marked him in the old days, but which we children had quite forgotten.

He had apparently given in to his wife to the extent of forbidding Michèle, not only to go to Baluzac, but even to exchange letters with Jean. I was staggered to learn that this ruling was to apply to me as well. As a safeguard against its possible violation, our father confiscated our bicycles for the time being. Sister Scholastique, the Superior of the Free School, who was under considerable obligation to my parents, was to be asked to superintend Michèle's studies during the holidays, when she would have a certain amount of time at her disposal. Actually, my father did not suspect his young daughter, and told her as much, kissing her tenderly. But he knew how merciless the people round Larjuzon could be, and wished to protect her against possible gossip. The whole affair, therefore, would have represented a victory for Madame Brigitte, had it not been for the fact that my father had told the Vignottes that they had better look out for another place. This decision struck directly at their patroness. She argued, but in vain, that her husband was running considerable risk by making enemies of such people, armed as they were. But my father assured her that he had a hold over the Vignottes and could find ways of stopping their mouths.

This scandal, then, which was destined to have serious consequences for so many of us, did produce one happy result at least, though it was unfortunately of short duration. It roused our father from the state of apathy in which he had been living for the past ten years. Brigitte suddenly saw herself opposed by an adversary with whom she had long ceased to reckon. Her husband's love for Michèle derived from the passion he had felt for the first Madame Pian. The real struggle was being fought over a dead woman's body. This, no doubt, my stepmother knew perfectly well—which explains her behavior during the days that followed.

In every circumstance of her life Brigitte Pian was sincerely anxious to do good. Or this, at least, was what she believed. That fact must never for a moment be forgotten by readers of this chronicle. I could have painted quite a different portrait of her from the one on which so pitiless a light is shed in these pages. I was made too clearly aware of her victims' sufferings to be altogether fair to her. But I feel that even when recounting what may seem to be some of her blackest acts, I ought not to yield to the too easy temptation of showing only one side of her forbidding character.

It is important to remember that when, before her marriage, Brigitte Pian used to spend the summer months at Larjuzon, she found herself involved in one of those marital dramas which may well go on, quite silently, for years without any violent arguments or outbursts of nagging, until one or other of the actors is safely dead. My father had always before his eyes the vision of his dearly loved wife Marthe. He had known that she was suffering because of someone else, had realized that he could do nothing to help, and had seen that the spectacle of his own pain merely had the effect of making her own sense of remorse the more acute. He was a simple man, not much given to introspection, and he had found comfort in Brigitte's clear-sighted analysis of the situation. A close tie had grown up between them. But when the circumstances in which it had had its origins no longer existed, it inevitably grew slack. Brigitte always claimed that she had saved him from suicide. However that may be, it cannot be denied that when things were at their worst he did relieve his feelings by confiding in an affectionate companion who had never been far from him, had even guided his footsteps during the most terrible moments of his ordeal. In her, too, he had found the only means he had of keeping in touch with his wife, whose cousin and childhood friend she was.

But when Brigitte Pian became the second Madame Pian, she quite honestly felt it to be her duty to finish the good work she had begun by delivering her husband from the obsessive influence of the dead—all the more so, since he had consented to this second marriage only in the hope that some

116

such cure might result from it. Possibly, at some later date, her actions were dictated by a sense of personal grievance, by feelings of jealousy which she would not admit even to herself. But at first she had a perfect right to believe in a mission to which no less a person than her husband had called her. When, after a few months, she realized that the influence of Marthe was still in the ascendant, that my father still believed that her virtue, in spite of all temptations forced upon her by an overwhelming passion, had never, never yielded, that the dead woman was still in his eyes a heroine who might have died for love but would never have been false to her plighted word, Brigitte thought it incumbent on her to make sure that this halo of sanctity had been truly merited. If only she could confront her husband with definite proof that the first Madame Pian had been guilty of adultery, that she had assumed the appearance of virtue only after her lover had abandoned her, and had finally taken her own life in an access of despair, then, and then only, she thought, would he be freed from the shameful spell. For a long while before any real evidence came her way, she had felt quite sure, as a result of what she had heard, that Marthe had in fact been guilty. Maybe her ardent desire to step into her shoes was in some sort influenced by her wish to discover this evidence. She knew that it would be easier to find, once she was free to come and go as she chose through all the rooms of the house, and to rummage in desks and drawers unseen by others.

This she did with a pleasure that one finds it difficult to credit. A very few weeks after her marriage she laid hands on a document that so far exceeded her wildest hopes that she thought it better, for the time being, to say nothing about it. This reluctance to make use of so tremendous a weapon shows that Brigitte was capable of pity. So long as any hope remained of effecting her husband's cure without opening his eyes, she resisted the temptation of telling what she knew.

Once the Vignottes had gone, it did seem as though he might perhaps be cured. Defeated on that issue, Brigitte got full satisfaction on every other. She could not but applaud a decision that my father made a few days later. From the beginning of the following term, Michèle was to go as a boarder to the Ladies of the Sacred Heart, whose school she had hitherto been attending as a day student. Octave Pian did not look on this as a punishment, but only as the best way of insuring that his young daughter would be removed from the influence of her formidable stepmother.

Madame Brigitte ought now to have declared herself satisfied. But she was far from feeling so. In defending his daughter, the father had, in reality, been defending his dead wife. His sudden return to the world of action had put the coping-stone, not on Brigitte's victory, but on Marthe's: had proved that he was still possessed, mind and soul, by the image of the dead woman. This, I have very little doubt, was the truth which my stepmother glimpsed in the dark recesses of her conscience, and it urged her to spring the mine that had been lying so long concealed, which, for so many months, she had refrained from detonating.

My sister and I were still, however, very closely watched. Unfortunately for us, the local postmistress was completely under Madame Brigitte's thumb, and must have received very precise instructions on the subject of our letters. Everything at Larjuzon intended for the post had to be put in the study each evening, to be collected next morning by the postman. Not an envelope could leave the house without our stepmother's knowing all about it.

Michèle, therefore, had to rely on me for getting messages to Jean. She had no wish to break the promise made to our father that she would not write to him, but she badly wanted to send him a little gold locket made in the shape of a heart, which she wore on her breast. It contained a piece of our mother's hair. I was shocked that she should give away such a relic to Mirbel, and showed no very great enthusiasm about making on foot a journey that would be all the longer and more tiring since I should have to go a roundabout way if I was to avoid being seen in the town and promptly denounced. Besides, so prolonged an absence would have aroused the suspicions of Madame Brigitte, who was keeping a more than usually watchful eye on me, though without any appearance of ill-will. At times she would give me a hug, would stroke the hair back from my forehead, murmur, "My poor child!" and heave a deep sigh.

The more insistent Michèle became, the more clearly did I show my dislike of undertaking such an adventure. And so it came about that the last weeks of vacation were spoiled by a series of fruitless arguments. I was deprived of the fun of long days spent with my sister, free of any third person to spoil our intimacy. I had so looked forward to them. As for Mirbel, I should see him again, I thought, when term began, for I did not then know that he was to spend the rest of the year at Baluzac. The fate awaiting me—the worst I could possibly have imagined—remained hidden. At school it was my pleasure to feel that I had to share Mirbel with nobody else. To be sure, it was as Michèle's brother that I should find favor in his eyes. But at least they would not be seeing each other, and would have no means of communicating, while I should always be at hand, the only one among all that tribe of boys whom he would deign to recognize.

One September day at about four o'clock, a priest riding a bicycle turned into the Avenue. Michèle cried: "The abbé Calou!" Brigitte Pian told us to go to our room, and, when Michèle began to protest, she was backed up firmly by our father. On this occasion, too, he stayed where he was, though as a rule, whenever a visitor was announced, he hid himself in the study. I am pretty sure that he wanted to make certain that his wife would say nothing about Michèle beyond what it had been agreed between them should be said. Since I was not present at the interview, I will here reproduce the notes that Monsieur Calou jotted down the same evening in his diary. I give them, succinct and dry, precisely as I found them.

*An extraordinary woman—quite a miracle of perversity. In her eyes the appearance of evil is as important as evil itself—when it suits her purpose. A deep nature, but she reminds me of those aquariums in which the spectator can see the fish from every side. Each one of Madame Brigitte's most secret motives, the intention behind her every act, is plainly visible. If ever that gift of judgment and condemnation which she now exercises at the expense of others is turned against herself, she's in for a bad time!*

*Much shocked that I should plead the case of these young people, and should anticipate nothing but good for Jean from this first love affair. She pursed her lips at me. Obviously thinks me a second "Savoyard Vicar." I ventured to warn her against being overzealous in her desire to act as the mouthpiece of the Divine Will. It is a fault to which* pious persons are only too prone. But how unwise of me to include the clergy in my criticism! It was simply asking her to hit back at me with a remark about my denying the rights of the Church to instruct its children! She's quite capable of denouncing me to the Archbishop—I can see her doing it! She's not so much concerned to find out what I think as to remember enough of what I say to incriminate me with the authorities. She would have no hesitation about ruining me if she thought it necessary to do so. I said as much, and though my attitude when I took my leave was respectful enough, hers was decidedly dry—not to say rude.

Just as I reached the door on the way out, Michèle emerged from behind the bushes. She was very flushed and wouldn't look me in the face. When I got to the bottom of the steps, she said: "Do you believe what they told you?"

"No, Michèle, I don't."

"I should like you to know that . . . if I were making my confession to you . . . I should have nothing to say about Jean."

She was crying. I stammered out—"God bless the two of you!"

"Tell him that I can't see him or write to him, that I'm going to be a boarder from the beginning of next term. I shall be closely watched. Can't you imagine the instructions that will be given about me? . . . But please tell Jean that I'll wait just as long as is necessary. . . . You will, won't you?"

I tried to turn the whole thing into a joke. "That's an odd sort of mission to give to an old priest, Michèle," I said.

"I don't care whether you're an old priest or not. Except for me, you're the only person in the whole world who loves him." She said this as though it were the most natural, the simplest, the most obvious thing that could be imagined.

121

*There was nothing I could say in reply. I had to turn my head away. Then she held out a little parcel addressed to him.*

*"I swore not to write to him, but I didn't say anything about not giving him a little remembrance. Tell him it's the most precious thing I have. I want him to keep it until we meet again. Tell him . . ."*

*She made a sign to me to go, and jumped back into the bushes. Sister Scholastique's coif appeared between the trees. . . .*

The abbé Calou found Jean just where he had left him, lying on a chaise-longue under the west wall of the house. A book was open on his knees, but he was not reading.

"Well, *you've* started a hornets' nest at Larjuzon, my poor boy."

"Have you just come from Larjuzon?" Mirbel tried, though in vain, to assume a detached and indifferent expression.

"Yes. That Brigitte woman is up to her old tricks again. Just imagine, Michèle . . ."

At the Curé's first words Jean could contain himself no longer.

"She ought to have sent me an answer," he burst out. "When one's in love, walls don't mean a thing. One takes any risk. . . ."

"She's only a little girl, Jean . . . though I've never met a braver one."

Without looking at Monsieur Calou, the boy asked whether he had spoken to her.

"Yes, for a few minutes. I've remembered everything she asked me to tell you. She can't see you or write to you: from the beginning of next term she's going as a boarder to the school of the Sacred Heart. But she will wait—for years, if necessary."

He spoke like someone repeating a lesson learned by heart. In this way he gave the maximum weight to each word.

"Is that all?"

"No, she asked me to give you this . . . it is her most sacred possession, and she wants you to keep it until you see her again."

"What is it?"

The Curé did not know. He laid the little object on Jean's knees and went into the house. Through the half-open shutters he could see the boy holding the little golden heart at the end of its chain in the hollow of his hand. He raised it to his lips as though he would drink it down like a draught of water.

Monsieur Calou sat down at his desk, opened the manuscript of *Descartes and the Theory of Faith,* and read over the last paragraph he had written. But he could not concentrate, and went back to the window. Mirbel's face was hidden in his two hands. No doubt the locket lay there, imprisoned between them and his lips.

For the past two days Jean had been taking his midday and evening meal in the dining-room. About seven o'clock, once more shut away in his old black mood of silence, he sat down at table opposite the Curé. Monsieur Calou had taken to keeping a magazine or a newspaper beside him while he ate. It was obvious from the moment the soup was brought in that the boy was shooting covert glances at his host. If he still maintained silence, that was because he was shy and embarrassed and did not know how to start on what he wanted to say. Nor was the Curé wholly at ease. He was

123

afraid that a clumsy word might ruin all. He therefore confined himself, as always, to keeping a watchful eye on Jean's rather capricious appetite. When, after the meal, they went out into the garden, he asked him what he would like to eat next day. Jean replied that there was nothing he had particularly set his heart on, but he spoke with rather less ill grace than usual. Suddenly he asked:

"Are you really bothered about my health?"

"My dear boy, what a question!"

Murmuring, "No, honestly, I mean it," in a childlike tone, Jean sat down in his chaise-longue and took the abbé's hand. The latter was still standing. Without looking at him, Jean said: "I've been pretty beastly to you . . . and then . . . you went and did a thing like that for me."

He started to cry, as a child cries, making no attempt to hide his tears.

The abbé Calou sat down beside him. He had not withdrawn his hand.

"You can't know what it means. . . . If Michèle had given me up, I should have killed myself. I suppose you don't believe that?"

"Yes, my boy, I do."

"You really believe me?"

How he longed to be reassured, to have his word believed!

"I knew from the very first that this was serious."

But when Jean murmured in a low voice—"Was I dreaming? Did I really see what I thought I saw at Balauze?"— the abbé interrupted him: "Don't tell me anything if it's going to hurt you too much."

"She lied to us. Do you realize that? It was all bunk about her sleeping at Vallandraut. . . . They had booked a room at Balauze, at the Garbet. . . ."

"It is the way of women to say one thing and do another
. . . it's a well-known fact. . . ."

"She wasn't alone . . . there was a fellow with her. I saw
them at the window of their room, in the middle of the
night."

He had seen them, and his staring eyes could see them
still.

Monsieur Calou took his head between his hands and
shook it gently, as though to wake him.

"It's no use trying to force one's way into other people's
lives, if they don't want one there: remember that, my boy.
Never push open the door of another person's life, for it
can be known only to God. Never turn your eyes upon
that secret city, that place of damnation, which is the soul
of another, unless you wish to be turned into a pillar of
salt. . . ."

But Jean still went on, his gaze fixed on some invisible
picture. He described what he could still see by the light of
memory, what he would go on seeing until his dying day.

"He was almost an old man. . . . I recognized him—a
fellow from Paris who writes plays. . . . Dyed hair, a
paunch . . . and . . . and . . . that mouth. . . . Oh, it was
horrible!"

"You must tell yourself that in her eyes he represents wit,
genius, elegance. To love another person means to see a
miracle of beauty which is invisible to the rest of the world."
A moment later he added: "We must go in. It soon gets
dark at this time of year, and you haven't got enough on."

Mirbel followed him without protesting. The abbé held
him by the arm until they reached the library, where the
boy was now sleeping. Jean lay down on the bed. Monsieur
Calou lit the lamp and went over to his armchair.

"And did they," he asked, "see you?"

"No, I was standing against the wall of the church, hidden in the shadow. I had gone before it was light. Then I slept in a mill. If you hadn't searched for me I believe I should have died like a sick dog. When I think of all you have done for me . . ."

"You could hardly expect me to sit here with my slippers on waiting for you to come back, could you? You are in my charge, and I am responsible for your welfare. Think of the trouble I should have got into. . . ."

"That wasn't the reason, was it? Not the only reason?"

"Little idiot!"

"Because you do like me, don't you—just a bit?"

"As if there were no one else but an old curé to care for Jean de Mirbel!"

"I don't believe it's possible: it can't be!"

"But look at that gold heart . . . where have you put it? Ah, hung it round your neck, as Michèle used to hang it round hers. Against your heart—that's the right place for it: like that, you can always feel it. When things get bad you've only got to touch it."

"But she's such a little girl. She doesn't know me, anything about me. She's so pure that she wouldn't understand me, no matter how hard I tried to explain. Even you don't know some of the things I've done . . ."

Monsieur Calou laid his hand on the boy's head. "You're not one of the virtuous, I know. You're not that kind. You are one of those whom Christ came into the world to save. Michèle loves you for what you are, just as God loves you because you are as He made you."

"Mamma doesn't love me."

"Passion blinds her to the love she has for you in her heart . . . but it exists all the same."

"I hate her!" This he said in the rather forced and arti-

126

ficial voice that he sometimes affected. "You think I don't mean it? But it's true: I hate her!"

"Of course you do, as we all of us *can* hate those we love. Our Lord told us to love our enemies. It is often easier to do that than not to hate those we love."

"Yes," said Jean, "because they can hurt us so frightfully." He leaned his head against the Curé's shoulder, and went on in a low voice: "If only you knew how terribly it hurt, and still does! It's as though I were touching an open sore. It hurts so much that I want to shriek—to die!"

"My poor child—we must forgive women a great deal. I can't yet explain to you why. Perhaps you will understand later: I think you will, because you have it in you to hurt them too. Even those among them who seem to have everything they want deserve our pity . . . not a corrupt and furtive pity, but the pity of Christ, the pity of a man and of a God who knows well from what imperfect clay He has made His creatures. But this is not the time to speak of such things."

"I'm no longer a child. You must realize that."

"I do realize it: you are a man. You have reached the age at which suffering begins."

"Ah, *you* can understand!"

They went on talking for a long time, the priest and the boy, even after Jean had gone to bed. And when weariness lay heavy on his eyes, he asked Monsieur Calou to say his prayers beside him there, and not to leave the room until he was asleep.

# 10

THE crowing of a cock woke me. Was it dawn already? I struck a match: it was not yet five. I decided to wait a bit. Though Michèle had never succeeded in making me promise to take that journey to Baluzac, I had made up my mind to go this morning on my own account. The evening before, after Monsieur Calou had gone, I had been told by my step-mother that Mirbel would not be going back to school for the rest of that year. Had she seen me tremble? Had she realized what a mortal blow she was striking at the pale little boy who pretended so hard not to mind? She added that it would make a great difference to her own plans, that she and my father had agreed to look for another school, so that I might be removed from the influence of so black a sheep. Now, however, that would not be necessary. I should find Monsieur Puybaraud gone, but about that, too, she was glad. I was quite sensitive enough as it was, and Monsieur Puybaraud had been altogether the wrong sort of master for me—a dangerous man.

Jean at Baluzac, Michèle at boarding-school . . . what on earth would become of me? On that day I looked for the first time straight in the face of loneliness. He is an old enemy now. We have learned to rub along together, to know each other. Loneliness has struck me every imaginable blow. There is no spot in me left to strike. It has set me many traps, and I have fallen into every one. But it torments me no longer. We sit now, one on either side of the fire on winter evenings, when the fall of a fir-cone and the sobbing of the night wind mean as much to me as the sound of a human voice.

Whatever happened I must see Jean again for the last time. . . . We must arrange to write. . . . It would be easy for me, but how should I address my letters? How does one have letters delivered *poste restante*? I must see him once more, must be convinced that I still existed for him, that Michèle had not entirely taken my place.

The roses on my curtains grew faintly pink: the day was breaking. I dressed, holding my breath. Not a creak did I make on the floor. A single wall stood between me and the huge room in which the two mahogany beds of Monsieur and Madame Pian stood as far as possible from each other.

I opened my door without a sound. The stairs, it is true, creaked a little, but Brigitte was no light sleeper. I would go out by the kitchen door so as to make sure of not being heard. The key was hanging in the scullery.

"Where are you off to so early?"

I choked back a cry. There she stood, at the turn of the stairs, erect in the dawn light. She was wearing an amethyst-colored dressing-gown. A great coil of hair, like a fat snake with a red ribbon round its snout, fell to her waist.

"Where are you off to? Tell me now!"

It did not occur to me to lie. She knew everything before I so much as opened my mouth. Besides, despair had sapped my courage. In a panic of escape I flung myself into its waiting arms. I sought safety in that very oversensitiveness which had only to show its face to terrify any aggressor, however formidable, and compel him to help rather than to punish me. I screamed, I choked: I went further than I intended, and could not stop. Brigitte lifted me in her strong arms and took me to her room, where my father, suddenly wakened, sat up in bed thinking that he was in the throes of a nightmare.

"Quiet, quiet . . . I'm not going to eat you. Drink a little water. It's flavored with orange."

She had laid me on her own bed.

"It was because I was never going to see him again," I stammered. "I wanted to say good-bye to him."

"It's that Mirbel boy all the trouble's about," said Brigitte to Octave. "See what a state he's in. I sometimes wonder whether it is not too late to do anything about these fits of his. He's so morbidly sensitive." And then, in a lower voice: "Poor child!—what an inheritance!"

"What do you mean, talking about 'inheritance' with him here?" asked my father in the same low tone. "What are you hinting at?"

"Hinting is not one of my failings."

"Oh, isn't it?" He chuckled, shook his head, and said: "Oh, that's rich!"

I had never seen him looking so pale. He was sitting on the edge of his bed. His legs, all covered with black hair, did not reach the floor. Large swollen blue veins showed in his feet with their malformed toes. A mat of gray hair sprouted from his open nightshirt. His thighs were terribly thin, almost emaciated. Brigitte, standing there in her ecclesiastical-looking robe, her hair drawn forward on her prominent forehead, with the long, fat, shining tress hanging down, brooded over him with an eye that was at once hostile and watchful.

My father got up, took me in his arms and carried me back to my own bed. I sobbed into his nightshirt. He tucked me in. A misty sunlight entered through the fleur-de-lis openings cut in the shutters. I can still hear the tone of his voice as he said: "Wipe your eyes, you little fool; blow your nose and go to sleep." While he was saying this he brushed the hair away from my eyes with his hand, and stared— stared as though he had never seen me before.

I ought never to have known what I am now going to relate—with overwhelming shame and embarrassment, but it must be done. Indeed, I did not learn it until immediately after the First World War, when I became reconciled with my uncle Moulis, one of my mother's brothers from whom I had been separated all my life as the result of a family quarrel into which I need not enter here. He had been devoted to his sister Marthe, and wanted to get to know me before he died. He was an architect, like my grandfather, practicing in the city, a Bohemian, artistic sort of man, of the kind that Brigitte Pian loathed. She always maintained that he was responsible for the influences that had surrounded my mother's early life and had led to her undoing. This cynical old bachelor, speaking more than twenty years after the events he was describing, told me about the circumstances that had attended my birth. He could not actually prove that I was not Octave Pian's son, but he thought it more likely that I owed my existence to a first cousin of my mother's, Alfred Moulis—"a regular Adonis," said my uncle. I could see no trace of charm in the photograph he showed me, and the idea that I may be the son of that curly-headed and rather sheepish-looking person gives me no sort of pleasure. From childhood he had adored his cousin, and she responded without reserve. I will not expatiate on this odious subject. I intend to say only what is absolutely necessary to an understanding of the document that my stepmother discovered very soon after her marriage.

According to my uncle Moulis, it was a sort of memorandum written in my mother's hand: a series of calculations and comparisons of dates, from which it seemed clear that, if Octave was really my father, I must have been born two months prematurely. It is true that at the time of my birth I was considerably under normal weight, that I had to be wrapped in cotton-wool, and that I was reared only with the greatest difficulty. But what had been the purpose of this paper? There seems little doubt that it formed part of a letter. That, at least, was what my uncle thought, though he could not be sure.

But Octave Pian had a reason, which he thought was known only to himself, for doubting whether I could really be his son, and to this the document in question lent strong support. Uncle Moulis had had the facts from his sister. . . . It is an extremely delicate subject, and I can broach it only in the most roundabout manner. What I gathered was that Octave belonged to that by no means rare species of men who, when desperately in love, are afflicted with impotence. Such a state of affairs must lead to atrocious suffering, especially when the love is not mutual, and the ridiculous despair of one partner is observed by the other with a cold and mocking eye.

I hope that the reader will realize how very repugnant it is to me to put all this down in words. But it does, at least, prove that what I am relating is true and in no wise invented. Subjects of this kind are as a rule instinctively avoided by the professional novelist, because he knows that most people find them repellent. But those who turn their backs on fiction, and set out to follow up the destinies of persons with whom they have actually been connected, are forever coming on the traces of these miseries and aberrations of the flesh. And even worse than the aberrations are the inadequacies. For those are just the things that we do not wish to hear about, because so many of us may have been to some extent their victims. Renan once said that the truth may well be depressing. He was thinking in terms of metaphysics. On the level of human affairs it may be not only depressing but ridiculous and embarrassing—so much so that decency forbids us to put it into words. Hence the silence in which such things are usually shrouded. Only when they result in a divorce or a suit for annulment at Rome does the glaring light of publicity beat upon them.

When, in October, I went back to the city with my stepmother, Octave Pian stayed on at Larjuzon. The separation of husband and wife had now become an accomplished fact, even though they had never discussed it in so many words. Everything happened quite naturally. My father had not yet seen the revealing document (though it had been left behind, as by accident, in a drawer of his room where he must sooner or later come upon it), but he had been sufficiently prepared and worked upon by Brigitte to see me go without any real feelings of regret. He preferred winter solitude in the depths of the country to life with a woman whom he hated and a son the very sight of whom opened old wounds. My last memory of him is of a man who had sunk back into the apathetic stupor from which he had roused himself for a brief spell in order to take up the cudgels on Michèle's behalf. It must have been about this time that he started drinking again, but it was only after our departure that the habit grew upon him.

Michèle was now a boarder at the Sacred Heart, and I was left alone with my stepmother. The two years that elapsed before I took my final examination were bleak and dreary, but I suffered a good deal less than I thought I should. Work came easily to me, and Brigitte had little cause to anticipate trouble from the silent schoolboy who spent his evenings studying his lessons and doing his themes without any need of supervision. During the first year my father came into town once every month on Michèle's free day, and took both of us to lunch at a restaurant. I can still remember vividly the peculiar pleasure it gave me to choose my favorite dish from the menu—oysters, jugged hare, or duck hash. The certain knowledge that Michèle and Jean were separated, probably forever, had the effect of diminishing not only my jealousy, but also my affection, though spasms of both would occasionally recur for a few brief moments. I have never been able fully to realize that I love anybody unless the emotion is accompanied by some degree of suffering.

Here, I think, I ought to recall two incidents which proved to me, once and for all, that my friendship for Mirbel was a thing of the past. One evening during that first winter, when I got back from school, my stepmother said, without raising her eyes from her book: "There's a letter for you." I was not taken in by her assumed indifference. "It's from Mirbel," I remarked, after one glance at the envelope, and immediately, with that instinctive cunning that the young sometimes show when they have to deal with difficult relatives, added with seeming frankness, "Do you think I ought to read it?" At first Brigitte Pian appeared to hesitate, but almost at once decided to leave it to me whether I ought to show it to her. She never so much as glanced at me as I opened it. Jean de Mirbel, after describing the "deadly existence" he was leading at the Baluzac presbytery ("and it's enough to make a fellow want to blow the lid off," he wrote), begged me to send him news of my sister. "Perhaps you could persuade her to scribble a few words at the end of your reply. It would make me awfully happy, and it wouldn't really be breaking her promise. Tell her that no one can imagine what it's like to live in a scrubby little country town tucked away in a pine forest, cheek by jowl with an old priest—though I don't deny he's a decent enough fellow and does what he can for me. The trouble is that *I'm* not decent. Tell her that three lines would make all the difference to me. She can have no idea how it would help. . . ."

I can remember my feeling of anger when I read on and found that the letter contained nothing whatever about my own affairs. I was more irritated than hurt. If that was how things were, I felt I'd much better think no more about him, but wipe the slate clean. How often in the course of my life have I felt a similar need to terminate some relationship, to throw some person or persons overboard!

I held the letter out to Brigitte, who read it at once, but without any display of haste. When she had finished, she folded it up, baring her large, horselike teeth in a smile. "The Reverend Mother," she said, "has forwarded me a whole packet in this young man's handwriting. He had the impudence actually to send a number of letters to your sister at the convent. Each one began, though you'd hardly believe it, with an appeal to Reverend Mother—or to whoever might first open the envelope—to deliver it to Michèle! Which goes to prove," she added sententiously, "that corruption of mind may walk hand in hand with stupidity, and that the two things are by no means incompatible." Saying which, she threw the pages into the grate, where they fell a prey to the flickering flames.

I am not sure that the second incident belongs to the same period. I have an idea that my meeting with the abbé Calou took place during the winter of the following year. One Thursday, just as I left the house, someone called my name.

135

I at once recognized the abbé, though he had grown much thinner. His old soutane flapped round his bony shoulders. He must have been watching for me to come out. I told him that I was on my way to Féret's bookshop, and he fell into step beside me.

"How pleased Jean will be when I tell him this evening that I have seen you!"

"Is he all right?" I asked with an air of indifference.

"No," he said; "no, the poor fellow is very far from being all right."

He waited for me to question him, but in vain, for I had stopped at the door of Féret's shop and was turning over the pages of several second-hand books on display there in the open. Was I really so hard? I don't think I can have been, for I was vividly aware of the poor old priest's distress as he leaned over my shoulder, and am even now conscious of the remorse that assailed me at that moment.

"Actually, I'm very worried about Jean. Do you know, he hasn't been home to La Devize once this year? His mother is spending the winter in Egypt. Of course, he's working very hard, and he gets a certain amount of shooting. I took him out after pigeon last October. He bagged a hundred and forty-seven. I've found a horse for him, too, at Du Buch's mill, a sorry old nag, but ridable. It's the lack of companionship that's so bad for him."

"But what about you?" I asked with the ingenuousness of youth.

"Oh, me . . ."

He made a vague movement with his hands, and said no more. He must have realized for a long time how helpless he was. He had none of the qualities that a boy of Jean's age needs for happy companionship. His pupil had no more use for his erudition than for his gentleness. What else could he be but a jailer in the eyes of a young man whom he would find, of an evening, curled up in a wicker chair by the kitchen fire, in precisely the same position as when he had left him after luncheon, with his book open at the same page. On these occasions Jean never so much as raised his eyes to the abbé's face. Nor did he find much amusement in going out alone on his old nag. When he was not in the house the abbé knew only too well where he had sought refuge. I was not at that time aware of this latest cause for anxiety. The truth was that Jean frequently stayed late in the enemy's camp—at the drugstore kept by that very Voyod who was the abbé Calou's declared foe. The master and mistress of the local school would join the party after school hours. There would be much drinking of coffee in the back shop, and discussion of an article by Jaurès or by Hervé.

Although I knew perfectly well what the abbé was after, I gave him no assistance. He had to launch into his subject without preliminaries.

"I much regret that I have had words with Madame Pian," he said. "I believe her to be quite incapable of yielding to bitterness, and I am sure that only the highest motives led her to act as she has toward Michèle and Jean. I have no wish to discuss her decision, and am perfectly willing to yield to her superior wisdom. But don't you think, my dear boy, that Michèle might occasionally write a few lines to the Curé of Baluzac? What harm could there be in that? I am not suggesting that she should send Jean any direct message, but she could tell me something about her life. That would be an enormous source of comfort to your young friend. I am prepared to go even further, Louis, and to say"—he almost whispered the words into my ear—"to say that it might prove his salvation. For things have got to that pitch now—he has got to be saved. Do you understand what I am talking about?"

I could see his childlike eyes close to mine, could smell his sour breath. But I did not really understand what he was talking about. Still, this time I was touched, and it was for his sake rather than for Jean's that I agreed to do what he asked. I gave him a promise that I would pass on his suggestion to Michèle, and I spared him the embarrassment of having to beg me to say nothing to my stepmother. I gave him that assurance unasked. He enveloped the back of my head in his great hand, and pressed my face to his stained soutane. I went with him as far as the streetcar. The men standing round him on the rear platform looked like a lot of midgets.

The correspondence between the abbé Calou and Michèle, which might perhaps have prevented or, at any rate, retarded much unhappiness, was interrupted after the third letter. Michèle had been foolish enough to give it to one of the weekly boarders, because she had not been able to resist the temptation to address it directly to Jean, though the name on the envelope was that of the abbé Calou. The letter was impounded by one of the nuns, who sent it to Brigitte Pian. She related the whole incident to me, though without attaching any blame to Michèle. "It was the priest who led her into temptation," she said; "there can be no doubt of that. Your sister has been guilty of a grave fault, but I thought it my duty to ask Reverend Mother to overlook it, and I must say that she has behaved in the whole affair with exemplary charity. But the account against the Curé of Baluzac grows daily"—she spoke with involuntary satisfaction—"and this letter is the last straw."

In some such words she spoke out her thoughts in my presence. Did she love me? For a long time I was quite

138

convinced that her show of affection was due to the fact that I was the living proof of the first Madame Pian's sin. But I have since changed my mind. I am inclined to believe now that she lavished on me all the love of which she was capable, and that I had, in some way, managed to touch that maternal instinct which is to be found in even the most insensitive of women.

# 11

FROM then on my existence was closely bound to that of Brigitte Pian. The small drawing-room where she worked and in which she received visitors separated my bedroom from hers. The door was always left half open until someone was announced; then she would close it. But no matter how low she kept her naturally vibrant tones, I could follow all conversations easily enough, especially in winter, when the windows were kept shut and only a dull rumble reached the flat from the Cours de l'Intendance.

Occasionally, when I recognized Monsieur Puybaraud's voice, I would go and say how-do-you-do to him, though not always. It was usually he who made the move. He would come into my room and give me a hug just before taking his leave. My behavior to him had changed in proportion as his position in the world had deteriorated. The poor, frail creature whose shoddy ready-made overcoat offered little protection against the wind, whose shoes were never shined, could not inspire in me the same deference as the frock-coated schoolmaster whose favorite pupil I had been.

In justice to myself I must add that his appearance moved

me to a sense of pity, or at any rate produced in me the sort
of moral discomfort which is always excited by the sight of
another's poverty, and which we are tempted to call by the
nobler name. But when I thought about Monsieur Puybaraud's misfortunes I could not but feel myself in agreement
with Madame Brigitte. I found it difficult not to despise him
for having yielded to an attraction which, though I had
never yet felt its power myself, I was already inclined to
view with suspicion and disgust. I should not have felt quite
so keenly repelled by the outward signs of his deterioration
if they had not stood in my eyes for a spiritual equivalent;
if he had not, by marrying, made himself deliberately guilty,
in my opinion, of disloyalty to a higher vocation. My views
on this matter have not greatly changed. I believe that all
the miseries of our human state come from our inability to
remain chaste, and that men vowed to chastity would be
spared most of the evils that weigh them down—even those
that seem to have no direct connection with the passions of
the flesh. From the lives of a very small number of human
beings I have derived an idea of what happiness might be in
this world if it were based on generosity and love. Wherever
I have found it, the movements of the heart and the promptings of the flesh have been kept under a strict discipline.

Monsieur Puybaraud came once every fortnight to receive from the hands of my stepmother the small allow-
ance on which his household depended. The rest of the time
he spent in running all over the city in search of employment that he never found. Octavia, now pregnant, but
threatened with a miscarriage, had to stay on her back
until the child should be born, and could be of no help to
him. I heard it said that a Little Sister of the Assumption
went in every morning to do their housework. That was all

I knew about the domestic arrangements of the wretched couple, and I was too incurious to ask many questions.

I did notice, however, that if the semimonthly interviews between Monsieur Puybaraud and my stepmother always ended with the passing of an envelope from one hand to another, they usually involved a long, low argument diversified by occasional muted outbursts. On his side the tone was that of an eager beggar, while my stepmother's replies were given in a voice I knew only too well. She was obstinate in her denials, undeviating in her refusals. And suddenly she would be left speaking alone, in the manner of one expounding the law to an inferior who had been talked down and reduced to silence.

"You know perfectly well that things will happen like that because I mean them to, and the sooner you reconcile yourself to the fact, the better." This she said one day loudly enough for me to hear every word. "When I say 'I mean,' I express myself badly, because we should do not what *we* will but what God wills. It is no use your hoping that I shall back you up in this matter any longer."

Whereupon, my former master, in spite of all that he owed to my stepmother and his utter dependence on her good-will, accused her of abiding by the letter of the law rather than the spirit, and so far forgot himself as to say that her neighbors always had to pay for her scruples, that it was always at somebody else's expense that she displayed her spiritual delicacy and the rigors of her conscience. He added that he would not go away until he had got what he was asking for. (I had not been able to make out through the door what all this was about.) My stepmother, by this time quite beside herself, exclaimed that if such were the case she had better leave him, and I heard her go out of the drawing-room, not without considerable commotion. A few seconds later Monsieur Puybaraud came into my room. His face was dead white. He held in his hand the envelope that she must almost have flung at him. His trousers were mud-spattered to the knees. He was wearing no cuffs. His black tie and starched shirt-front were the left-overs of his old school outfit.

"You heard?" he asked. "Louis, dear boy, you shall judge between us. . . ."

I don't think that many youngsters can have been asked to referee between older persons quite so often as I was. The trust that I had inspired in my master on that evening, now long past, when he gave me a letter to post to Octavia Tronche, urged him once again to have recourse to my good offices. It was a rational trust deriving from that cult of the young which he had always professed. According to him (and he had been foolish enough to develop his views in my hearing), boys between the ages of seven and twelve are the privileged possessors of a remarkable clarity of mind, of something that at times amounts to the inspiration of genius, though older persons find it hard to believe this. It vanishes, however, with the approach of puberty. In spite of the fact that I was now fifteen, I had retained, in his eyes, all the glamour of childhood. Poor Puybaraud! Marriage had not improved him physically. He was now almost bald. A few sparse strands of fair hair waged a hopeless struggle against the encroaching nakedness of his skull. His flushed cheek-bones alone gave color to his bloodless face, and he was continually coughing.

He drew a chair up to mine as he used to do when he explained some Latin text to me in the old Larjuzon days.

"*You* will understand. . . ."

He used the second person singular. This he did only in moments of emotional outpouring, and when he was speaking to one of those young persons whom he regarded as the possessor of an infallible genius. He told me the doctor believed that Octavia could have a child in the normal way only if she were assured of complete rest, both mental and physical. He had thought it best, therefore, to calm her most harrowing anxieties by keeping from her the origin of the small sum of money he brought back to her each fortnight. She did not know that it came from my stepmother, but believed that her husband was earning his living and had succeeded at last in getting some post in the diocesan organization.

"Yes, I lied to her, and I do still, every day, though at the cost of how much shame and moral agony God alone knows! But surely fibs we are obliged to tell a sick woman can hardly rank as lies? I refuse to admit that they *are* lies, in spite of anything that Madame Brigitte may say!"

He gazed fixedly at me, as though expecting some oracular pronouncement.

I shrugged my shoulders. "Surely it doesn't matter what she says, Monsieur Puybaraud, so long as you are easy in your own conscience? . . ."

"It's not so simple as all that, Louis, my boy. You see, Octavia is surprised and worried that Madame Brigitte has never been to see her since she has been confined to bed. Up to now, your stepmother has always refused to come. She won't come—so she had the effrontery to write—until I have repudiated what she calls my 'offense against the truth.' Consequently, I have been led into a series of explanations to Octavia of which I will spare you the details. Lies beget lies. I know that I ought to give way. I am in a maze from which I can find no way out. But so far I have managed, more or less, to save my face. Now, however, Madame Brigitte is beginning to use threats. She says that her conscience forbids her to remain my accomplice any longer in this deception. She insists that I tell Octavia where the money comes from. . . . Can you imagine such a thing?"

I could, very easily, and I told Monsieur Puybaraud that what really astonished me was that my stepmother should have consented to keep Octavia in the dark for so long. I made it pretty clear that I admired this scrupulous honesty on the part of my stepmother, though I did not say so in words. I was just then beginning to make the acquaintance of Pascal in the little Brunschwieg edition. The Brigitte Pian type appealed to me. I found it beautiful. It reminded me of Mother Agnès, of Mother Angélique, and of those other proud ladies of Port-Royal. I can see myself now, implacable in my youthful fervor, seated beside the log-fire in front of a little table loaded with dictionaries and notebooks with, opposite me, that poor, worn-out figure stretching two small, grubby white hands to the blaze, his uncobbled shoes smoking in the heat. There, in the flames, his gentle and defeated eyes could see the image of a woman lying in bed with her precious, menaced burden. That was a reality that Brigitte Pian refused to recognize, a reality that he could not make me see. My stepmother had said to him more than once: "I warned you before it all happened: you have no cause of grievance against me." It was true that everything was turning out precisely as she had foreseen, that in the light of events she could feel no doubt of the illumination which had descended from God upon her spirit.

"She left me with a threat. She warned me that she would call on Octavia late tomorrow afternoon," said Monsieur Puybaraud in a gloomy voice. "She is going to bring her some broth, but she insists that between now and then I shall prepare Octavia for the news of my real situation.

What am I to do? I want to spare my poor wife the spectacle of my shame. As you very well know, I am incapable of self-control. I shall not be able to keep myself from crying. . . ."

I asked him why he didn't get some pupils. Couldn't he do some tutoring? He shook his head. He had no degree, and his marriage had closed against him most of the houses in which he might have found some chance of employment.

"What a pity that *I* don't need a tutor," I said in a self-satisfied voice; "but you see, I am always top of the class."

"Oh, you!" he answered on a note of tender admiration. "You already know as much as I do. Pass your examination: get as many diplomas as you can, my boy. You don't need them now, but one never knows. . . . If only I had a degree!"

Child of a poor family, and educated out of charity by his future colleagues because they saw great possibilities in him, Léonce Puybaraud had found no difficulty in learning, and might have gone far, had he not been asked, when he reached the age of eighteen, to deputize for some of the teachers when the school happened to be short of staff. He had to continue his own education while acting as a teacher, and knew no more of literature than what he had managed to pick up from anthologies and school textbooks. On the other hand, he had read more deeply than most university students in the great classic writers of Greece and Rome. But today all his erudition could not help him to earn the three hundred francs a month which was the minimum on which his family could live.

I longed for him to go, and began turning over the pages of my dictionary in an effort to make it clear that I had no time to waste. But he allowed himself to relax in the warm,

145

cozy atmosphere of the room, in the presence of the youth to whom he was devoted. He sat there, wondering and wondering what he could do to disillusion Octavia without causing her too great an emotional disturbance.

"Why tell her yourself?" I suggested. "Couldn't you get somebody else to do it for you?—the Little Sister of the Assumption, for instance, who comes every day?"

"What a good idea, Louis!" he cried, slapping his skinny thighs. "No one but you would have thought of such a solution! She's a little saint, that girl. Octavia is devoted to her, and she to Octavia. It is quite curious to see two human beings each so convinced that she is inferior to the other. I only wish that Madame Brigitte could share the spectacle with me. It would teach her the nature of true humility. . . ."

He stopped because I pursed my lips. He felt that I was more completely under the influence of Madame Brigitte than he had ever been.

Next day, about the middle of the afternoon, Brigitte Pian descended from a landau in front of the house in the rue du Mirail where the Puybarauds lived in furnished rooms which she had chosen for them and whose rent she paid. Her arms were so loaded with a variety of parcels that she could not lift the hem of her skirt as she climbed the appallingly squalid staircase. The water from the household sinks ran in an open gutter. The smell was not unfamiliar to her: she met it constantly in the course of her charitable visits. The prevailing stench of urban poverty is always the same: a mixture of stews and privies. But it is not my intention to underrate what was best in Brigitte Pian's life, tempting though it is to do so. Whatever her true motives may have been, she was always a great giver of alms, and at times, when visiting the genuinely sick, showed herself capable of real personal devotion. She worked on the principle that it was better to provide solid help for a few than to spread inadequate relief over a wide field. I remember that when I accompanied her on her shopping rounds, she would buy cotton or groceries at out-of-the-way shops kept by protégés whom she had helped out of their difficulties, and would send her friends on similar errands. She spared these petty tradespeople neither advice nor criticism, and was forever complaining of the ingratitude of those who resolutely refused to make a success of their lives, no matter how much pecuniary aid she might bring them.

She had been less generous than usual with the Puybarauds and, though she kept them alive, left them to struggle along as best they could. I find it hard to say whether this was deliberate policy on her part. It is conceivable that she did not know the full facts of the case. I am inclined to think she considered it a good thing that they should remain in the state of penury which she had always predicted for them; should so obviously suffer the punishment that had come upon them as a result of their refusal to follow her advice. She never ceased to find a source of triumphant satisfaction in her knowledge that they were entirely dependent on her. Had she recognized the true nature of her feelings for Octavia, they might have caused her a passing tremor.

The first object that caught her eye as she entered the sick-room was an upright piano standing at right angles to the bed, close to the pillow. It took up so much space that it was difficult to move freely between the wardrobe, the table, and the dresser, on top of which lay a litter of bottles, cups, and dirty plates. (Each morning Monsieur Puybaraud in his haste would destroy the order that the little Sister of Mercy left behind her.)

While the first courtesies were being exchanged and their visitor was inquiring about the patient's health, the Puybarauds noticed—with what anxiety may be imagined—that the piano had already "caught Madame Brigitte's eye." They realized that at any moment she might begin to ask them about it. The shop from which they hired it had promised to take it away, but had not done so. That very morning Monsieur Puybaraud had started another hopeless discussion on the subject. How were they ever going to explain to Brigitte Pian that they had been guilty of so absurd an act of self-indulgence?—absurd, because neither of them could play a note, although they both loved picking out hymn tunes with one finger on the keys. Even had they not been in the last extremes of poverty, their hiring of the instrument would have been difficult to excuse: but dependent as they were for the very means of life on another's charity . . .

Octavia hurriedly embarked on a subject designed to divert Madame Brigitte's attention. She thanked that lady from the bottom of her heart for not having allowed Léonce to deceive her any longer about the source of the money that he brought home every other week. He had acted as he had with the best possible intentions and out of consideration for her. But for some time now she had suspected a trick, and had thought at first that it was of Madame Brigitte's own devising, since, as all the world knew, she would do good by stealth as others did evil. (Octavia was not wholly innocent of a fault, so widespread in the circles in which she had been brought up, where flattery causes few pangs when it is addressed to rich and influential patrons with the power of life and death over those around them.) She added that she

understood and shared Madame Brigitte's scruples of conscience. That lady listened with but half her mind. Her
eyes kept constantly returning to the piano. She interrupted
the invalid to say how sorry she was that she had caused
Monsieur Puybaraud any distress of mind. She might, she
said, have been weak enough to yield to him had she been
dealing with one of those many worldly persons who know
nothing of the ways of God. But she had decided that a
Christian like Octavia ought not to remain ignorant of the
consequences of her acts, that she ought to face the trials
that Providence had seen fit to lay upon her. "Since it was
clearly part of the Divine plan that you should live on the
charity of a devoted friend and that Monsieur Puybaraud
should be unable to find suitable employment, I felt that I
had no right to spare you the effects of so salutary a lesson."

Monsieur Puybaraud, having noted these words in his
diary, and stigmatized them as "damnable," adds: "I won't
swear that she spoke them with conscious irony, but I am
pretty sure that she felt considerable satisfaction at being
able to find a watertight excuse (from the religious point
of view, I mean) for the pleasure it gave her to know that
she had such a hold over us: that nothing stood between us
and starvation but the little envelope that I had to accept
from her twice a month."

"It is odd," she said, "but somehow I don't remember that
piano in the inventory sent me when I took these rooms for
you."

"No," replied Octavia in a voice that trembled; "it is a
piece of silliness for which I alone am responsible."

She looked at the elder woman with that sweet, disarming
smile which few could resist. But the expression of hauteur
on the face of her patroness showed no sign of softening.

"Forgive me, darling," broke in Monsieur Puybaraud; "it was I who suggested it, and I was thinking more about my own pleasure than yours."

It was foolish of him to call his wife "darling" in front of Brigitte Pian. She had always hated the lack of reserve in married couples who, presuming on the legitimacy of such endearments, stressed by word and gesture the fact of their squalid intimacy. In the case of this particular pair it was quite intolerable.

"Am I to understand," she inquired in tones that were suspiciously gentle, "that you have hired this piano?"

The accused nodded.

"One of you, then, must be capable of giving music lessons. I had an idea that you were both so ignorant of the art as not even to know your notes."

Octavia explained that they had agreed to give themselves this small indulgence.

"What indulgence? Picking out tunes with one finger as I often used to see you doing at school, though it made you ridiculous in the eyes of the girls?" Madame Brigitte, who scarcely ever laughed, emitted a sort of sharp bark.

Octavia hung her head. Her faded yellow hair was parted in the middle and drooped low on either side of her face. Her breast rose and fell rapidly beneath her coarse cotton slip.

"I know that it was wrong of us, Madame Brigitte," said Monsieur Puybaraud; "but please do not distress Octavia"— he dropped his voice to a whisper—"we will discuss the matter, if you don't mind, on the occasion of your next visit. I will explain it all. . . ."

"Yes"—she had adopted the same low tone—"we will go into it another time. You can tell me then where the money came from. . . ."

"It is yours: I am not denying that. . . . I realize that for people who are living on charity it is unpardonable to spend twenty francs a month on a piano that neither of them knows how to play. But I'd rather not discuss it now. . . ."

"What is there to discuss? You have already made the whole matter abundantly clear." Brigitte was still speaking in the same low voice (but Octavia had not lost a single word). "There is nothing you can add. You neither of you seem to realize that you have done anything at all out of the ordinary. It is not the money I am worrying about. . . . It is not a question of money. . . ."

Monsieur Puybaraud broke in by reminding her that she herself had remarked that there was no more to be said. He put his arms round Octavia, who was choking back her sobs. But Brigitte Pian, alarmed by the woman's tears, was in the grip of one of those fits of temper which she found it extremely hard to control, and regarded, in all humility, as a sign of that volcanic temperament with which it had pleased Heaven to endow her. Though she tried hard not to raise her voice, the fury of her mood came from behind clenched teeth in a spate of words.

"Well, I suppose I've got to make the best of it, but there is a limit, even to virtue! It is my duty not to be weak: however charitable I may have been toward you, I am not going to push kindness to the point of idiocy!"

"I beg of you either to stop talking or to go! Can't you see that you are distressing Octavia?" Monsieur Puybaraud so far forgot himself as to seize her by the arm and push her towards the door.

"How dare you lay a finger on me!" This attempt at physical interference with her movements had had the immediate effect of once more seating Brigitte Pian on the familiar throne of her perfection.

"No, Léonce!" groaned Octavia. "She is our benefactress. It is I whom you hurt when you fall short of the behavior she has a right to expect from us."

At this, Monsieur Puybaraud allowed himself to be carried away by one of those sudden outbursts of temper to which weak natures are prone. Seeing that Brigitte was already on the landing, he exclaimed rather too loudly: "After all, darling, this is our house, isn't it?"

My stepmother, framed in the doorway, drew herself to her full height. "*Your* house, indeed!"

Such an easy triumph enabled her to recover an almost divine complacency. The statement with which she had just silenced her wretched adversary stood in no need of being elaborated. But she could not resist the temptation of leveling a parting shot.

"Would you like me to send you the lease? You will find, I think, that the name in which it is drawn up is not yours!"

Monsieur Puybaraud slammed the door and went across to the bed where Octavia lay with her face in her hands, sobbing.

"It was wrong of you to act so, Léonce. We owe everything to her . . . and, really, you know, that piano . . ."

"Calm yourself, beloved: you'll do some injury to our child."

They always spoke of "our child" when referring to the still unborn life, the adored baby which might never come into the world. Holding his wife's head pressed close to him, he said, more than once: "Horrible creature!"

But Octavia protested. "No, Léonce, no; it is wrong to speak like that. Temperament is a stumbling-block to us all. It is easy enough not to commit crimes for which God has seen fit to spare us the opportunity. But only a special gift of Grace can enable us to overcome in our daily lives the real weaknesses of character with which we are burdened. It would have been better, perhaps, if Madame Brigitte had lived under convent discipline."

"If she ever had, she would soon have bossed the whole community. She'd have made them all tremble, and she'd have had plenty of time to pick out her particular victims. We ought to rejoice, rather, that she is not in a convent where she would have had complete authority over the lives and thoughts of the sisterhood. A woman like Brigitte Pian would be in her element there. We, at least, are free to starve, free never to set eyes on her again! . . ."

"I agree with you that she would have made it her business to insure the sanctity of the Sisters," said Octavia, still tearful, but with the faint glimmer of a smile. "You must have noticed that the history of the great Orders is full of instances of Superiors like Brigitte Pian. They have always helped the Community to take the stoniest way to Heaven—and the shortest, for people subjected to that sort of discipline do not live long. . . . But I oughtn't to talk like this," she added; "after all she *is* our benefactress. . . . Oh, it's wicked of me!"

For a while they said no more. Monsieur Puybaraud, seated on the bed, began to nibble one of the biscuits that Brigitte had brought with her. At last: "What's going to become of us?" he asked.

"You must go and see her tomorrow morning," replied Octavia. "I know her. She will spend tonight wrestling with her scruples, and will be the first to ask forgiveness. In any case, things will be different when little Louis arrives."

He could not share her conviction. Never, no, never, would he expose himself to such treatment again!

"It is hard to have to humble oneself, darling; for a man, and a really good man like you, it's the hardest thing in the world. But it is what God asks of us."

"What I find hardest to bear is her assumption that God has justified her belief that things would turn out exactly as they have. Do *you* think we are being punished for what we have done?"

"No," she exclaimed with eager passion. "Not punished but tested. We were right in what we did. Our lives belong together. Madame Brigitte does not understand that we were meant to suffer together."

"You're right. From our suffering has come all our happiness."

She flung her thin arms round his neck. "You regret nothing?"

"I suffer because I cannot support us . . . but once the child is born, nothing else will matter. Our happiness will be complete."

She whispered in his ear: "Don't set too much store on it, don't be too hopeful."

"What makes you think . . . Has the doctor said anything you haven't told me?"

He pressed her with questions, but she shook her head. No, the doctor had said nothing; it was only that she had an idea that the ultimate sacrifice might be asked of them. "No," said Monsieur Puybaraud again, as she went on to say that he must be ready to accept whatever God might think best for them, must acquiesce wholeheartedly in the possible ordeal, as Abraham had acquiesced, and that then, and then only, their Isaac might be given back to them. Monsieur Puybaraud continued to say "No," but more gently now, until at last he slid to his knees, pressed his forehead against the bed, and in a strangled voice made the responses to the evening prayer which Octavia had begun to recite.

When it was over she relapsed into silence and closed her eyes. Then her husband lit a candle, went over to the piano, the keys of which reflected the light, and, with one hesitating finger, tried to pick out her favorite hymn, the hymn sung by little children at their first Communion. As he did so he whispered the words:

"Heaven has come down to earth, my beloved rests in me."

# 12

BRIGITTE PIAN was no sooner in the street than she turned what remained of her anger against herself. How could she so utterly have lost control of her temper? What would the Puybarauds think? They did not, as she did, see her perfections from within, nor could they measure the height, breadth, and depth of her virtue. They would judge her in the light of an outburst which, if the truth were told, had made her feel thoroughly ashamed. How could human nature be relied upon, she thought as she walked up the rue du Mirail towards the Cours Victor-Hugo, if, after a whole lifetime spent in the conquest of herself, at an age when she might reasonably expect to be exempt from the weaknesses that disgusted her in others, the mere sight of a piano was enough to break down all her self-control?

Though the maintenance of her armor of perfection was one of her most constant preoccupations, there was nothing so very extraordinary in a link's occasionally working loose.

She could always console herself for such an occurrence—provided there had been no witness. But the Puybarauds, and especially Octavia, were the last people in the world before whom she would willingly have shown signs of weakness. "They'll take me for a beginner," said Brigitte to herself, and the idea was painful, because she measured her progress in the spiritual life very much as she would have done in the study of a foreign language. She was made furious by the thought that the Puybarauds should have no idea how she had "moved up" in class during the last few months; should, on the evidence of a moment's ill-humor, rank her with ordinary church-going females. Just how far Brigitte Pian had been "promoted" it was not for her, conscious of the need for humility, to say, but she would gladly have climbed all the way upstairs again to the Puybarauds' rooms just to remind them that even great saints have sometimes been the victims of bad temper. Was she a saint? She was making great efforts to be one, and, at each step forward, fought hard to hold the ground she had gained. No one had ever told her that the closer a man gets to sanctity the more conscious does he become of his own worthlessness, his own nothingness, and that he gives to God not from a sense of duty but because the evidence is overwhelming, all credit for the few good activities with which Grace has endowed him. Brigitte Pian pursued an opposite course, finding each day ever stronger reasons for thanking her Creator that He had made her so admirable a person. There had been a time when she was worried by the spiritual aridity that marked her relations with her God; but since then she had read somewhere that it is as a rule the beginners on whom the tangible marks of Grace are showered, since it is only in that way that they can be extricated from the slough of this world and set upon the right path. The kind of insensitiveness that afflicted her was, she gathered, a sign that she had long ago emerged from those lower regions of the spiritual life where fervor is usually suspect. In this way her frigid soul was led on to glory in its own lack of warmth. It did not occur to her that never for a single moment, even in the earliest stages of her search for perfection, had she felt any emotion which could be said to have borne the faintest resemblance to love: that she had never approached her Master save with the object of calling His attention to her own remarkably rapid progress along the Way, and suggesting that He give special heed to her singular merits.

Nevertheless, here, on the pavement between the rue du Mirail and the Cours de l'Intendance, as she made her way up the rue Duffour-Dubergier and the rue Vital-Carle, all blanketed in their customary fog, Brigitte Pian found herself yielding to a mood of spiritual discomfort which was far more profound than could be accounted for merely by the fact that she had cheapened herself in the Puybarauds' eyes. A sense of suppressed anxiety (which, though it was sometimes in abeyance, never wholly vanished from her consciousness) made her aware that the balance-sheet of her soul had not been truly audited, and that she too might one day be weighed in those unchanging standards of the Infinite by which, so she had always understood, the Uncreated Being was in the habit of judging the world of men. There were days—more particularly those on which she had been to see Octavia Tronche—when a flash of lightning would tear holes in the mists that shrouded her soul, and show her to herself as she really was. When that happened, she realized beyond all possibility of denial (the mood never lasted for more than a moment) that her way of life was not the only way of life, nor her God the only God. The sense of satisfaction in being Brigitte Pian, which as a rule was so

157

overpowering, fell away from her suddenly, and she shivered, feeling herself naked and miserable, cast upon an arid waste of sand beneath a copper sky. Far away she could hear angelic choirs, and, mingled with them, the hateful voices of the Puybarauds. The feeling soon passed, and she always managed, by dint of certain impromptu prayers of proved efficacy, to recover her spiritual equilibrium. When the need for such rehabilitation came on her, she would pause before an altar somewhere (as now in the Cathedral) until silence once more filled her heart. She not only felt the silence, but adored it as a sign sent to her from her hidden Master that she had again found grace in His eyes. But today, first before the Holy Sacrament and, later, before the statue of the Virgin which stands behind the choir (looking for all the world like the Empress Eugénie), she was conscious of a voice within her that spoke in tones of disapproval. "It has been sent to try me," she thought; "I must submit in all humility"—which was her way of saying: "Notice, I beg, O Lord, that I do not kick against the pricks, and enter my acquiescence, please, on the credit side of the account." But since peace of mind still would not come to her, she went into a confessional and accused herself of violence of thought, though not of injustice (for her anger had been fully justified), of having failed to keep her legitimate indignation within the bounds of a duly disciplined charity.

If, after luncheon next day, Monsieur Puybaraud had seen Brigitte in her own home, he would have found himself in the presence of a woman now utterly defenseless and only too willing to exhibit herself as an object-lesson in humility. In the matter of humility she feared competition with none. But when, pale with emotion, he asked the servant whether her mistress was at home, he was told that she had been summoned back to Larjuzon by telegram, and that the young people had gone with her. Monsieur Pian had been taken suddenly ill, and the wording of the telegram had been sufficiently alarming to make Madame pack at once; she had taken "the nearest thing to mourning that she happened to have."

There was nothing suspicious about my father's death. Saintis (who had been re-established in the vacancy left by the dismissal of Vignotte) had found him early in the morning, lying on his face by the side of his bed and already cold. Like many of his comfortable country neighbors, Octave Pian had always eaten and drunk too much; but after he had been left alone in the house, his drinking had taken on frightening proportions. The evening before his death he must have surpassed himself, for the bottle of Armagnac which he had opened that day was found empty in the study, where it was his custom to sit smoking by the fire until the stroke of midnight.

I know today that Brigitte Pian's scruples had crystallized around the paper to which I have already referred. Rightly or wrongly, she held that it must strike a final blow at my mother's memory. I long believed that when she went from Larjuzon she had deliberately left that document in a drawer where she was certain that sooner or later my father must find it. That was, doubtless, to let my imagination outstrip events. Knowing what I do today, I can read their true meaning into the phrases my stepmother endlessly repeated as she lay in her bedroom through the long nights that preceded and followed my father's funeral. Lying wide-eyed in the dark, I listened in a state of terror, firmly convinced that Brigitte Pian had gone mad. Beneath the door, whose woodwork had been gnawed by rats, the light showed, obscured at regular intervals by the passage of her body as she paced up and down. Though she was wearing bedroom slippers, the floor creaked beneath her tread. "I must think, I must think," she kept on saying in a loud voice. I can hear the words still, words spoken by someone intent on getting order into the confusion of her mind at any price. She could have shown him the paper, but she had not done so. She had always hesitated to cause him anxiety, although it would have been a simple matter for her to destroy the kind of worship with which he surrounded the memory of Marthe. But she had never allowed herself to do so. It was far from certain that he would open that drawer. The only thing for which she can be truly blamed is that she did not burn the paper. . . . She never did, but it was not because she still had a lingering hope that one day he would discover it. "Into Thy hands, O Lord, I commit myself." God must be the judge. Whether or no Octave opened the drawer must depend on God, and even if he did, it must still depend on God whether the poor man would understand the meaning of what he read, would attach any significance to it. There is nothing to prove that he *would* have caught its drift. "I know, of course, that the document is no longer in the drawer, and that the stove in the hall is full of the fragments of papers that he burned. But he got rid of everything that had belonged to his first wife, and of that paper along with the rest. . . . He didn't know what he was doing. He was drinking hard at the time, had made up his mind to get as drunk as possible. . . ."

These are not, I need hardly say, her actual words. I have reconstructed them from memory, giving full weight to what I have learned since, but did not know at the time. I have set myself the task of getting at the heart of her scruples. The only ones to which I can bear witness are "I must think," which expressed the eager necessity to which her wandering mind still clung during the long night.

Michèle pretended not to see Brigitte—poor Michèle, who had to face the torment of her own remorse, a remorse which I shared with her, which for some time had been a part of both our lives, but of which now in the evening of my days I can recapture no trace. However genuine Michèle's sorrow may have been—and she had loved her father dearly—her chief preoccupation just before the funeral, when she was at Larjuzon, was to wonder whether she would see Jean at the service. And when it was all over, her grief as a daughter was dominated and, so to speak, eclipsed by her disappointment at not having caught a glimpse of Mirbel in the congregation.

Because she was afraid that the thick crape that veiled her face might prevent her from noticing him, she had given me the task of telling her the moment I caught sight of Jean de Mirbel. So wholly had I identified my wishes with hers that my own personal feelings counted for nothing in the curiosity with which I scrutinized the faces of the local shopkeepers and countryfolk who crowded the church. Among all these animal faces, with their ferrety noses, their foxy or rabbity masks and cowlike expressions, some of the women's eyes looking dead or vacant, others bright, glittering, birdlike, and utterly stupid, I sought for the familiar features, the powerful brow beneath its shock of short curly hair, the eyes, the laughing mouth—but all in vain. No doubt Jean had been afraid that he might have to pass in front of my stepmother, but, since it was not customary for the widow to accompany the coffin to the graveside, I still had hope that he might pluck up courage and join us.

The morning had promised well, but later a mist had

blown across the face of the feeble sun. Up to that very last moment when we stood by the open grave, while the trowel was passing from hand to hand among a crowd of living persons who looked in the shrouding fog as though they were already half-dead themselves, while skimpy handfuls of earth were falling on the coffin of that Octave Pian who had perhaps never been my father after all, I still hoped to see Jean's figure emerge from the ghostlike figures that surrounded me. More than once Michèle thought she had seen him, and pressed my arm. For years afterward we shared a feeling of shame when we remembered that day. Still, the very pain it caused us was in itself a proof that we had genuinely loved our father. I no longer feel indignant now at the thought of that convention which claimed my sister's obedience in the little cemetery of Larjuzon. She was one of those human beings whose temperaments are so surely balanced, their hearts so pure, that their instincts are almost always at one with their duty, so that their natural inclinations lead them to do precisely what God expects of them.

In the afternoon my stepmother retired to her room, where we could hear her pacing up and down until the evening. Contrary to custom, we none of us appeared at the funeral meal, but the din reached us upstairs where we had taken refuge. In the absence of any near relation, our guardian, Monsieur Malbec, the local solicitor, did the honors. He came up to us after coffee, red in the face and almost merry. We knew that there were clients waiting for him, and that we should not have to endure his presence for long. If I were writing a novel, I should find it amusing to sketch in the character of Malbec, who was the sort of man of whom it is said that "he might have stepped straight out of the pages of Balzac." But he played no other part in our lives than that of a man who relieved us of all those responsibilities which might have served to divert our attention from what was going on in our hearts and minds. He bored me to extinction. Whenever I had to visit him in his office to hear him read documents which I then signed with my initials, I used to tell myself stories in an effort to alleviate the tedium. During all the period of my youth I believed (or behaved as though I believed) that people like him, with their bony skulls, their pince-nez and their whiskers, middle-aged men of business who looked as though they were made up for a part, knew nothing of the human affections and were utter strangers to the emotions of every day.

When Monsieur Malbec had left us, and the last carriages had driven off, we gave ourselves over to what at that moment seemed to us no less than sacrilege—to a discussion, in fact, of Mirbel. We sat there talking of him and smoking, in a room that was separated only by a partition from the one from which our father's body had been so lately taken. We realized then that we should have no difficulty about going over to see Jean at Baluzac. The cemetery, which we were to visit again next day, lay beyond the village and directly on the Baluzac road. We could easily make the journey to the presbytery on foot. Brigitte Pian seemed to be in no state to keep an eye on us, and the death of her father had released Michèle from her promise.

When the next day came, the fog was thicker than ever. If we kept to the woods it was most unlikely that we should meet anybody. At the grave, with its panoply of already faded flowers, Michèle insisted on saying the *De Profundis* twice over. I thought she was never going to finish. Then, with a strong sense that we were abandoning our poor dead father, we began walking so fast that in spite of the mist the sweat began to stand out on my forehead in great drops. Michèle led the way. She was wearing a white beret (the only mourning hat she had was the one she had worn at the funeral), and a short jacket cut close to her waist which, in those days, most people would have thought was rather thick. Her shoulders were too high. Those physical blemishes are still vivid in my memory. But her dumpy little figure radiated strength and an overmastering vitality.

The few houses composing the township of Baluzac seemed stricken with death. They formed no street, and there was nothing that bore any resemblance to a market-square. The presbytery was separated from the church by the graveyard. Beyond it was the new school; opposite, a combination inn and grocery-store, the blacksmith's forge and Voyod's drugstore, which on this particular day was shut. Two-thirds of the abbé Calou's parishioners lived in isolated farms lying some miles outside the hamlet.

The kitchen-garden appeared to be abandoned. "Wait till I've got my breath before you knock," said Michèle. She did not make the gesture she would certainly make today, for she owned neither powder nor lipstick. For that matter, she had not even a handbag, but only a pocket in her skirt.

I lifted the knocker. The sound echoed through the house as though it had been an empty sepulcher. Half a minute passed, and then we heard the sound of a chair's being pushed back, followed by the noise of dragging clogs. The door was opened by what might have been a ghost. It was the abbé Calou. He was already much thinner than when I had met him last in the Cours de l'Intendance.

"Ah, my dear young people . . . I was just going to write to you. I ought to have come to the funeral . . . but I didn't dare—because of Madame Pian, you know."

He led the way into the drawing-room and opened the shutters. It was as though an icy cape had fallen about our shoulders. When he asked us, rather hesitatingly, whether we weren't afraid of catching cold, I said that, as a matter of fact, we had got very warm, and perhaps it would be wiser if we went upstairs. He seemed put out by the suggestion, begged us to forgive the untidiness we should find there, and then, with a faint shrug, signed to us to follow him.

I could feel Michèle go tense in anticipation of the longed-for meeting. Jean would appear, leaning over the banisters. He was, perhaps, behind the very door that the abbé Calou was even then in the act of opening—still to an accompaniment of muttered apologies.

"The bed is not made. Maria is growing old, and I never feel really up to the mark in the morning. . . ."

What a mess! Books were scattered all over the gray-looking sheets. On the mantelpiece, in a confusion of papers, stood a plate with the remains of a meal. The coffeepot was wedged in the dead ashes of the grate.

The abbé Calou pulled two chairs forward and himself sat down on the bed.

"I should like to be able to tell you that I share your sorrow, but for the moment I am incapable of thinking of others. I am the prisoner of my own misery. Perhaps you know where he is? There must be rumors going round. I know nothing at all, and it looks as though I never shall, because it is not very likely that his family will keep me informed of the result of their search—as you may well imagine! Forgive me for talking like this. . . . Since the whole wretched business started, I have not exchanged ten words with a single living soul. . . . The people here turn their backs on me, or, worse still, laugh at me. . . ."

"What wretched business?" I asked.

But Michèle had understood. "What has happened to him? Nothing serious?"

165

The abbé Calou kept hold of the hand she had stretched toward him. He repeated that he was the last person in the world to be able to give her an answer. He was the one person who must expect to be told nothing. . . . At length he became aware of our amazement.

"You didn't know he had gone? You weren't told? It'll be a week ago tomorrow."

We exclaimed with one voice: "Gone? but why?"

The abbé raised his arms and let them fall again. "Why? . . . boredom, of course. . . . Living here with a priest, an old priest. . . . But the idea would never have occurred to him if someone hadn't started meddling. . . . No, I can't speak out to you . . . you're both of you only children. Ah, Michèle, you alone could have . . . you alone . . ."

I had never seen a man of his age, let alone a priest, cry. His tears were not those of a grown-up person. His drowned blue eyes were just like those that his mother must have wiped sixty years before, on some occasion when he was terribly unhappy, and there was something childlike in the way his mouth was twisted awry by grief.

"I thought I had done everything possible. . . . I ought to have run after you, Michèle, got hold of you by hook or by crook, brought you here by force. But my judgment was at fault. What an idiotic arrangement that was of mine that you and I should exchange letters! Naturally, you couldn't resist the temptation of slipping a note to Jean into an envelope addressed to me. I ought to have foreseen that. You probably don't know that, so far as my part in the affair is concerned, a complaint has been made to the Archbishop. That dear woman, your stepmother, has lodged a formal charge against me. Fortunately, Cardinal Lecot is not so formidable as he looks. I have no doubt that His Eminence has had a good laugh at my expense. He referred to me as

'Love's messenger' and quoted some Latin verses. But that was because he wanted to treat the whole thing as a joke instead of taking it seriously. The Cardinal is a hard man, and his mockery is terrible, but he has the heart that usually goes with a fine intelligence. I realize that he has behaved very well. . . ."

Monsieur Calou hid his face for a moment in his two enormous hands. Michèle asked him what she ought to do. He lowered his hands and looked at her for an instant. A smile spread over his tear-stained face.

"Oh, it's very simple for you, Michèle. So long as you and he are still alive, all is not lost. Do you know what you mean to him—really know? But it is different for me. I can suffer: I know that. One can always suffer for others. . . ." Then he muttered, as though to himself: "Do I really believe that?" He seemed to have forgotten our presence. "Yes, I do. What an appalling doctrine it is that acts count for nothing, that no man can gain merit for himself or for those he loves. All through the centuries Christians have believed that the humble crosses to which they were nailed on the right or the left hand of our Lord counted for their own redemption and for the redemption of those they loved. And then Calvin came and took away that hope. But I have never lost it. . . . No," he said, "no!"

Michèle and I exchanged glances. We thought he was going out of his mind, and we were frightened. He had taken from his pocket a huge purple-checked handkerchief. He wiped his eyes and made an effort to steady his voice.

"You can write to La Devize, Louis," he said to me. "It is natural that you should ask the Countess for news of your friend. You'll have to read between the lines of her reply, of course, for no one can lie as she can. . . . Perhaps he's back home already. They can't have got far," he added.

"Then he wasn't alone?" asked Michèle.

The abbé kept his eyes on the fire to which he had just added a log. I pointed out that one couldn't travel without money, and that Mirbel was given practically nothing by his family.

"He was always complaining of that. You can't have forgotten, sir?"

The abbé went on picking red-hot embers from the fire as though he had not heard my question. We stood there waiting, while he, obviously frightened of being interrogated, hoped that we would go. Michèle brought no pressure to bear on him. She gave one last look round the dirty, untidy room, and then slowly went downstairs, her hand touching the rail on which Jean's must so often have rested. The paper on the wall showed damp patches, the very tiles of the hall floor were wet.

"Please," said the Curé, "write as soon as you hear anything, and I will do the same."

"I'm not asking you the name of the person he went away with," said Michèle suddenly. (I heard later that she had picked up from Saintis the rumors that were going around about Hortense Voyod and the odd young fellow who was living up at Monsieur Calou's.) "Though it's not hard to guess," she added with a laugh.

I remember that laugh very clearly. The Curé had opened the front door and the mist had drifted in, smelling of smoke. Monsieur Calou began talking very fast, without looking at us, and still keeping his hand upon the latch.

"What has that got to do with you? It is a matter of no importance, Michèle, because he cares about no one in the world except you. You were his despair. What has it got to do with you," he repeated, "if another woman took the chance that came her way simply because you were not on

168

the spot? Have some pity on me and don't ask questions. . . . You'll hear all you want to know from the people round. You won't even have to ask them. It is not for a poor priest to speak of such things. You are a couple of children. All I am permitted to say, Michèle, is that if Jean is to be saved, it will be through you. No matter what happens, he will never forsake you. He has not in any real sense betrayed you. . . . He was to me as the son of my old age, but I made no attempt to force his confidence. The office of fatherhood, which I had myself assumed, put no obligation on him. He is guilty of an offense against God alone, that God whose presence I so signally failed to make him feel, of whom he knew no more after all these months spent under my roof than he did on that first day when the three of you were quarreling in the garden: do you remember?"

Yes, I remembered. Young though I was, the past had already become for me an abyss in which even the most trivial events of my childhood were transformed into lost delights.

It may have been on this very evening, after we had closed the door behind us and had plunged into the fog, that Monsieur Calou wrote the lines that are now lying before me.

*If we want to know in what relation we really stand to God, we cannot do better than consider our feelings about other people. This is peculiarly the case when one person above all others has touched our affections. If he is seen to be the source of all our happiness and all our pain, if our peace of mind depends on him alone, then, let it be said at once, we are separated as far from God as we can be, short of having committed mortal sin. Not that love of God condemns us to aridity in our human friendships, but it does lay on us the duty of seeing that our affection for other human beings shall not be an end in itself, shall not usurp the place of that utterly complete love which no one can begin to understand who has not felt it. During the retreat I made before I was ordained, I sacrificed to Thee, O God, all hope of human fatherhood. I sought to find it again in my feeling for this boy. How could I hope to overcome in him and conquer those natural instincts of the young animal, if I found them so attractive? It is easier to hate the evil in ourselves than in those we love.*

Michèle led the way. Each time I tried to catch up with her she quickened her pace as though she wanted to be left undisturbed. She held her head high and gave no sign that what she had just heard had beaten down her high spirit. All that really mattered to me was that we should get home before our stepmother should have noticed our long absence. This anxiety blotted all other considerations from my mind.

As we crossed the hall on the way to our rooms, Brigitte opened the door of the small drawing-room and called to us. "Wouldn't you like some tea? It will warm you after your long walk."

Michèle replied that she was not hungry, but, faced by the insistence of our stepmother, she felt, I think, that she mustn't seem fearful or anxious to conceal anything. We entered the room, therefore, and found the tea things laid. Brigitte Pian's face was void of the expression that I knew so well when she was girding herself for battle. I was pretty sure, however, that she knew where we had been, and I found it hard to square with her actual appearance of fatigue and defeat the mood of anger that should normally have been hers. She filled our cups and buttered some slices of bread. These she offered first to Michèle, after which she asked us, as though it had been the most natural thing in the world, whether we had seen the abbé Calou. Michèle nodded assent, but the crash of thunder that I fully expected to follow never came.

"In that case," said Brigitte in a sad and sympathetic voice, "I suppose you know . . ."

Michèle, keen to carry the fight into the enemy's camp, interrupted the sentence. We knew all that there was to know, but she would rather not discuss it. . . . As she moved towards the door, my stepmother called her back. "Please stay here a little longer, Michèle."

"If you are going to preach to me, I tell you plainly that I am in no mood . . ."

The note of defiance in the girl's voice seemed to make no impression on Brigitte Pian, who doubtless was pursuing her own train of thought. What was it?

"You need not worry. I haven't the heart to preach to you. I only want you to be fair to me. But I want that very much."

Michèle, her face set in hard lines, was wondering how the attack was going to develop. She raised her cup to her lips and slowly sipped her tea, thus avoiding the necessity of answering Brigitte, and forcing that lady to show her hand.

"You will tell me that it is useless to look for justice to our fellow men, and that the approval of our own conscience should be sufficient for us. But, like all other human beings, I am weak. I have no wish to triumph over you, my poor child, but, for my own peace of mind, I want you to admit that I was right in scenting danger for you. You do see that, don't you? This young man has turned out to be even worse than I feared. I knew how to protect you as well as your real mother, if not better. . . ."

We were so used to the fact that Brigitte Pian never spoke

aimlessly that our first instinct was always to wonder what lay behind her words. I think she had never been more sincere than she was at that moment. There was nothing to tell us that the question which she had put to Michèle was the expression of an agony of mind which had not left her for a single instant since our father's death. We knew nothing of that. What she wanted was to be reassured. She did not see how Michèle could possibly avoid the necessity of admitting that she had been right.

My sister had no idea of the strength of the blow she was leveling at her enemy when she exclaimed: "You want me to recognize that you were stronger than I was. Well, I do. It was you and you only who separated us. It was you who drove him to desperation. If he is a lost soul, you are the cause of his damnation, and if I . . ."

The sky did not fall. Brigitte Pian remained seated in her chair: or rather, contrary to her usual habit, she lay slumped in it. She scarcely raised her voice.

"Sorrow has unhinged your mind, Michèle. Either that, or you have not been told all. If anyone is the cause of his damnation, it is that Voyod woman."

"A letter from me would have sufficed to turn him from his intention, just one letter. If only I had been able to speak to him, if only you had not put yourself between us with the same merciless obstinacy that has led you to ruin the abbé Calou in the eyes of his Superiors. . . ."

Sobs prevented Michèle from going on. It was the first time that she had ever cried in her struggles with Brigitte. It was as though some instinct prompted by hatred had told her that tears would spoil the older woman's triumph and leave her beaten and bewildered.

"Come now," said Brigitte Pian, "come now." She spoke in the same voice that she had used during the night when

I had heard her muttering to herself. "You can hardly deny that the young man has shown himself to be a black sheep, an evildoer. . . ."

"An evildoer because at eighteen he has let himself be led away . . . ?" Michèle hesitated to add "by a woman."

"Yes," Brigitte insisted, with the concentrated passion of someone seeking to gain peace of mind. "I mean what I say —an evildoer. We will leave the woman out of it, if you so wish. The fact remains that this young man of good family has behaved like a ruffian, and that if there was any justice in this world, he would be behind bars at this moment."

Michèle shrugged her shoulders. This kind of talk seemed utterly absurd to her. Its very excess did something to disarm her indignation. She replied that, as everyone knew, Brigitte Pian was quite unable to control herself when she had to deal with a matter of this kind. The prisons would have to be enlarged if all the young men guilty of such crimes were to be locked up.

"It isn't every young man," retorted Brigitte, "who breaks open desks and runs off with his benefactor's savings."

She had flung this remark at my sister with no definite intention, thinking that we knew all the circumstances of Jean's flight. The look of horror on Michèle's face warned her too late of her mistake. She jumped up and hurried to the girl's assistance, but Michèle pushed her away and sought comfort on my shoulder. I was standing close to the wall.

"That's a wicked lie!" She spoke so fast that the words tumbled over one another. "An invention of the Vignottes!"

"You didn't know it, my poor dears?" She fixed on us a long gaze of happy astonishment. Never had she addressed us in tones so quiet, so almost gentle. She felt reassured. We should have to admit that no mother could have acted otherwise.

Evening was deepening into night. Brigitte stood there illuminated only by the flickering flames.

"I should have realized that that wretched abbé wouldn't have the courage to tell you of his pupil's villainy. I am sorry I gave you such a shock, Michèle. But now do you understand? It was my duty to protect you against a criminal. I knew what I was about. The necessary information was given me by the Comte de Mirbel . . . but too late, alas, and for that I ask your forgiveness. My great fault lay in ever letting you associate with that young ne'er-do-well. I should never have regarded the presence of Monsieur Calou as providing a sufficient guarantee. I fear I was wrong, too, in my estimate of him. . . ."

She took our silence for acquiescence and proceeded to yield utterly to her craving for self-abandonment and surrender.

"There are moments in one's life," she went on, "when one fails to see clearly. More than once I have questioned myself, have felt myself oppressed by doubts. . . . Your father's death had a greater effect on me than you will ever realize. We are responsible for every one of the souls with which God brings us into contact on our way through life. 'What hast thou done to thy brother?' That question, put by God to Cain, I asked myself when I looked at the dead body of the man whose soul had been so suddenly withdrawn. Sudden death is a fearful warning. . . . Each day I become more aware of all those for whom I shall have to answer. There may have been times when my judgment was wrong, but God is my witness that I have always striven for His greater glory and for the welfare of men's souls. . . . What was that you said, Michèle?"

My sister shook her head as a sign that she had said nothing, moved away from the wall, and left the room. I made as though to follow her, but my stepmother kept me back.

"No, better leave her alone with her thoughts."

Time passed. Brigitte Pian poked the fire, and every now and again a flame leapt upwards, setting her large face in a warm glow, and then died down, until nothing but her forehead and the pale mass of her cheeks was visible in the gathering dusk.

"No," I said suddenly, "it would be better not to leave her alone."

I went up to Michèle's room and knocked, but there was no reply. I opened the door, thinking that she was lying in the dark as it was so often her habit to do. I called to her in a low voice, for I was frightened of dark rooms. But she was not there. I looked for her high and low, scouring the house from the kitchen to the linen cupboard. But no one had seen her. I went out onto the steps. The cold darkness was lit by an invisible moon. I went back to the small drawing-room.

"I don't know where Michèle is," I cried; "I have looked for her everywhere."

"Well, she's probably gone out—into the town, perhaps. What is there so tragic about that, you little silly?"

My stepmother had risen from her chair. With the tears pouring down my cheeks, I replied that there was nothing to take Michèle into the town at this time of night; at which, in a wild sort of voice, she murmured that these children would drive her mad. But already she had hurried before me to the steps. Someone was walking along the path.

"Is that you, Michèle?"

"No, ma'am: it's Saintis."

Saintis, her enemy, had been reinstated, and she could not,

with decency, dismiss him until some further time should have elapsed. He was out of breath, and we could hear him panting in the darkness. He told us that Mademoiselle Michèle had borrowed a lamp from him for her bicycle. She had asked him to tell Madame not to wait dinner, as she had something very important to see to.

"Where can she have gone?"

"Gone? To Baluzac, I don't mind betting."

"I suppose it is just as well," said Brigitte Pian when we had returned to the little drawing-room, where a lamp was now burning. "She probably hopes that the abbé Calou will explain everything satisfactorily, will be able to gloss matters over. . . . Still, theft with breaking and entering is theft with breaking and entering: nothing will alter that."

She started to stroke my hair: "What an example for you, my poor boy," she sighed. "At your age you should know nothing of such horrors. But what a lesson, too, Louis! Look at your sister, a good girl if ever there was one . . . yet nothing can keep her from roaming the woods and fields on a winter's night. That is what passion does to human beings—just swallows them up. Promise me that you will be different, that you will never let yourself be changed into a wild beast."

She tried to kiss me, but I turned away my face and went to the other end of the room, where I sat down out of reach of the circle of lamplight.

# 13

I SAID nothing that could betray the hatred with which she filled me. But she must have felt its presence there between us as we sat together at dinner, and later still, while we waited for Michèle. It was eleven o'clock before she got back. This time Brigitte called to her in vain. Michèle went straight upstairs without pausing at the drawing-room. I replied in monosyllables to the remarks that my stepmother made as she gave me my candle.

Just as I was bracing myself to stretch my legs beneath the icy sheets, she came into my room. She had on one of the purple dressing-gowns she liked to wear, and—as usual after she had undressed—her lusterless hair hung in a thick braid.

"It's a cold night: I've brought you a hot-water bottle," she said.

She slipped it into my bed and touched my feet. For the first time in my experience she kissed me good night and tucked me up.

"The poor child didn't dare admit that Monsieur Calou had finally opened her eyes to what really happened. I think I know how she must be suffering. We must be gentle with her. She will realize later that I was right. . . . Don't you think she will?" she asked, raising the candle above her head the better to see me.

Sheer exhaustion offered me a way of escape. I closed my eyes and turned my face to the wall, taking refuge in a state that was half waking, half sleeping, like a swimmer struggling between conflicting currents.

She sighed. "Asleep already!" she murmured. "How lucky you are!" and went back to the loneliness of her own room.

I was awakened in the night by the creaking of her floor. I told myself that she was brooding over her scruples, and the thought gave me an unworthy sense of pleasure. I did not realize then the full horror of the torment that they inflict upon themselves, those servants of God who do not know the true nature of love.

Next day at breakfast, Michèle, looking pale and heavy-eyed, avoided my questions.

"According to Monsieur Calou it is ridiculous to say that he stole anything," she told me. "The abbé was in the habit of making small advances to Jean when he wanted money. This time Jean helped himself, but he knew that his mother would pay it back at once. He left a note in the desk, and the abbé knew perfectly well that he would be reimbursed."

I asked whether it was true that Mirbel had broken open the lock. My sister was forced to admit that he had, but she was annoyed by the face I pulled, and turned her back on me, refusing to say any more. The odd thing was that though I regarded such an act as monstrous, it somehow reawakened my feeling of affection for Mirbel. I could never willingly turn from him or deny him, and I trembled to think that I was thus indissolubly bound to a boy who could wallow in crime.

It was only much later, and then in fragments only, that the details of this adventure were imparted to me, not by Monsieur Calou but by Michèle herself. Even today, the old Countess sometimes talks of that time when I go to see her, but without the slightest sign that she finds the memory of it in any way embarrassing. "It would make a good subject for one of your novels," she says, savoring her words as though they were something good to eat. "I might have kept it for myself, but you can have it. I'd only spoil it. It's not really my genre. It has nothing to do with love, you see. . . ." For her, only fashionable adultery has any right to the name of love.

The origin of this theft and of this flight which lay so heavily on Michèle's destiny was to be found in a "good deed" that the abbé Calou had performed many years earlier during his first few years at Baluzac. He was suffering at that time from the worst form of spiritual discomfort to which a priest is subject. He felt convinced that the great mass of the people with whom he was brought in contact had no need of him. It wasn't that they cared nothing for the Kingdom of God: they did not even know that it existed, had never been stung to awareness by the good news of the Gospel. For them the Church was merely an organization which carried out certain prearranged rites suitable for special occasions, using for the purpose a class of men called priests. That was the most they would admit. What, then, was left for a priest to do but turn in upon himself and tend in his own heart the flickering flame that lit his footsteps, and those of a very few others, until such time as God's intentions for His world should be manifested with glory?

Such was the abbé's state of mind when, after twelve years spent in a seminary, he had to give up the Chair he occupied because of certain charges that had been leveled at his orthodoxy. Very humbly he had accepted the cure of souls at Baluzac, a place situated on the border of the heath country, and one of the most unpopular livings in the whole diocese. Study and prayer made up the tale of his days. He decided that he would devote himself entirely to the small flock entrusted to him without looking for any results. On the very first Sunday after his installation he spoke as simply as he could—such was always his habit—to about forty faithful parishioners, but without any deliberate attempt to put himself on their level. The subject with which his sermon dealt was the priest's mission. What he really did was to meditate out loud, speaking to himself rather than to them. The next day he found, slipped beneath his door, an anonymous letter of eight pages. A woman had heard him and had understood. She must be a person of education. She had come to church, she said, out of curiosity, and because she had nothing else to do. She had gone away completely overwhelmed. But she complained that priests had fallen into the error of waiting until the lost sheep came to them. They should imitate their Master who sought them out and carried them home upon His shoulders. She alluded to something shameful that could not be put into words, to a state of despair from which the human soul could not free itself unless God took the first steps towards achieving its release.

That morning the abbé Calou believed that a sign had been vouchsafed to him. He was by temperament inclined (like Pascal) to expect from God perceptible signs, materia' evidence. This cry which, on the very first day of his new life, had reached him from the wastes of a forgotten countryside, he interpreted as an answer to his prayer for comfort, it is true, as a reply to his questing heart, but also as a gentle reproach. He prepared his sermon for the following Sunday with all his usual care, but, while couching it in general terms, he weighed its every word so that the unknown writer of the letter might hear in it an answer designed for her in particular. As he glanced round the congregation, he saw two brown eyes fixed on him from behind a pillar, and noticed that they were set in a young, fresh face that lacked something of firmness in its contours. Later that same day he discovered that it belonged to a schoolmistress from Vallandraut who came frequently to Baluzac for reasons that his informants would not specify, though they shook their heads a good deal and chuckled. The abbé Calou noted in his diary how fierce a struggle he had had to wage with himself before delivering his sermon, but after that single entry there are no further references to the incident, or only such indirect and obscure hints as would have meaning for no one but himself. This was due to the fact that the schoolmistress had almost at once become his penitent, and that he felt himself bound by the secrecy of the confessional.

I will set down, as discreetly as possible, what I know of the affair. This young and innocent woman had, very early, fallen under the fascination of Hortense Voyod—a type of amazon not wholly unknown, contrary to general opinion, in country districts. There are people who set their toils and are prepared to go hungry for a very long while before any prey lets itself be caught. The patience of vice is infinite. One single victim will content such people, and a brief moment of contact will insure them long years of happy repletion. When at the end of September Monsieur Calou entered on his cure at Baluzac, the apothecary's wife had just completed a different kind of cure at Vichy. Though she was fully aware that her new young friend would be a difficult catch to land, since she was a girl with an excessively scrupulous conscience, she was far from supposing that her influence would be seriously menaced. She could think of no one within a radius of ten miles whose interference she need fear. Consequently, she attached little importance to the letter she received one morning putting an end to the friendship, though it did have the effect of making her hasten her return. No sooner had she got home than she discovered the identity of her adversary. She told herself that it would be mere child's play to get the better of him.

Here, once again, if I am to be faithful to my promise to invent nothing, I cannot describe a struggle about the progress of which I have no precise information. It must have been hard, since the abbé Calou, who never asked favors and hated meddling, managed to get his penitent transferred. The young girl, in spite of the fact that she was sent to another school, was still exposed not only to Madame Voyod's letters, but also to her frequent visits that lady having recently bought a car, the first to be owned by anyone in Baluzac. But on the very eve of the day that she had chosen for her second trip, the post brought her a short note dated from Marseille. In it the girl announced that she had entered the novitiate of a missionary order, and said farewell to her friend until such time as they should meet in another world.

Although no scene ever took place between the druggist's wife and the abbé, he realized before very long that he had roused in her a degree of hatred which no mere passage of time would serve to allay. The knowledge did not much worry him on his own account, because it seemed impossible that she could get any hold over him, but it did on hers, for he was a man who could well understand the depths of her misery, no matter how shameful its causes might be. He had always had an eye for the unforeseeable repercussions, the mysterious consequences, of our actions when we intervene in the destinies of others, for no matter what good reasons.

His adversary was not slow in opening her attack. At first it was confined to the only field in which she could come to grips with him. Anticlerical feeling was running high at that time. Together with the schoolmaster of Baluzac and his wife, Hortense Voyod set up a sort of committee of propaganda, the activities of which very soon extended to the whole neighborhood. But in Baluzac itself her reputation was so bad that the offensive made very little headway. For the space of two or three years the Curé seemed to be justified in his belief that he had very little to fear. For all that, he never felt comfortable when he had to pass the apothecary's shop, and, if he happened to meet the woman in the street, it was he who looked away, so violent was the effect upon him of her cold, implacable glare.

She had waited years for her victim. Her opportunity for revenge was not so long in coming. The abbé had every excuse for being caught off his guard, since she was known not to be interested in young men, and was not likely to be physically attractive to them. She often showed herself arrayed in the "bloomers" which at that time were fashionable among women cyclists. She sported a low-cut bodice confined by a belt which was adorned in front by an enormous silver buckle engraved with her monogram. Her hair, arranged "à la Cléo," was parted in the middle, arranged in two shining bandeaux over her ears, only the lobes of which were visible, and caught, at the nape of her neck, into a huge yellow "bun" which rained innumerable pins. Her face was a mass of freckles which were thickly clustered on her nose and cheekbones, thinning out above.

The abbé Calou had profited by Jean's convalescence to complete his conquest of him. Or that, at least, was what he thought. In this, he was the dupe of an illusion from which we all suffer in spite of the lessons of experience. In dealing with human beings, no position is ever permanently won in either love or friendship. Jean de Mirbel, betrayed by his mother and weakened by illness, was in the mood to feel a shock of passing gratitude and to surrender before a show of tenderness. But from his very first day at Baluzac, a hard core of resistance to the priest had grown up in his mind. It was still there, though Monsieur Calou did not realize it. The relation of priest to layman is never a neutral one: he either attracts or repels. Mirbel was always conscious of an instinctive repulsion, a feeling of disgust for the man who was professionally chaste. Against this instinct he struggled as hard as he could, but was unable to keep himself from hating the very smell of a house that had no woman in it. He held it as a grievance that Monsieur Calou should think it natural for a young man of his age to subscribe to the same rule as himself, and his brooding rancor was the greater since neither in mind nor in heart was he susceptible to the attractions of piety, purity, and divine love. Those who live by the light of divine love find it hard to understand that the majority of mankind are complete strangers to it. They can form no idea of a state of mind in which it plays no part. The monotony of his solitary life, his losing fight against seeming to be ungrateful to a man who had done so much for him, combined to reawaken in Jean de Mirbel the old slumbering devil. The very affection that Monsieur Calou showed to him played into the enemy's hands, for Jean was by nature just the kind of young man who instinctively sets himself against any display of tenderness. Many and many a time in afterlife I have heard him say: "How I hate being loved!"

As the result of an inward contradiction which he never attempted to resolve, Mirbel resented the fact that the abbé seemed willing to relax in his favor the rigors of a moral and religious rule which he nevertheless hated. The priest shut his eyes to a number of things, and refrained from bothering the boy where the mere letter of the law was concerned. Far from feeling grateful for this latitude, Jean drew strength from the old man's weakness, and began to "run wild." On several occasions he went to the local inn, but he was not naturally sociable and he made no friends there. On the other hand, he was definitely attractive to women, and had had his first "adventure" before the winter was out. The girl's parents complained to the abbé, who intervened, though in rather a tactless way. Like most chaste men he believed that a serious love affair was the best way of protecting a young man from the passing temptations of the flesh. He had no doubts about Jean's loyalty to Michèle, and felt sure that he would never be false to her. Now, however true it may be that a great many young men are capable of remaining faithful to the young women they love, there are plenty of others, and Mirbel was one of them, who think of "being in love" and indulging their senses as two totally different things. They really care for one woman and for one woman only, and it exasperates them to think that the same standard should be applied to the genuine adoration of true love and to the trivial affairs in which the body is all that matters.

This subject was the occasion of the first real quarrel that took place between the abbé and Mirbel. In the course of it the latter let himself go with a violence which until that moment he had kept under strict control. He took advantage of the fact that the priest did not dream of condemning him on grounds of Christian morality, but appealed rather to an outworn code of sentiment in which no one outside the walls of a seminary any longer believed. Jean went so far as to forbid the abbé to speak of Michèle, adding that he would let no one mention her name in his presence. The angrier Mirbel became, the less did the abbé press his argument. But Jean felt no gratitude for this consideration, and resented the other's obvious, if unspoken, grief. "He makes it a point of grievance that I behave to him much too like a complacent father," the abbé noted in his diary that evening. "However little of a Christian a man may be, he wants to be loved in and for God alone—even though he does not believe in God."

Though Mirbel has never confessed to me precisely what it was that he said in the heat of anger, I imagine that this sentence of the abbé Calou's referred to something very cruel that he had let slip that evening. Jean knew that he had been cruel, and though part of him was horrified by the realization, he drove ahead along the same road with a sort of fierce intensity and displayed a needless spitefulness. It was, however, neither out of malice aforethought, nor with any intention of dealing his benefactor a final blow that he became entangled with the druggist's wife. It was the schoolteacher and his wife who first took him to visit Hortense Voyod. On that rainy February day when the young man whom she had watched for so long from behind her window blinds crossed the rain-soaked little courtyard wrapped in his schoolboy's cape and hood and entered the shop, she could at last heave a sigh of relief, even though her revenge was as yet far from complete.

Many were the discussions held by the light of an oil lamp and in the warmth of a roaring stove, with Armagnac loosening the assembled tongues. Jean would have found it impossible to say precisely what satisfaction he derived from the presence of this pallid woman and from the sound of her voice which, for all its hoarseness, was gentle and quite unmarked by any local accent. While the schoolmaster's anticlerical passion, when it was expended on the politics of the moment, had no manner of interest for Mirbel, the mocking sallies of the pharmacist's wife roused an immediate response in him. She spoke a language which he had never heard till then, but which he at once recognized.

On that first evening she insisted that he should come to her shop only after nightfall, and should never enter the door until he was quite certain that no one had seen him. For, said she, the Curé, with whom she had had several passages of arms, would certainly not approve of their friendship; but it would be easy to keep secret. He protested against being involved in his tutor's quarrels. During the next few days they began to realize how deep was the sentiment that bound them.

The ruling passion of this woman (who was without any real education, though she had read a number of modern books both good and bad) was a hatred of—a sense of grievance against—the God whose very existence she denied. The lack of logic in such an attitude did not bother her in the slightest degree. Against an unknown Being in whom she did not believe she leveled the reproaches of a class of creatures for whom there can be no release in this world save in complete destruction.

It is most unlikely that she ever spoke to Mirbel of this private and festering sore. But it so happened that, though there was no particular reason why he should share the special bitterness of a woman twenty years his senior, he did suffer from a wild sense of anger against the Fate that had made him what he was. That he was a Mirbel, the heir to a patrician name, made it all the stranger that he should be animated by so hostile, so stubborn a feeling of resentment against all ordered living, against all constraint where his own happiness was concerned. Hortense Voyod was well aware from what poisoned source her own hatred proceeded, but for no consideration in the world would she have imparted this knowledge to Jean, though she could have done so had she wished. The young man, on the other hand, had no idea why it was that everything in life seemed hateful to him with the exception of one young girl whom he would probably never see again, and a priest whom he detested.

Perhaps Hortense Voyod would have reached her goal less easily had not Jean been an instrument ready to her hand. But the understanding that grew between them from the occasion of their very first meeting, the link that bound them so tightly together, facilitated her maneuver. No longer was it necessary for her to feign a sympathy which, in fact, she genuinely felt. The youth had walked willingly into her spider's parlor and seemed to take pleasure in the consciousness of his imprisonment. No trickery on her part had been necessary to attract him thither.

It was the abbé Calou's habit to go into the church each evening with the object of finishing the reading of his breviary before the Holy Sacrament, and he stayed there until dinner-time. As soon as he was out of the way, Jean used to leave the presbytery by the door that faced away from the main road, and make his way round the outskirts of the village. It was not necessary to go into the shop at all. He could reach Hortense's house by jumping over the fence that surrounded the kitchen garden.

Even had he not wanted to avoid meeting stray customers, Mirbel would have been careful to keep out of the way of the druggist, who was a little old man forever occupied in wrapping up bottles of medicine as though the lives of all the invalids in the neighborhood depended on him. His manners were excessively humble, but his way of laughing and the expression of his eyes gave them the lie. He looked after his wife's property (that he should do so formed the essential clause of their secret compact: he made no claim on her person, but, in return for this concession, had insisted that her property be consigned to his charge). Consequently he was absent every afternoon, and, on returning home, never ventured into the back shop when what he called "the club" was in session.

Scarcely a fortnight passed before Monsieur Calou got wind of these secret meetings. This time he did not yield to his first impulse, and, when at last he mentioned the subject to Mirbel, did so without any show of anger, and only after giving much thought to the problem of how best to deal with the situation. Far from reproaching the boy, he realized that solitude is a vocation that can hardly be expected to appeal to youths of eighteen. But he had good reasons—reasons that he could not mention to Jean—for holding that Hortense Voyod was a woman bent on his destruction. What he did, therefore, was to make an appeal to his loyalty. To enter into close relations with such a woman while he was living under her enemy's roof would be tantamount to treachery. If Jean felt it impossible to remain at Baluzac without constant visits to the apothecary's shop, they had better face the fact, and the abbé would make arrangements for the boy to go home. But this was what Jean dreaded above all else, since it would mean that he would be sent to board at some Jesuit college. Moreover, his master's tone in mentioning the subject had touched him. He could not deny that Hortense Voyod wanted to injure the Curé—not that she had ever attacked him in Jean's hearing (he would never have permitted such a thing), but her sentiments were obvious in every word she spoke; so much so, that each time he left the back shop and found himself again in the presbytery dining-room, looking across the steaming

189

tureen at the abbé's childlike gaze, and returning his smile, he felt deeply ashamed. He gave his word that he would discontinue his visits. He told me later that he spoke in perfect good faith and fully meant to keep his promise.

It was about this time that Monsieur Calou arranged for him to have a horse, and stopped me in the street with the proposal that he and Michèle should exchange letters, with what disastrous results I have already explained.

Separated as he was from Michèle, and forbidden to correspond with her, Jean had been suffering from a sense of being exiled even before he made the acquaintance of Hortense Voyod. He felt it still harder to endure his isolation when he was deprived of the distraction provided by the discussions to which he had grown accustomed, and those readings aloud by the schoolmaster of articles by Hervé, Gérault-Richard, and Jaurès. (On these occasions Hortense would toss off her glass like a man, light a cigarette, and hold the company by those bursts of bitter, lively talk which, as Mirbel told me many years later, still remained in his memory as having been curiously exciting.)

The abbé Calou would far rather have faced some active show of resentment by his pupil. How could he deal with this sullen gloom, as of some caged beast?—especially after the Superior of the Sacred Heart had dryly intimated that all correspondence between him and Michèle must cease? Jean no longer occupied his time with reading, but roamed the woods on foot and on horseback until darkness fell. After some weeks he took to paying frequent visits to the schoolmaster. The abbé shut his eyes to all this. He had a pretty shrewd suspicion that the boy found a letter from Hortense Voyod awaiting him each time he went there, and that he left one for her when he said good night. But nothing had been said about writing. Without these almost daily exchanges, it is probable that their relations would never have taken a passionate turn—that it was the young man's romantic effusions that gave Hortense her great idea. She began to think that certain developments might be possible of which hitherto she had never even dreamed; for Jean was young enough to be her son.

She proceeded with the utmost caution. At first she confined herself to the language of friendship, a sentiment she was adept at using for her own purposes, though quite incapable of feeling in fact. Since her days at boarding-school, where she had remained until she got her diploma, friendship had never been anything for her but an alibi for desire. And now it was her desire for revenge that was at stake. She had no illusions about the kind of feeling she inspired in Mirbel. He had not confided in her, but she knew perfectly well that he was very unhappy, and that his heart belonged to another. But, more clear-sighted than the abbé, she soon realized how strong·the animal was in him, and how wholly dominated he was by the blind and irresistible cravings of his senses.

Hortense Voyod had begun by getting a clear picture of this side of his nature. The two or three letters from her which Jean kept, and which he showed me later, were not so much sentimental in tone as carefully composed with the sole object of stirring, without any touch of coarseness, a young imagination condemned to loneliness. One of the few notes left by the abbé on the subject of Hortense shows the extent to which the priest was preoccupied, even obsessed, by the thought of this woman. "It is difficult to account for such knowledge of the human mind in a mere country-bred woman," he wrote. "The explanation is, I suppose, that vice itself has a certain educational effect. It is not given to all of us to look evil in the face. Our petty individual weaknesses, to which we give the name of 'evil,' have nothing in common with this violent determination to destroy the soul. . . . The spirit of evil, as the eighteenth century knew it and expressed it in the *Liaisons Dangereuses,* exists, as I know now, actually within a few miles of my presbytery, behind the shutters of an apothecary's shop. . . ."

Spring came early. Jean, though he would have to face his finals before the year was out, continually played truant. Hortense knew that she could contrive a meeting with him as soon as she thought that the right moment had come. All she had to do was to take a walk along the banks of the Ciron. But she was in no hurry and wanted to avoid all unnecessary risk. First of all, she must so arrange matters that the boy was haunted by the thought of her, obsessed by dreams in which she was the central figure. Her plans were beginning to extend further than the mere satisfaction of a desire for vengeance. It was not enough for her to deal the abbé Calou a mortal blow. Ever since she had lost her girl friend she had been seeking a pretext to get rid of her old husband, whose days of usefulness were over. She reckoned that this young Mirbel could not only help her to her revenge, but could serve as a stage in her fight for freedom, provided he was willing to face the scandal. But she was still uncertain what steps to take.

As soon as the first fine weather came, the abbé Calou, as was his custom, made a tour of the district and the outlying farms on his bicycle. He had to round up the children for his catechism classes and visit the sick, especially the old men whom their sons kept hard at work until they dropped down dead. Very often, as they lay helpless in bed, there would be some virago of a daughter-in-law to grudge them the very black bread they mumbled with their toothless gums. Here was to be seen humanity with very little pity for itself and none whatever for others. The general view in such houses was that all priests are sly and lazy. "What's the use of the clergy, anyway? Much better . . ." What it would be much better to do with them was never clear in the speakers' minds, but it had some connection with an idea, so precious at that time to the abbé Calou, of what that stationary cross bearing the figure of the nailed God really meant. The priest, fastened to the same instrument of torment and exposed to the same derision, confronts mankind with an enigma which it makes no effort to solve.

One afternoon toward the end of April, when the Curé got home before dusk, he was met by Maria who had been on the lookout for his return. She told him that Monsieur Voyod the pharmacist had been there for half an hour. She had thought it her duty, she said, to light the fire.

This was the first time that Hortense's husband had crossed the threshold of the presbytery. The abbé, much moved by curiosity, found his visitor seated beside the smoking grate. As the priest entered he rose from his chair. He was wearing his Sunday-best. A narrow black ribbon failed to conceal his shirt stud, and it would not have been difficult to insert a hand between his collar and his skinny neck. When he smiled he revealed a mouth entirely empty.

He apologized for not having come before this to pay his respects to his parish priest. He had feared that he would not be too well received. Most people, however, knew that he did not share all his wife's ideas. When his first wife had been alive he had always gone to church on feast-days, and had sung in the choir until he was nineteen. He was very anxious that the Curé should not look on him as an enemy, and hoped that he would be good enough to give him his custom. It was a nuisance to have to go into Vallandraut every time one wanted a few lozenges.

All this was spoken glibly, like a lesson learned by heart, and the abbé could not think what it was that the man really wanted. He referred once again to the principles expressed by Madame Voyod, which, he said, he was far from approving. Things weren't any too easy for him, as the Curé might well imagine. He had sacrificed much in order to be a father to the daughter of his old friend Destiou when she was left alone in the world with no one to look after her property. He fully realized, he said, that people had imputed interested motives to him . . . but what advantage had the marriage brought *him?* All the troubles of ownership without any of the rewards. The ideas of Madame Voyod had lost him quite a number of customers. She had been a trial to him from the beginning, and now the cloven hoof was beginning to show. It wasn't for him to give the Curé advice, but he couldn't help feeling rather surprised that that young pupil of his should be allowed to see so much of a woman who was known to be an enemy of the Church. However that might be, he, as her husband —though he was more a father to her than a husband—was getting a trifle worried about the meetings between the two. All Baluzac was talking. He knew that the boy was just a young scamp, and that at his age such things weren't very important . . . still . . .

At this point the Curé interrupted him with an assurance that his pupil would pay no further visits to the shop; but the old man went on to talk of meetings in the woods, which couldn't do the young man much good, and which she'd be a great deal better without, as was shown by the fact that she had taken his remarks on the subject with a very bad grace. As though he had forgotten that he had already represented his marriage as an act of disinterested devotion on his part, he began to snivel, and to say that it was very hard that after a lifetime of work for others he should find himself threatened in his old age with the loss of everything that he had struggled to build up. When a man has spent years looking after a property, has got it into good shape, has sown the waste land, cleared the brush, and fought off encroaching neighbors, it's a bit rough, just when everything is going smoothly, to find himself threatened with dismissal like a servant.

Monsieur Calou pointed out that all this had nothing to do with his pupil. The druggist admitted that it was hard to believe the situation had taken so serious a turn. It was the last thing that would ever have entered his head because, after all, it was only fair to Hortense to say that she had never run after men, and no one could say there'd ever been any reason why she should . . . (here the old man shot a quick glance at the Curé, but hastily veiled his eyes behind their inflamed lids).

The abbé had taken up the tongs and was paying very self-conscious attention to the fire. He said that the chimney was cold, that they hadn't burned so much as a handful of twigs there all winter. The smoke was making the visitor cough. He urged the Curé to give a word of warning to his pupil. . . . Of course there was nothing in it all . . . but why arouse unnecessary gossip? . . . Hortense was getting to the difficult age. . . .

The tongs shook in the priest's large hands. He got up. He had to bend his head in order to see his visitor's face.

"You can be perfectly easy in your mind, Monsieur Voyod. There shall be no more wandering in the woods—from tomorrow: I give you my word for that."

His visitor was of the opinion that the Curé was not in

the best of tempers. He said later that he had never seen a man so beside himself, so capable of giving someone a bad half-hour. He felt very glad not to be in that young man's skin when he came in for supper.

As soon as Monsieur Calou was alone he went up to his room, poured some water into the basin, and bathed his face. Then he knelt down, but the words got no farther than his lips. Thoughts swarmed in his brain like dead leaves in a high wind. In his brother's family there was a saying: "That was during the holidays in 1880, the year when Ernest saw red. . . ." The last of these terrible fits of temper had delayed his ordination as deacon by twelve months, and since that time he had always managed, aided by the gift of Grace, to keep his outbursts within bounds.

On this particular evening he knelt at his *prie-dieu* and held his head in his hands. "There is danger . . . you may do him irreparable harm. . . ." But stronger than this appeal to his sense of prudence was an angry longing to take the boy by the scruff of the neck and force him to his knees until he begged for mercy. That done, there should be an end to this business of not taking things seriously. He should be treated as Uncle Adhémar had always hoped he would be. Since he would obey nothing but superior strength, and yield to nothing but fear, the Curé of Baluzac would find some way of breaking his will and making him as obedient as a whipped cur. "Go on praying, give yourself time," went on the tireless inner voice.

Suddenly he heard the well-known footstep on the stairs. He went to the door and opened it.

"Come in here: I've got something to say to you."

And when the other replied, "Later," he remained stern and insistent. "Now, at once."

Jean shrugged his shoulders and started up the second flight. But a hand gripped his collar, he felt the pressure of a knee in the small of his back, and found himself lying on the divan-bed where he had been thrown like a parcel, all among the books and pamphlets.

Staggered, he sat here, conscious of two enormous fists in close proximity to his face. He could do nothing but stammer: "What on earth's up?"

The abbé was breathing hard and wiping his damp brow with the back of his hand. Thank Heaven, he had not given way to violence. For the time being, at least, the worst was over.

His voice was icy but completely under control. He told his pupil that he had been within an ace of getting a sound thrashing. He added that in future he would keep a watchful eye on him until such time as the Mirbel family should see fit to relieve him of his responsibilities. He hoped, he said, that the boy would not compel him to have recourse to physical violence, because he was apt to lose control of himself, and was a hard hitter.

Having delivered himself of this warning, he ordered his pupil to his room, and remarked that supper would be sent up to him.

"All the time he was behaving like a brute," wrote Jean to Hortense Voyod, "the Curé kept his eyes shut. Perhaps he was praying, though his lips did not move. . . . Priests always manage to get away with things in that way!"

The abbé kept his word. He never let Mirbel out of his sight except when duty called him away, and then he left Maria in charge. No doubt Jean managed to slip away quite often, and not for a moment did he discontinue his correspondence with Hortense Voyod. This he managed, thanks to the visits of the schoolmaster who came to coach him in mathematics. But, for all that, he was completely dominated by the priest, and was forced to bow to his inflexible will. Besides, the examination was approaching and he had to keep his nose to the grindstone, which meant that he must postpone until later any plans of revolt that he might have formed. He satisfied the examiners on his written work, but failed in his orals. He did not return to Baluzac until September, having spent a month with the Countess at La Devize. It was the first time that he had met his mother since the terrible revelation which had come to him at Balauze.

"My Jean has changed," wrote the Countess to the abbé Calou. "He was always a handful, but he never used to be cynical. Now all that has changed! I can't utter a word of advice, or even try to raise the tone of our conversations (hard though I try to do so), without the little wretch's laughing in my face. I don't want to question the excellence of your methods, but I hope you won't mind my saying that they seem to have misfired entirely in the case of my son."

Almost every day during the vacation Jean got a letter from the druggist's wife. No sooner had he returned to the presbytery than her plans began to take shape. In October a fresh cause of frustration occurred, and he hesitated no longer. The necessity of making his Retreat had obliged the abbé to be absent for some days. During all that time Jean was constantly in the company of Hortense. The abbé found on his return that the boy seemed much calmer, almost mild indeed, and consequently he somewhat relaxed his watchful attitude. Relations between the two had become merely those between master and pupil. They hardly ever spoke except about work, and avoided all controversial subjects. The priest was giving himself with renewed confidence to his little flock. The children were beginning to talk freely to him and even showed some signs of affection. He failed to notice the new barrier that had arisen between Jean and himself. Illogical and hard to believe though it may seem, the young man was irritated and hurt by Monsieur Calou's attitude of detachment, and this fresh wound had a good deal to do with the fatal resolution that he was so soon now to take. Its gravity was cunningly concealed from him by Hortense Voyod.

It is by no means uncommon for human beings to set great store by the affection of those for whom they themselves feel no love, and whom they may even think they despise. Jean was quite incapable of understanding how it was that the abbé Calou should keep for him the first place in his heart and mind. Mystics obey the law of an economy that they find it impossible to explain in words to those who are not themselves initiates. How should the priest not feel easy in his mind about Jean? How could he help believing that they were quits, seeing that he had already offered his life for the boy, and daily renewed his sacrifice? The discipline of exchange, of compensation, of transference which Grace imposes on the true believer was far removed from the world of the flesh into which the adolescent was slowly being introduced. Jean felt that he had been rejected by the one man who held the key to all his secrets, who knew what he had suffered and was still suffering because of his mother and because of Michèle. If *he* deserted him, what was there left but flight from a hateful world that held no place for him? He knew, of course, that his relations with Hortense would not last very long . . . but he had vowed himself to the vocation of misery, and what most attracted him in the whole of this adventure was the thought that it was so utterly hopeless, so completely beyond any power to solve; that it would compel him to set sail from his sheltered harbor and commit himself to a course from which there would be no turning back.

# 14

WE were to stay at Larjuzon until the celebration of what, in the Gironde, is called the Mass of the Octave. On the very day before it occurred my stepmother received a letter from the Sister who was looking after Octavia. It had been found impossible to prevent a miscarriage, and double phlebitis had set in. The patient's temperature remained high, and her heart was growing weaker. The doctor feared the worst. There was a complete lack of everything in the rue du Mirail. Though Monsieur Puybaraud had forbidden her to make any appeal to Madame Pian, the Sister felt compelled to disobey him, because the baker and the pharmacist were turning nasty.

This news seemed to overwhelm my stepmother. She could, no doubt, have managed to get to Bordeaux and back before the Mass of the Octave, but she felt that my former master would probably not welcome her. So with her customary generosity, she telegraphed a money order in the name of the Sister, and had it addressed to the convent.

Brigitte asked my advice, and thought her thoughts aloud in my presence, as though she had quite failed to notice the coldness of my attitude. "If they hadn't had *me!*" she kept on saying, and then proceeded to rehearse all that she had already done for the Puybarauds. "I warned them how it would be. Everything is turning out exactly as I said it would. I didn't dare say anything about this final mishap, to warn him that Octavia would almost certainly die, though God knows I felt that something of the kind was bound to happen. . . . It wasn't for a poor weak woman like me to dot their i's for them. Their spiritual director has been very lax. He was the only person who might have been able to keep them from the abyss, instead of doing which he pushed them over the edge! . . . But Monsieur Puybaraud will hold *me* responsible: you see if he doesn't! . . . Your sister, as it is, thinks I was the cause of your father's death, as well as of the flight and house-breaking escapade of young Mirbel. . . . Really, it's hard to believe."

She gazed into my face, and the anxious laugh with which she wound up this catalogue of grievances was an invitation, a piteous invitation, to me to say something, to offer her some crumb of comfort. But I remained obstinately silent, and, by so doing, showed clearly enough that I was on the side both of Monsieur Puybaraud and of Michèle in every single instance that she had quoted. She had no one to fall back on but herself. She spent her time dragging from room to room or wandering aimlessly round the table, strengthening her defenses against an attack that could come only from herself. Should I, I wonder, be quite so ready today to put the weight of responsibility for so much unhappiness on the shoulders of a woman so lashed by the Furies of the new dispensation, so torn by those scruples which, ever since the coming of Christ, have been the stock-in-trade of tortured consciences? Brigitte Pian's scruples urged her to return as soon as possible to town in order that she might see Monsieur Puybaraud in person and so be reassured. But since there was only one train a day, we had to wait until the Mass of the Octave was over.

It meant getting up in pitch darkness. During the whole journey Brigitte had to submit to the presence of Michèle who, at Larjuzon, was for long periods out of her sight. During the whole three hours which we spent cooped up in a second-class carriage, the young girl, swathed from head to foot in crape, played a wicked game. Not once did she so much as look at our stepmother, although she knew that she was being wordlessly implored to do so. Today I am filled with pity for the poor woman who has been dust these many years. But at the time I felt none. The train, a slow one, was insufficiently heated by hot-water tins which the porter had given us, and I had to kneel on the seat to get a little warmth into my frozen feet. But I began to be aware of what was passing through Madame Brigitte's mind. I fixed my eyes with keen curiosity on the imposing presence, on the great brazen statue whose shadow had darkened my childhood, but now, before my eyes, was toppling on its base. Cracks were opening here and there. Perhaps in a moment I should see it fall. When she got up to leave the carriage she gave me the impression of a small woman. I was astonished. It never occurred to me that it was I who had grown.

She gave the cabman not our address but the Puybarauds'. It was a gloomy morning, and the noise of the conveyance filled the melancholy rue du Mirail. We glanced up to the floor on which my old master lived, and saw that the shutters were closed. The concierge poked her bony face out of the lean-to which served her as a lodge. From her we learned that the end had come on the previous evening, that Monsieur Puybaraud would not see anybody, and that no one knew when the funeral was to be. We were informed that he had issued very harsh instructions about us. "Misfortune very often makes people ungrateful," she said; she had often noticed it. When we were once again in the cab, Michèle's attitude underwent a sudden change. She no longer kept her eyes averted, but stared so long and so relentlessly at our stepmother that the latter was compelled to turn away her own and look out of the window. Though her lips scarcely moved, I knew that she had already begun to recite the prayers for the dead. I am pretty sure that she could not resist the temptation of crying across the spaces of eternal silence: "Well, my poor Octavia, who was right?"

No doubt she surrendered to the temporary satisfaction of finding her views and those of Providence in such complete agreement. But by the time we reached the Cours de l'Intendance an air of gloom had settled on her face. Michèle went to her room and we saw her no more that day. Brigitte Pian came into mine to plague me with questions, but I scarcely answered her. She left the communicating door open. Even though I was in a hostile mood, she found my presence necessary to her peace of mind. After a few moments she came back, and once again went over the whole story of her relations with the Puybarauds during the past two years, making a point of praising her own conduct except on the occasion of her last visit to Octavia's sickbed. She only hoped, she said, that Monsieur Puybaraud would not take it into his head that the little argument they had had then had been injurious to the patient! She rehearsed all its ins and outs: she even tried to remember the actual words she had used. I listened with icy politeness, and gave her not one sentence of either comfort or approval.

At last she could stand it no longer, and begged me to go back alone to the rue du Mirail. Monsieur Puybaraud would be sure to receive me, and would say when the funeral was to be.

But the concierge would not let me go up, no matter how

hard I begged, and I had to get the information I wanted from the Church of St. Éloi, where I was told that there would be no requiem but only the absolution. This would be given at eight o'clock next day.

Our stepmother had fully expected that we should be the only people present, but we were not. A great many of Octavia's old pupils had come, and several of the mistresses from the Free School. Almost everyone was crying, and so thick was the air with prayers that I felt something like a sense of physical oppression. Monsieur Puybaraud, wearing the old black overcoat that had been so familiar to me on winter days in the school playground, stood stiffly upright. He neither knelt nor wept. His face was as white as Octavia's must have been within the four wooden walls of her coffin. Since he appeared to see no one, we might have been able to persuade ourselves that there was nothing hostile in his attitude to us. At the gate of the cemetery he seemed not to notice the hand I held out to him, and I had to take hold of his. He withdrew it at once. As to my stepmother, she did not dare even to make the gesture, for he bowed his head without giving her a glance or making the slightest movement with his arm.

That evening after dinner, in my room, whither she had followed me, she said that she feared that Monsieur Puybaraud had listened to the promptings of rebellion. It was much to be regretted that she had not been able to have a word with him, for she might have succeeded in softening his hard heart and helping him to achieve a mood of resignation and submission. To this I objected that the enmity he had shown us was no proof that he felt the same way toward God, and I added hypocritically that, since he had been the husband of a saint, my stepmother could ask her intercession for all those particular manifestations of grace of which Monsieur Puybaraud stood in need.

"A saint?" said Brigitte Pian. "A saint?" She looked at me without anger, but with a sort of concentrated gaze that might have been taken for stupidity. For a moment or two she moved about the table, and then withdrew, taking with her, doubtless, an added load of trouble and anxiety upon which to brood during the night.

All through the days that followed Octavia's funeral she made no attempt to see the widower again, though she continued to help him surreptitiously, with the connivance of the Sister. Michèle had gone back to the Sacred Heart, and my stepmother and I resumed our old life of shared solitude. She did everything she could to please me, showing an eagerness in the task that might almost have deserved the name of humility. It was as though her sole hope of succor lay in a young man whose attitude to her was one of frightening correctness.

Following the suggestion made to me by the abbé Calou, I wrote from Larjuzon to the Comtesse de Mirbel asking for news of Jean. I found her answer awaiting me in Bordeaux. Every word of her letter had been carefully weighed, with the sole intention of minimizing the scandal.

*I am not at all surprised, my dear young friend, that you should be anxious about Jean, or that you should have been influenced by the ridiculous tittle-tattle that has been going the rounds. He has returned to us here much surprised and considerably disturbed by all the talk there has been about his little escapade. The Curé and the pharmacist are the two persons chiefly responsible. Both are guilty of having stirred up public opinion. For the second of the gentlemen in question there is some show of excuse, but the former has shown a lack of judgment and moderation which is really quite intolerable in one of his cloth, to say nothing of the fact that he claims to be an educator of youth! I said as much when I went to pay back the money he had advanced to my son. It has been the subject of fantastic gossip. I can only hope that if it came to your ears you refused to believe a word. The priest had nothing to say to my charges, and I must admit that my feelings as a mother led me to express myself with what may have been rather excessive warmth.*

(Much later I was able to realize how sublime the abbé's silence had been. With a single word he could have crushed the woman who was hurling insults at his head, for she did not then know that her son had spent a whole night shivering beneath the windows of the Balauze hotel, that he had very nearly died as a result of that adventure, and that his mind had been permanently scarred and poisoned by what his eyes had seen on that occasion, and by what his ears had heard.)

The Countess told me, in conclusion, that Jean was to spend the rest of the year in England, and that he would have to be in Bordeaux for a few days before starting on his journey. She hoped that he would be permitted to come and say good-bye to us.

This letter left me with a feeling of embarrassment and uncertainty. Ought I to send it on to the abbé Calou in accordance with my promise? I had to relax my attitude of reserve toward my stepmother in order to ask her advice on the point. As a matter of fact, I anticipated a certain amount of pleasure from watching her reactions. But if I had expected her to rail violently against the Curé of Baluzac, there was a surprise in store for me (as there had often been on previous occasions). She adopted an entirely unexpected attitude. She gave it as her considered view that I should do nothing that might unnecessarily wound a man who had recently been so sorely tried. Since, on the other hand, the document might be useful to him, she advised me to forward it, but with a covering note to the effect that we none of us believed the Countess's allegations. This was the first time, so far as I knew, that my stepmother had ever gone back on a verdict once given, and when I wrote to the abbé Calou I did not hesitate to draw his attention to this extraordinary change in her. I allowed myself to indulge in an expression of irony which he did not at all approve. His answer reached me only a week later. I insert a copy of it here with feelings of respect and admiration. I can truly say that, having read it, I was never quite the same again.

*Dear Louis:*

*I have delayed replying to your letter because it arrived after I had left Baluzac, and was forwarded to me at my brother's house where I shall be for some time to come. I shall not beat about the bush with you. You know too much about what has happened for me to be able to deceive you successfully. I am no longer Curé of Baluzac. I am no longer even permitted to live there. I was told to leave the parish as soon as possible, and to retire into the bosom of my family. The long and the short of it is—I am in disgrace, and circumstances compel me to attach rather more significance to that phrase than it usually bears. The Mirbels and old Voyod have agreed to saddle me with full responsibility for the scandal. But that is not all. The report that Madame Brigitte did me the honor of compiling some months ago and sent to the Vicar-General appears to have anticipated in every detail precisely what did in fact occur. Events have fully justified the weighty and truly remarkable*

*survey which your dear stepmother then prepared of my
character and general tendencies. I write this in no spirit
of irony, my dear boy, and I will take this opportunity of
saying that I did not greatly care for the tone that marked
your letter to me. As you know very well, I do not believe
in chance, and I do not believe that it is mere chance that
all Madame Brigitte's prognostications were borne out by
the facts. I will not go so far as to say that her interpretation
of the facts or of the motives of others is always very judi-
cious, but she does have a sort of gift for unearthing evil intentions. She would probably be quite genuinely surprised
if I told her that my mistake and hers are at bottom identi-
cal. They pursue different roads, only to reach the same end.
Both of us, she ruled by her reason, I by my feelings, have
been inclined to believe that it is our duty to interfere in the
destinies of those around us. I do not deny that it is the first
duty of the sacred office conferred by priesthood—as, indeed,
it is part of the duty of every Christian—to preach the Gospel: but that does not mean that we should try to turn our
neighbor into a replica of ourselves, or force him to see with
our eyes. Of ourselves we can do nothing. Our concern
should be limited to walking before the Divine Grace as the
dog goes in front of the invisible hunter. This we can do
with greater or less effectiveness in proportion as we are
more or less attentive and obedient to the Will of our Master, more or less willing to let ourselves be molded by it,
more or less ready to ignore our own. So far as I am concerned, Madame Brigitte has been perfectly justified in her
attitude. What she condemns in me is the lack of any sense
of proportion, of any genuine power of judgment. She points
out, with striking truth, that this lack, when found in a
priest, and in the highly developed form it has assumed in
my own case, is apt to produce worse disasters than any low,*

*criminal passion. It led me to interfere rashly, heatedly, and ill-advisedly, in the concerns of others. Naturally, these activities of mine have to some extent served the purposes of Grace, because such is the Love of God that it turns all things to the greater good of those on whom it is lavished. But when it comes to measuring the havoc that accumulates about what we conceive to be our mission, we must give full weight to all those unadmitted interests, all those secret desires whose existence in our hearts we scarcely realize. That is why we should allow full play to the spirit of compassion.*

*I am afraid, my dear boy, that all this will seem very obscure to you. We will talk about it again some years from now, should the Father not have seen fit meanwhile to call unto Himself his very useless, nay, his sometimes actively dangerous, servant. For the moment, let me give you the following word of advice in regard to Madame Brigitte. You must not sneer at the way her spirit moves nor look on her ordeal as something petty and unimportant. Up to now she has seen only the edifying aspect of her activities. Suddenly, and without any warning, her eyes have been opened on to a new and horrible view of herself. When Christ makes us see clearly, and we become aware of our actions pressing in upon and surrounding us, we are as much astonished as was the man born blind who, in the Gospel story, saw "men as trees walking." But it is important that Madame Brigitte should understand the truth of what I have discovered for myself as a result of my present degradation, which is a great deal worse than you can possibly know. There is no form of calumny that has not been heaped upon me. People believe of me what they will, both in the Archbishop's palace and out of it. I can say without fear of contradiction that now, in my old age, I have lost every scrap of that honorable reputation I once enjoyed in men's eyes, that, in my own person, I have allowed outrage to be done upon that Jesus who has marked me as His own. My family is humiliated and vexed as a result of the shame I have brought upon it, to say nothing of the material embarrassment that my constant presence in this house has caused to its inmates. My youngest nephew has had to give up his room to me, and share with his brother. I need hardly say that they are all very kind to me. But my sister-in-law is just a little too insistent with her questions. What am I going to do with myself? she asks, and I can answer only that I do not know, for, truth to tell, I am good for nothing, and can be of use to none. . . . It would be foolish to deceive myself further. I stand now in the presence of my God, as naked, as much stripped of all merit, as utterly defenseless as a man can well be. Perhaps that is the state in which those of us should be whose profession it is—if I may so express myself—to be virtuous. It is almost inevitable that the professionally virtuous should hold exaggerated ideas of the importance of their actions, that they should constitute themselves the judges of their own progress in excellence, that, measuring themselves by the standards of those around them, they should at times be made slightly giddy by the spectacle of their own merits. I should like to think that Madame Brigitte is drawing from her present testing-time an assurance that her feet are set upon the road to a great discovery.*

Some may think that the abbé Calou, by thus addressing a youth of seventeen, was merely showing that he had not made much progress towards bettering his judgment. I did not dare to show this letter to my stepmother, though she no longer made any effort to keep her state of mind from me. I lived continuously now in the intolerable atmosphere created by her condition of spiritual torment. About this time, an anarchist weekly rag called *The Battle*, which flourished on scandal, published a number of poisonous paragraphs about the "abduction of a pharmacist's wife." I was amazed when Brigitte Pian asked me to get this scurrilous production for her each week. She would never have dared buy it for herself, nor would she have sent a servant to buy it for her. I could not understand the curious pleasure she seemed to get from reading it, especially after learning at school that Monsieur Puybaraud had been taken on as editorial secretary, and that, rightly or wrongly, the general view was that all the antireligious muck that it contained came from his pen.

She spent the whole of each Saturday evening reading this paper. I know, for I was always there, and I suspect that she carried her perusal of it far into the night. It was as though she wanted to saturate her mind in the vileness of a man whom she had herself driven (or thought she had) by despair into a state of rebellion and hatred. Children (and adolescents too, for that matter) are not as a rule conscious of the physical changes that take place in the grown-up persons with whom they live. But I did become aware that Brigitte Pian was growing a little bit thinner each day. The amethyst-colored dressing-gown now hung loosely upon her body, as though the thick, bloated snake of braided hair were indeed feeding on the very substance of her flesh. The oddest thing of all was that after the lapse of a few months, Monsieur Puybaraud not only left the paper and shut himself away in the Trappist monastery of Septfonts for a retreat, but that he stayed there for good and all, and, in the habit of a novice, accomplished that destiny which my stepmother had always urged on him. Once again the views of

Brigitte Pian had coincided with those of Providence. . . . But she could not, at the time of which I am speaking, have foreseen such an unhoped-for issue, and if at moments her anxious mind ceased to concern herself with a renegade, it was only because she was obsessed by thoughts of her other victims—of her husband, of Octavia, both of whom might still have been alive (or so she believed) had they not met with Brigitte Pian on their way through life. She thought too of Michèle, of Jean, and of the abbé Calou whom she had denounced.

On one point I am still not clear: whether she could have derived comfort, during her time of crisis, from a spiritual director. I did not know who hers was, and was not even certain that she had one. I have an idea, moreover, that even at the period of her life when she was deriving the most satisfaction from the thought of her progress in virtue, and when there was no reason to suppose that she would one day become a prey to the furies of scruple, she did not take the sacraments as often as might have been expected of so convinced a church-goer. The quarrel centering about the question of "frequent communion," which had been loosed upon Christendom two and a half centuries before, was, in my childhood, still very much alive. There are today few Christians, however devout, who have recourse to the Eucharist as often as they might. Forty years ago a spirit of fear and trembling still ruled the minds of certain persons in their relations with the Incarnate Love, who, so they had been taught by Jansenism to believe, was implacable.

One thing is beyond doubt. All through Lent that year, and the closer we drew to Easter, Brigitte Pian's worries took on more and more the character of sheer terror. One evening she came into my room without knocking. I was already in my bed, reading *Dominique,* and the eyes I turned

212

on the intruder were still full of the imaginary sights from which I had been snatched.

"Aren't you asleep?" she asked in a shy, imploring tone. She saw from my face that I resented being disturbed. If I had not been in bed, I should have clasped my head in my hands, stuck my fingers in my ears, and buried myself in my book in such a way as to discourage her from persisting in her interruption. But there beneath the sheets I was, as it were, quite defenseless.

"I want your advice, Louis. . . . It may seem odd to you that I should say that, but there are moments when I can no longer see my way clear before me. Which do you think is worse: to disobey the Church by not communicating at Easter, or, by obeying, to expose oneself to the risk of receiving the Eucharist in an improper state of mind? . . . No, don't answer at once: take your time and give me a considered reply. Remember what Saint Paul said when he spoke of those who do not fully realize the presence of our Lord's body. . . ."

I told her that my answer didn't need much thought, and that there was really no dilemma at all, because the confession of her sins to a priest would insure her recovering a state of Grace. . . .

"That may be true for you, Louis, my dear: true enough for the heart of a child. Indeed, I am sure it *is!*"

She sat down heavily on the edge of my bed. I was in for a long visit! I must give up all thoughts of *Dominique*. Instead, I had to listen to the outpourings of a haggard old woman.

"For that to be true, the sins must in the first place be simple, easily recognized and defined, capable of being fitted into a formula. But how do you think I could ever make intelligible to a priest the problems that are tormenting me?

How could he understand my relations with your father, with the Puybarauds, with Monsieur Calou, with Michèle? I have tried three times already. I have been, in turn, to a Secular, to a Dominican, and to a Jesuit. All three regarded me as one of those overscrupulous females who are the bane of confessors, and against whom they use the one weapon most calculated to increase the torments of their penitents by speaking as though they did not take their self-accusations seriously. On such occasions one leaves the confessional convinced that one has not been understood, that one cannot be pardoned for a sin that has made no real impression on the priest. . . . Well, that is *my* position," she added suddenly, after a moment's silence. "The whole problem is to know whether one's scruples are justified. Surely, the mere fact of suffering as I am suffering *must* mean that my sins are real."

"In such a case," said I priggishly, "scruple is the wrong word. What you mean is remorse."

"You have put your finger on the sore place, Louis. We try to comfort ourselves by using pretty words. It is true that I am tormented, not by scruples but by remorse: yes, remorse. You, with that quickness of mind that poor Monsieur Puybaraud so much admired, have understood me at once. But I despair of making myself clear to those inexperienced men who look on sins as so many easily defined gestures; who entirely fail to grasp the fact that evil can sometimes poison a whole life, that evil may have many shapes, may be invisible, incomprehensible, and, consequently, incommunicable—impossible to put into words. . . ."

She stopped speaking. The weight of her body was crushing me. I could hear her heavy breathing.

"I have an idea," I said. (I now felt as excited as I used to

feel in the old days when Monsieur Puybaraud asked me
questions as though I had been an oracle, and I tried to
dazzle him by an answer that should be at once unexpected
and full of wisdom.) "The only priest who can restore your
peace of mind is one who not only has known you for many
years, but is familiar with the happenings that are causing
you so much uneasiness." I warmed to my task, while she
watched me with the same kind of eager attention that the
seriously ill show as soon as the doctor opens his lips. "The
abbé Calou knows everything already. In his last letter to
me he described all the details of the trouble from which
you are suffering. Scruple or remorse—the name does not
matter. He will know what is on your mind and, because
he knows, will be in a position to give you absolution."

"The abbé Calou? Do you really think so? Do you think
I could make my confession to him after everything I have
done to him?"

"That's just the point: after all you've done *to him*."

She got up and began to pace about the room. She kept
on groaning that she could never bring herself to do it. . . .

"It will be hard, of course," I said (I was becoming
crafty); "but by so much the more will you acquire merit."

That word "merit" made her raise her head.

"It would be beyond the strength of most people, but
you . . ."

She straightened up still more. "After all . . ." she muttered, and then went on: "I should have to seek him out in
the bosom of his family. But is it certain that he has the
right now to hear confessions?" She addressed the question
to herself rather than to me. "Yes, surely he has, provided
it is within the limits of the diocese."

She started walking up and down again. I yawned noisily
and burrowed down under the sheets.

"Sleepy, aren't you? Lucky you: nothing will keep *you* awake."

She leaned over me, and her cracked lips touched my forehead.

"It *is* a good idea, isn't it?" I asked in a self-satisfied voice. She made no reply, but stood turning the matter over and over in her mind. She put out the light, but I lit it again as soon as she had closed the door. Once more, *Dominique* drew my thoughts far from the concerns of that hag-ridden woman.

# 15

WHEN she left the train that had brought her back from the abbé Calou, it was still two hours before dinner-time. Instead, therefore, of taking a cab, she walked back along the gloomy rue Saint-Jean. It was foggy and she was jostled by the crowd. But today she was indifferent to all that usually she most disliked, for she carried within her the assurance of pardon. She pursued her way with a light heart and, for the first time, the impulse of gratitude that set her in the presence of God had in it something of a tenderness that was at once humble and very human. Her evil had been taken from her. She no longer suffered, no longer found it difficult to breathe. Occasionally, as a sharp reminder, the prick of her old anxieties returned. Had she confessed everything? Yes, of course she had: and anyhow, he who had listened to her had known it all before.

She let her mind dwell on what had been said in the fireless, whitewashed, almost bare room in which the abbé Calou had received her. He had offered her no words of comfort. Instead, he had made her feel ashamed because she had attached so much importance to her faults, as though she didn't know that it is God's way to turn even our sins to His own purposes. The abbé had begged her to dwell on her own insignificance, and not to substitute for the illusion that she was a person well advanced along the way of perfection, that other, no less vicious, illusion that she was a notable sinner. He had added that she could do much for those to whom she thought she owed reparation; for the dead, naturally, but also for the living. "As, for example," he said, "you can be of great help to me with the Cardinal. . . ." (She realized that he was saying this to help her, from a feeling of charity. . . .) To be taken back into favor was not what he desired, but to be allowed to settle, at his own cost, somewhere between Bastide and Souys, in the poorest, most solitary part of the country he could find, there to take premises where he might be permitted to teach the catechism and to say Mass. Brigitte Pian, walking so light-heartedly along the pavements damp with fog, decided that she would shoulder the expenses of this enterprise. Already she saw in imagination a new parish arising around the abbé Calou.

She had just time to go into the Cathedral before the doors were locked, and remained there for a few minutes, motionless, like someone who has been blessed by a miraculous cure and can find no words of gratitude. Then she set out again and reached her own front door, scarcely conscious of what streets she passed along.

In the hall an unusual smell of tobacco brought her back to earth. Who could it be who dared to smoke in her house? She recognized a voice, Michèle's, mingled with another which she could not identify. Yet, for all that, she knew at once who had penetrated, had dared to penetrate, into her drawing-room. The Countess's letter had hinted that young Mirbel might pay us a visit, but Brigitte had not seriously believed that the young thief would have the effrontery to show himself. But he had come! We had actually received him! There he was, behind this very door, talking freely to Michèle.

Brigitte Pian drew herself up. There, in the hall lit by a single gas-burner in a frosted globe, she became once more her old self, a woman strong in her assurance of Grace, convinced of her right to interfere in the lives of those over whom she had authority. At the same time she heard within herself the low rumblings of that righteous anger which she found it so difficult to resist, which showed itself whenever her orders were flouted and anyone dared to question or evade something she had determined and laid down. With her hand on the latch, she hesitated once more. In spite of her anger, in spite of this blow administered to her newly acquired sense of peace, the deep call of her spirit was still operative. She knew that the people there in her drawing-room felt that she had done them a wrong. On that point, however, her conscience did not reproach her. What else could she have done? She had protected Michèle, who was still a child, and any mother would have done the same. The abbé Calou, however, saw things in a different light. She knew what young Mirbel meant to him, even though he had never once that day mentioned his name in her hearing. But certain words he had spoken came back now into her memory, and doubtless put her in mind of the lost sheep. Each one of us, he had said, has his own peculiar destiny, and it is, perhaps, one of the secrets of that compassionate Justice which watches over us, that there is no universally valid law by which human beings are to be assessed. Every man inherits his own past. For that he is to be pitied, because he carries with him through life a load made up of the sins and merits of his forebears to an extent that it is beyond our power to grasp. He is free to say yes or no when God's love is offered to him, but which of us can claim the right to judge what it is that influences his choice? It was while talking of the Puybarauds that the abbé had said: "We must not interfere blindly between two persons who love one another, even when they do so in sin. The important thing is that we should understand what their being brought together means, for the ways of human beings do not cross by chance. . . ."

As Brigitte Pian listened outside the door she could hear two voices intermingled: that of the young girl, which sounded depressed; the other, virile, uncertain in its register, with occasional rising passages which were muted by distance. No longer annoyed, but still uncertain, she sat down on the wooden chest. That it might not be thought that she was listening at keyholes (though she could not hear what was being said in the drawing-room), she went up to her room a few minutes later, and remained there a long time alone and on her knees in the darkness.

Jean de Mirbel had chosen Thursday for his attempted meeting with Michèle, because he knew that she would be free in the afternoon. It was I whom he asked to see. My first thought was to tell Michèle, and I saw at once that she knew that Jean was there. Her school uniform made her look plain. Her hair, half caught up into a "bun," was tied with a mauve ribbon. Her high shoes gave her ankles a thick appearance. I was not taken in by her assumed air of calmness. It was essential that this visit should not be made an excuse by our stepmother for a show of malevolence, and we agreed that even should Jean ask me to do so, I must not leave them alone together at any time during his visit.

That settled, we went down into the drawing-room. It was not yet four o'clock, but the heavy, fringed lace curtains made the room dark, and the wall-lamp had been lit. A smell of lamp oil hung about the "occasional tables" with their pyrographed tops, and the painted screens. The gilded chairs caught the light. Mirbel was taller than of old and had filled out, but his face was thinner. His hollow cheeks threw into relief the nose that had always been aquiline, though we had thought of it as small. His forehead was more lined than befitted his eighteen years. He was wearing a new ready-made suit, the shoulders of which were too much padded.

The two young people who had fallen in love before the lines of their physical development had become fully determined looked at one another with astonishment. There was what seemed to me a long interval of silence. The poor human insects had to trace backward the stages of their metamorphosis in order to see once more the child whom each had loved in the other. But their eyes had not changed, and it was those, I am sure, that first gave them the clue to their identities.

My boyish jealousy had long ago vanished. I wanted only to get away, to make myself invisible. It was no difficult task, for as soon as they began to speak, they were conscious only of each other. But their conversation dragged. It was as though they did not know what to talk about. Michèle sat down, but Jean remained standing with his back to the window. He had lit a cigarette without asking her whether she minded. From my corner I could not hear them very well, especially Jean, who kept on saying in angry, impatient tones, "But that's not the point . . . that's not of the least importance," to which Michèle replied with an air of mockery: "Really?" I gathered that they were discussing

220

the druggist's wife. Jean, his hands in his pockets and his shoulders hunched, was rocking backward and forward on his feet. It was obvious, he said, that she did not want to have anything more to do with him, that she was taking the first excuse that came to hand to send him packing. Not that it wasn't perfectly natural. The only surprising thing was how she had ever come to believe that she cared for him.

Michèle interrupted the flow of his words. She spoke as she used to do in the days of their childhood quarrels. "So *you're* accusing *me!* I must say, I like that: after all, you started it!"

To this, Jean in a fit of exasperation replied: "Why must you harp on that idiotic story? I do wish you'd try to understand that it meant absolutely nothing to me. It was merely my way of smashing things up and breaking loose. I just had to get out of that house . . . because of you, because life had become intolerable. Yes, it was you who were the cause of it all. . . . What about the woman? you say. Well, you'd have laughed if you could have seen us in the hotel at Biarritz. Why, everybody thought I was her son, and she didn't dare say I wasn't. As a matter of fact, she didn't much mind . . . she was laughing at me the whole time . . . but I can't explain. . . ."

And when Michèle struck back with, "I wouldn't try, if I were you!" he assured her that it was the Curé and no one else who had mattered to Madame Voyod from beginning to end of the business. "She kept on talking about him: 'He'll be just about getting home now,' she would say. 'He must have been told by this time. What will his first reaction be? D'you think he's capable of crying? Have you ever seen him cry?' Those were the questions she asked me. She wanted to play him a dirty trick, or to revenge herself on him. What for? Oh, I suppose the mere fact that he wears a soutane makes her want to hurt him. . . . However that may be, *I* didn't count for much with her."

Michèle replied that she was quite prepared to believe that the woman had been laughing at him. But what she could never forgive was that he had allowed himself to be caught like that.

To this burst of temper Jean replied with a show of tenderness. It gave the measure of his exhaustion. "What's the good of arguing?" He realized, he said, that everything was over between them. She didn't know what he had had to stand. There were things he couldn't tell her. He had trusted her, believed the promise she had made to be faithful to him whatever happened. . . . But naturally he understood now that she had overestimated her strength. A young girl shouldn't get mixed up with a fellow like Jean de Mirbel. If she did, she ran the risk of being lost for ever.

"You're getting away from the point," insisted Michèle, who kept on mulishly returning to the subject of the Voyod woman.

Jean groaned: "You don't understand. . . ."

But I, sitting there alone, and more or less outside the arena, could see clearly into both their minds. Michèle was the victim of the same sort of evil mood that used to afflict me on their account when I was little more than a child. She could never have been sure that she had loved this emaciated young man whom she scarcely recognized, were it not for the fact that he had caused her so much pain during the last few weeks. And he, indifferent to her jealousy, was calling from the depths of his loneliness: "Take me as I am: I am sick; I am only a boy; take me, look after me!" But she was deaf to his appeal. She had become a woman, the kind of woman who cannot see beyond the outrage done to the craving of her senses, a woman practical and positive.

"I'm really very sorry for you," she said. "To hear you speak, one would think you were an outlaw . . . you, Jean de Mirbel."

He could find no answer to that, or rather, he could not find the only words that might have broken down her obstinacy. He was amazed that she should speak to him of his birth and fortune. . . . How could he make her see what was going on inside him? that he was repudiating something, longing for something, and had no idea what it was all about? . . . After a fairly long silence, he said:

"Tell me, Michèle, why was it that I was always in trouble at school, always being pointed at? Why did my brute of an uncle want to break my spirit? . . . As I said before, there are things you know nothing about."

"What things?" she asked.

He shook his head: not, as I supposed, as a sign that he couldn't answer, but to free himself of an image by which, as he told me later when we had become inseparable, he was obsessed at the time of which I am writing: the picture of a narrow street in Balauze, of nettles growing against the wall of the Cathedral, of the stocky figure of a man at a window, of the white, wraithlike form of a woman who could scarcely find room to slip between his shoulder and the wall.

After another silence, he went on: "I must give you back . . . you know what, surely?" He was thinking of the locket.

She protested: "No, keep it!"

But he had already undone his collar, and was trying to take off the chain. After a bit of fumbling he gave up, sat down, and remained, saying nothing, his head drooped forward.

I did not notice at once that he was crying, but it was to his tears that Michèle at last surrendered. They had moved no nearer to one another. This visible sign of a misery at whose cause she could not guess overcame Michèle's resistance, though she had stood out against everything else. She had not forgotten a single one of her grievances. She would have a whole lifetime in which to brood on them. She would add many others to them, storing up ammunition for future quarrels. But he was crying, and this she found impossible, physically impossible, to bear.

She went close to him and, bending down, wiped away his tears with her diminutive handkerchief. At the same time she laid her hand on his head.

Though I had turned away, I could see what was happening in the mirror. I saw, too, the door into the hall open. It remained open. No one came in. Jean de Mirbel had got up from his chair. Then, Brigitte Pian appeared, carrying a tray loaded with cups and bread and butter. I realized that she must have put it down on the chest in order to open the door.

Only her lips smiled, and she looked at us from a pair of somber eyes.

# 16

SHE served tea with an eagerness of humility very different from the eagerness she had displayed when it was her object to edify us in the old days. Or perhaps I should say that if some concern for our edification was still discernible in her attitude, it made less impression on me than did my feeling, which increased as time went on, that her nature was, as it were, turning back upon itself. People do not change. At my age one can have no illusions on that point: but they do quite often turn back to what they were once and show again those very characteristics they have striven tirelessly, through a whole lifetime, to suppress. This does not mean that they necessarily end by succumbing to what is worst in themselves. God is very often the good temptation to which many human beings in the long run yield.

This was not at once the case with Brigitte Pian, although we were to see her, under the abbé Calou's influence, rid herself in the course of a few weeks of her old tendency to dominate. Clearly, she was seeking the sources of a deep, personal religion. But it was precisely in those things that she was now trying to suppress that she had formerly found that religion, in all that could satisfy her craving to direct others—to rule. She had always been unwilling to take second place to no matter whom in purity of intention or perfection of virtue.

I can see her still, upright in the middle of that hideous room, a cup of tea in each hand. During the few moments in which she imposed the fact of her presence on us, everything that separated Jean from Michèle and from me vanished. We formed a compact block of youth confronted by an aging woman. Three stars that are separated by vast distances of space may seem to be quite close to one another when seen in relation to a fourth, more distant, star.

She looked at us with a sort of hungry concentration. At first I did not understand its full significance.

"We're on top all right now, she'll have to give in!" exclaimed Michèle as soon as our stepmother had left the room. But no, that was not what chiefly emerged from this incident. It is true that Jean was asked, in the most friendly tone possible, to remember us to his mother. Brigitte even went so far as to express a hope that he would let us hear from him when he got to England, which was tantamount to admitting his right to correspond with my sister. This seeming defeat showed its true significance only in the course of the two or three years that elapsed before I went off to Paris. During all that time Jean wrote regularly, several times a week, to Michèle from Cambridge. To say that our stepmother acquiesced in all this is to put the matter too mildly. Every day she studied the girl's face, trying to read in it whether she had received a letter, and whether it had told of pain or happiness. Not one detail of this love affair, of this interminable succession of storms and stresses, the story of which I must some day tell, was lost on Brigitte Pian.

"She is pleased when I suffer," complained Michèle. But that was not true. Brigitte was not pleased, only interested, passionately concerned.

Another thing that Michèle said was: "Now that she can no longer torment anybody, she has become like those people who find their only sexual satisfaction in watching others make love. . . ." And that I found nearer to the truth. The whole center of Brigitte Pian's interest in life had shifted. She no longer worked at her old task, adding link by link to the armor of her false perfection. Consequently, she had time now to study others, to observe the strange game they played under the name of love, that game from which, for so long, she had averted her gaze in horror, without attempting to fathom the mysteries the word conceals.

Michèle, so far from being touched by the interest that our stepmother was showing in her, suspected every kind of evil intention, and was careful not to reveal anything that concerned her relations with Jean. But Brigitte interpreted in her own way the girl's fits of ill-temper, and drew her own conclusions from her least sigh, and even from her periods of silence.

Doubtless she was more regular now than she had been in her religious duties, and may even have taken the sacrament more often, for her scruples had at last vanished. But from now on she led two lives. When she was not in church, she spent her time exploring a world which had no connection with the one illuminated by Grace. At the age of fifty she had suddenly discovered the joys of imaginative literature, and I often came on her in my room taking down some book from the shelves. Her method of reading was more like eating—like the greedy eating of a child who stuffs its mouth with food. She had to make up so much time that she had wasted on printed nonsense, the worthlessness of which she was too intelligent not to have realized at the time. I remember the way in which, in the old days, she used to open the regular parcel of "Good Family Reading." She would pick out some volume at random, turn several pages at once, sigh, shrug. Now she showed a similar eagerness in her approach to *Adolphe, Le Lis dans la vallée, Anna Karenina.* I indulged her taste for books that dealt in the precise analysis of sentiment. All love stories appealed to her, provided they did not falsify reality. In just such a way will a man condemned to lead a sedentary life cram himself with tales of travel, but always with a keen eye for the veracity of the writer. She scarcely ever saw the abbé Calou now. The attempt to get permission for him to occupy himself with a "cure of souls" at Souys had come to nothing. Already he was suspected in high places (though quite wrongly) of being responsible for certain venomous comments in *The Battle* on the diocesan administration. He was one of those innocent souls who cannot always resist the temptation to say something amusing, the kind of man who would rather be hanged than miss the chance of some biting rejoinder. Unfortunately for him, the man who had succeeded Cardinal Lecot in the office made illustrious by the Primates of Aquitaine was a cleric of limited intelligence, who therefore became an implacable foe. One of these days I may, perhaps, tell the story of the sainted abbé Calou's road to Calvary. He was already on the point of being suspended, and wore out Brigitte Pian with the tale of his miseries. But it was to talk of herself and not of him that she made the necessary train journey. She always came back from these trips in a disappointed frame of mind. But by next day she had forgotten all about it, and would concentrate her attention once again on Michèle's love affair, or become completely absorbed in some book which she read far into the night.

Not that the pharisee was dead in her. She took pride in the very clarity of mind which enabled her to sit in judgment upon herself and condemn her own conduct. She did not believe that there were many instances of a Christian woman capable at fifty of realizing that her feet had been set on the wrong road. Not that she ever admitted in so many words that she would like never again to meddle in the affairs of her neighbors. Sometimes she would be caught up into a mood of deep nostalgia when she remembered the years gone by. One day it happened that we had just come back from the funeral of my old trustee Maître Malbec. He had been carried from the house of his mistress with his mouth twisted sideways. His affairs were in bad shape, for, unknown to all, he had led a very dissipated life. "All the same," said Brigitte as we were driving home, "he did live."

I protested. Was that what she called living? My stepmother seemed to be embarrassed by my question, and assured me that I had mistaken her meaning. One said of a man that he had lived when he had done things on the grand scale; that was all she had meant to say. I do not doubt for a moment that she was sincere. My studious existence was a matter of surprise to her. "All men are beasts," she said more than once, not in her old, bitter tone, but with a smile. When I settled in Paris to read for a degree in political science, I had to endure endless sessions of acute, subtle questioning whenever I returned to Bordeaux for a short visit. She was convinced that I was leading a life of intrigue and smoldering passion, and she kept up a regular correspondence with the Comtesse de Mirbel of which Jean and I were the constant theme (for, from 1910 on, my old friend had joined me in the capital). Here, too, I must refrain from anticipating the story of these Paris years, though I may tell it later. I will mention one incident only, and that because Brigitte was mixed up in it, and because it illustrated the sudden flowering of the extraordinary change that had come over her.

Very early my mind began to play round the idea of marriage. The thought had obsessed me ever since the days when I was quite a boy, and it still did so at that time of my life when I was better placed than thousands of young men to try my hand at winning happiness. It was due to my fear of losing my way in the chaotic wilderness of my sensibilities. I might well have applied to myself the wise words of Nietzsche which he wrote about the French seventeenth century: "It contained much of wildness, much too of that will to asceticism which was so necessary if it was to remain master in its own house."

One day a friend spoke to me of his cousin, a young

woman of wealth, who had spent all her childhood in a world inhabited by writers and painters. He extolled her charms, and I snapped at the hook almost as soon as it was dangled before me. Living as I did in such close communion with God, believing as I did that nothing ever happened to me which did not spring from His direct purpose, and that no one could cross my path without being, in some sense, a delegate of the Infinite, I was prepared to find in this young woman an angel of liberation. *Their eyes all full of light, they walk before me.* . . .

As it turned out, this girl, whom I saw as a sort of combination of Madonna and Muse, hesitated a great deal longer and was far less easy to capture than I had either expected or wished. She was anxious not to make up her mind until she had traveled extensively in Europe. My love was, on the whole, flattered by the thought of our coming separation and by my knowledge of her perplexities, which I regarded as a merit in one who lived always in the regions of the sublime.

So taken up was I by this idea of sublimity that I quite failed to see her as she was: a rich, middle-class young woman who was in no hurry to bind herself by a definite engagement, who carefully weighed the pros and cons of the situation, with a wary eye on me. It was known that I had money, but my family came from the provinces and was no more than decently respectable. Did I represent someone who could be relied on? Her parents belonged to a world of sophisticated Parisians who knew that art and literature represented no bad investment. . . . Even in those days they were taking a chance on Matisse. But was I a sound proposition? They could not make up their minds, were suspicious of my impatience, and regarded me as, on the whole, a great blockhead—which I was. They did all they could, therefore, to keep me hanging on. When I threatened to give up the whole idea, they redoubled their friendliness. My stepmother had picked up some disturbing rumors about their medical history, and they went so far as to beg me to go and see their doctor, whom they had, so to speak, released for the occasion from his oath of professional secrecy.

That ridiculous, rather sordid errand of mine seems now like a dream. I have a picture of myself facing, from behind his desk, the eminent practitioner who waited, icily polite, to answer the questions I wanted to put to him. The whole business ended in a final family conclave from which I emerged definitely engaged, and received from the young woman a rapturous letter. But by the next day the whole situation had changed, and I found myself cast off without a word of excuse or explanation. I blamed myself. The fact was clear to me that, in spite of all the solid proofs of my worthiness which I could produce, she did not like me. In view of this check to my hopes, every other encouraging sign went for nothing. Something about me, I did not know what, had come between me and the Angelic Being. Was it a sign in me of the incurable romanticism of youth? The men of my generation were born with a sense of personal guilt. They imagined that they were destined for a life of solitude and despair.

I told my stepmother, without going into details, that my engagement had been broken off. I had expected a letter of condolence from her, but what was my surprise to see her arrive in person on my doorstep! She seemed to have taken my misfortune very much to heart. She carried her attitude of pity to excess, and gave me to understand that she feared I might have contemplated some desperate act. Her tactless efforts at cheerfulness bored me. They also had the effect of making me realize that I was considerably less unhappy than I had seemed to be in the first moments of disappointment. I saw that what I was really suffering from was wounded vanity. Brigitte took me back with her to Larjuzon. I felt that she resented the fact that I was being so reasonable. But all through that tropical summer of 1911 the evidence was too plain for her to mistake. Far from being mortally wounded by my disaster in love, I found it a stimulus, and was driven by a wild desire to get what compensation I could from life. That summer I found a wonderful antidote in the prolonged reading of Balzac. An author is neither moral nor immoral in himself. It is our own attitude of mind that decides what his influence on us is to be. In my then state of mind, Balzac put me in love with life, though at the same time he infected my still childish mind with a strong dose of cynicism. I was enchanted by the coldly calculating tricks and subterfuges of his young heroes.

It was about this time that Brigitte began to cut herself adrift from me. I had disturbed the idea of love that she had built up for herself. There was nothing she had come to dislike more in anyone than an absence of passion. She could not bear to think that I had recovered from my disappointment so quickly. She did not dare admit this to me, but I could feel that she suspected me of not belonging to the true race of tormented lovers. I did not then know how far her self-deception had gone.

Michèle spent the summer vacation of 1911 with the Mirbels at La Devize. The only resource, therefore, left to me and my stepmother was reading. Her gloom deepened. Already she had begun to grow slack in the performance of her religious duties. Her talk was more and more concerned with one subject only. Human passion had become an obsession with her. Occasionally she spoke to me of my mother in a tone of hostility that betrayed both admiration and envy. But for the most part she remained silent, lying on the veranda, a faint flush staining the dead white of her face.

I have always had a horror of neurasthenics, and that year I welcomed the necessity of having to go back to Paris. It was a way of escape. I still wrote to my stepmother, but our letters were trivial and colorless. Michèle, who was planning to marry Jean after he had done his two years of military service, was still living at the Cours de l'Intendance. In her letters to me she mentioned "something quite unbelievable that has happened to Brigitte," but waited to tell me what it was until she should come to Paris, where she was due to stay with the Mirandieuzes.

When at last I heard the details, the whole thing did indeed seem so unbelievable that I could do nothing at first but shrug my shoulders. I thought that Michèle was giving rein to her imagination when she told me that my stepmother had fallen in love with her doctor, a man well on in his sixties. But at Bordeaux I was confronted by evidence that would not be denied. It was not merely a question of a sick old woman developing a liking for her medical attendant. No, she had fallen a prey to a fierce, exclusive, and (what was really odd) a thoroughly happy and reciprocated passion. Not that there was anything "wrong" in their relations. Dr. Gellis, a fervent Huguenot with a practice that included all the best Protestant families of the city, was beyond the reach of any scandal. But, separated from a wife who had dragged his name in the mud, and plagued by a horde of children, most of whom were married, embittered, and needy, it had been a matter of delight for him to discover

233

in the evening of his days that he had become an object of exclusive concern to a woman who was far stronger-minded and better fitted to face life than he was. He saw her every day, and took no decisions without first consulting her. The two lonely old things were perfectly unashamed about talking of their mutual attachment, and it never seemed to occur to them that they were making themselves ridiculous. They found in each other's faces not the signs of old age, but of tenderness. They lived for one another like two old innocents, blissfully unaware that their irritated relatives were laughing at them, and that the neighbors were gossiping at their expense.

It was the last year of Jean's military service, and his marriage was to take place in October. The families exchanged dinners, and the contract was drawn up. Brigitte Pian had to act to Michèle as a mother, but did so with a bad grace. Her stepdaughter's passion no longer interested her. What chiefly worried her was the imprudent promise she had made to divide the family estate during her lifetime. This was a sacrifice that she had once gladly envisioned as, in some sort, making up for the wrong she had done the girl. Brigitte's personal fortune was less than ours. She scarcely had enough capital left (though she realized it too late) to enable her to buy a small property adjoining Dr. Gellis's clinic. The Comtesse de Mirbel expressed it as her view that this "entirely changed the whole situation. . . ." In her eyes, the loss of half a million francs only underlined the fact that her son was making a mésalliance. Brigitte played deaf, pretended not to understand the hints, but avoided any open warfare and anything that might have disturbed her strange, deep happiness. This happiness, seen in terms of the human figure, was a stout gentleman of sixty-odd years, with short legs. He wore a tight-fitting frock-coat and had a dyed beard which, taken in conjunction with his austere gestures and bald head, gave him a certain resemblance to the Chancellor Michel de l'Hôpital. He talked a great deal and listened to no one except Brigitte, though she preferred to stay silent so as not to lose a single word that might drop from the lips of the beloved. Most of their conversation was concerned with serious subjects, not excluding theology. She showed herself responsive to the logic of Calvinism, though neither gave the least sign of wishing to convert the other, either because of a mutual tenderness for their respective beliefs, or because they were no longer greatly interested in the matter of creeds. Age made them conscious of the value of every fleeting moment. Not a minute must be diverted from the one essential thing—their love for one another.

From now on Brigitte's life and ours lay apart. I got out of the habit of dropping in at the Cours de l'Intendance when I visited Bordeaux. My room had become a pied-à-terre for Dr. Gellis on those evenings when he took Brigitte to the theater or to a concert and slept in town. Their love of music was a great bond. The doctor had no car, but sported one of those ancient broughams that say "doctor" a mile off. It took a long time to cover the distance between the town and his clinic.

It is not always the case that graybeards fall for young girls, or aging women for growing youths. It sometimes happens that a man and a woman who have vainly sought one another through a long life meet by chance when the shadows begin to fall. When that happens, their passion takes on a peculiarly intense quality of isolation. Nothing else seems to matter. There is so little time left! The world may laugh, but, then, the world knows little of the secrets of the heart. When I did pay one of my infrequent visits to the Cours de l'Intendance, Brigitte's attitude to me was one almost of pity. I, not she, was the one who stood in need of sympathy. The old, formidable side of her character still showed at times when she conjured up the memory of my mother or of the Puybarauds; of all those people whom she no longer needed to envy, who, unlike her, had never known the delights of a love that was truly shared. The sight of that cruel flame flickering beneath the thick eyebrows that almost met across Brigitte's forehead got on my nerves, and I was goaded into dropping allusions to the kind of love that she would never know. I had discovered a chink in the armor of her proud and throned emotion. Passion, I hinted, is but the ghost of itself when it cannot take bodily form. So long as we cannot lose and find ourselves again in the beloved, we merely intoxicate ourselves with words and with the gestures of love, but we can never know whether what we have is the reality.

Brigitte broke in upon my monologue: "You don't know what you're saying, what you're talking about. . . ."

Her face had assumed the same familiar expression of disgust as in the old days whenever the forbidden subject was mentioned in her hearing. I have a feeling of remorse now when I think that I may have spoiled their happiness with these insinuations of mine because, about the time that I was indulging in these bouts of rhetoric, I learned from Michèle of occasional stormy scenes between Philemon and his Baucis. Could it be that Brigitte was conscious of regret? Could it be that she made certain demands upon her lover? One dares not attempt to visualize the squalid little efforts and contortions of those two bodies whose powers had not kept pace with the sentiments that stirred them. When youth suffers (as I was suffering then) it cannot bear the sight of age's placid contentment.

Dr. Gellis had his children and the parents of his grandchildren forever yapping at his heels. The purchase of the little property adjoining the clinic, which Brigitte concluded on the day before Michèle's marriage, set a match to the powder barrel. One of the pastors of Bordeaux made representations to the doctor, while his family begged Michèle to persuade her stepmother to see some priest in whom she had confidence, and to whose criticism she would listen. This was just about the time that the abbé Calou had been deprived of the right to say Mass. Since, however, he was merely suspended and not excommunicated, his poor, humiliated soutane could be seen among the black dresses of the old women each morning when communion was administered in the small chapel that stands close to the Faculty of Letters. He would go back to his seat followed by the curious or pitying glances of the congregation, and his face was as the face of an angel.

The Gellis family had no time in which to enlist his help. To use one of the cruel and futile sayings of which the Comtesse de Mirbel was so fond—"the whole thing was taken out of their hands." One evening, close to the clinic, a motor-car struck the doctor's brougham a glancing blow. He was killed on the spot. My stepmother saw the news next day in the paper. A number of no doubt highly colored stories spread through the town to the effect that Brigitte Pian had arrived, haggard and hatless, at the house where the Gellis children were living. It was said that the eldest son had tried to keep her out of the room where the body lay, but that she had thrust him aside, had broken through the barriers erected in her path by the rest of the family, and had thrown herself upon the corpse with never a tear or a cry, and that she had had to be pulled away by main force.

I was living at that time with friends at Cap Martin. I did not feel that so unofficial a case of mourning necessitated my presence. I merely wrote a letter. It was a difficult letter to compose, and it remained unanswered. But Michèle and Jean were away in Algeria on their honeymoon, and the thought of Brigitte haunted me. It was not in my power just then to make the trip to Bordeaux in order to assure myself that my stepmother had not gone out of her mind. I was due back in Paris. I therefore postponed the difficult duty until the beginning of spring.

The servant did not know me, and I was left waiting in the hall. I could hear my stepmother's exclamation: "But of course! Show him in." I was much relieved to find that her voice sounded as usual. She was sitting in her accustomed place by the writing-table, which was no longer, as of old, littered with circulars and invitations to charity sales. She had grown no older in appearance. I noticed, after the first few minutes, that she had gone back to the old way of doing her hair—raised high, puffed out with numberless little curls, and so arranged as to leave her large ears and well-modeled forehead free. A photograph of Dr. Gellis stood on the mantelpiece, shaded by a bunch of lilacs. There was nothing about Madame Brigitte to indicate nervous disturbance or mental unbalance. Her shoulders were covered by a knitted woolen shawl. As I came in, she had just put back on her desk the rosary she had always used when I was a child. She began the conversation by apologizing for not having answered my letter. She made no attempt to deceive me, but said that for several days she had been in a condition of prostration from which she had recovered only with considerable difficulty.

"And now?" I asked.

238

She looked at me thoughtfully. "If Monsieur Puybaraud were here, he would insist that you were the only person capable of understanding. . . ."

There was calm certainty in her smile. "You see, the real, secret truth is that I have not lost him . . . but there is no one I can tell. Dear Monsieur Gellis was never so close to me as he is now, not even when he was alive. He had already embarked on his mission to me while he was in this world, but we are all of us poor mortal flesh, and our bodies were a barrier. But there is nothing between us now."

She talked at length on this theme, and at first I suspected a trick of sorrow seeking to cheat death of the dear doctor. But at the end of a few days I realized that the sun of human love had not risen too late on the arid destiny of this woman of the Pharisees, that the "whited sepulcher" had been unsealed and stood open at last. Perhaps it still contained a few dried bones, a trace of corruption. Occasionally the formidable eyebrows met in a frown above the smoldering eyes. Some grievance, long mulled over, now and then brought a bitter word to her lips. But "dear Monsieur Gellis" was never far away, was always there at the critical moment to lead Brigitte Pian into the calm ways of God.

An urgent letter from the Comtesse de Mirbel called me to La Devize, where Michèle and Jean were going to return, some considerable time before they were expected. This hurried return of theirs worried me. I set off without delay, and was at once caught up into their drama, the story of which I shall some day tell. I became the satellite of their system, and was whirled about in the constant eddy of strife and reconciliation that made up their existence. I had no leisure in which to think of the old woman I had left in the Cours de l'Intendance, embalmed, as it were, in the posthumous adoration of "dear Monsieur Gellis." It was my strange destiny to become the go-between for Jean and Michèle—continually warding off the blows that they blindly aimed at one another—a rôle especially strange for a young man who had his own private misery and suffered in a solitude that no one in the world could break.

The mobilization of August 2nd, 1914, woke us from our dream. That thunder-clap disturbed thousands of personal dramas, all of them much like our own. We struggled up from the depths of our dark passions, all our saps destroyed, stupefied and dazed by an appalling disaster which was so infinitely greater than the one we were inflicting on ourselves. I left Jean and Michèle, who, now that they were to lose one another, could do themselves no further hurt, and faced the full extremity of my loneliness when I realized that there was no one in the world, except Brigitte, to whom I could even say good-bye.

She looked small now, and had grown thin. She drew me to her, and her tears surprised me. The name of Dr. Gellis was never once mentioned between us. She looked after me as a mother might have done. I found out later that she was seeing a great deal of Monsieur Calou at this time, and was doing much to help him. He had been taken back into favor by the diocesan authorities, but was already near his end.

All the time I was at the Front I was overwhelmed with parcels and letters and with inquiries about my health and my needs. I spent my first leave with Madame Brigitte. A few days before it fell due, Monsieur Calou had died in her arms. She told me about it quite unemotionally, and without making any attempt to point a lesson. Monsieur Calou, she said, had certainly not grown less in spiritual stature, though toward the end he had scarcely been of this world. He had suffered from agonizing attacks of angina pectoris—

the kind that drive the sufferer to the open window in a terrifying struggle for air. But as soon as he had recovered his breath, he would say that he was ready for still greater suffering. He had on his table a photograph that I had taken long ago in the kitchen garden at Baluzac. It showed Jean and Michèle, barefooted, their eyes screwed up against the sun, clinging to the same watering can. Brigitte added that, in spite of the pain he had to endure, he never gave one a feeling of pity.

When I alluded to past events, she talked of them quite openly. But I could feel that she had become detached from even the consciousness of her faults, and that she had decided to lay everything at the throne of the Great Compassion. In the evening of her life, Brigitte Pian had come to the knowledge that it is useless to play the part of a proud servitor eager to impress his master by a show of readiness to repay his debts to the last farthing. It had been revealed to her that our Father does not ask us to give a scrupulous account of what merits we can claim. She understood at last that it is not our deserts that matter but our love.